IN THE BETWEEN

OTHER PERSEA ANTHOLOGIES

AMERICA STREET: A MULTICULTURAL ANTHOLOGY OF STORIES
Edited by Anne Mazer and Brice Particelli

IMAGINING AMERICA: STORIES FROM THE PROMISED LAND
Edited by Wesley Brown and Amy Ling

VISIONS OF AMERICA:
PERSONAL NARRATIVES FROM THE PROMISED LAND
Edited by Wesley Brown and Amy Ling

PAPER DANCE: 55 LATINO POETS
Edited by Victor Hernández Cruz, Leroy V. Quintana, and Virgil Suarez

SCRIBBLERS ON THE ROOF:
CONTEMPORARY AMERICAN JEWISH FICTION
Edited by Melvin Bukiet and David G. Roskies

IN THE COMPANY OF MY SOLITUDE:
AMERICAN WRITING FROM THE AIDS PANDEMIC
Edited by Marie Howe and Michael Klein

POETS FOR LIFE: 76 POETS RESPOND TO AIDS
Edited by Michael Klein

THINGS SHAPED IN PASSING:
MORE "POETS FOR LIFE" WRITING FROM THE AIDS PANDEMIC
Edited by Michael Klein and Richard J. McCann

SHORT: AN INTERNATIONAL ANTHOLOGY OF FIVE CENTURIES
OF SHORT-SHORT STORIES, PROSE POEMS,
BRIEF ESSAYS, AND OTHER SHORT PROSE FORMS
Edited by Alan Ziegler

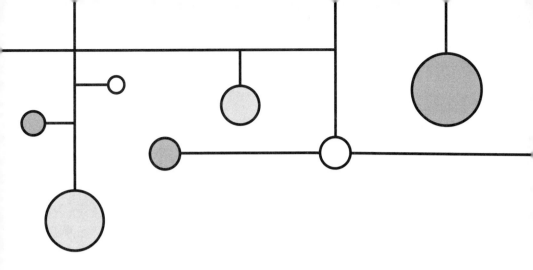

IN THE BETWEEN

21ST CENTURY SHORT STORIES

EDITED BY BRICE PARTICELLI

A KAREN & MICHAEL BRAZILLER BOOK
PERSEA BOOKS / NEW YORK

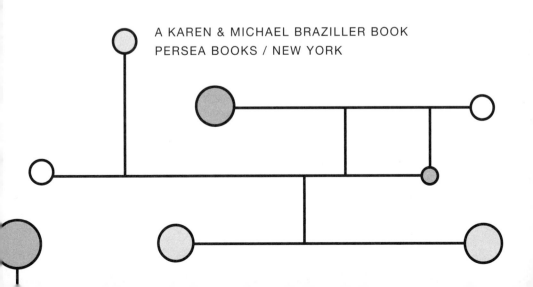

Permissions Department
Persea Books
90 Broad Street
New York, NY 10004
Email: permissions@perseabooks.com

Library of Congress Cataloging-in-Publication Data

Names: Particelli, Brice, editor.
Title: In the between : 21st century short stories / edited by Brice Particelli.
Description: New York : Persea Books, [2021] | "A Karen & Michael Braziller book."
Identifiers: LCCN 2021044011 (print) | LCCN 2021044012 (ebook) | ISBN 9780892555468 (paperback) | ISBN 9780892555482 (ebook)
Subjects: LCSH: Short stories, American. | American fiction—21st century. | LCGFT: Short stories.
Classification: LCC PS648.S5 I53 2021 (print) | LCC PS648.S5 (ebook) | DDC 813/.010806--dc23
LC record available at https://lccn.loc.gov/2021044011
LC ebook record available at https://lccn.loc.gov/2021044012

Design and composition by Rita Lascaro
Typeset in Carat
Printed and bound by Maple Press, Pennsylvania

First Edition

CONTENTS

Introduction by Brice Particelli   *vii*

Accepted   VANESSA HUA   3
The Thing Around Your Neck   CHIMAMANDA NGOZI ADICHIE   16
The Right Imaginary Person   ROBERT ANTHONY SIEGEL   25
Navigation   BRYAN WASHINGTON   39
Juba   RION AMILCAR SCOTT   45
Sugar Babies   KALI FAJARDO-ANSTINE   59
To the New World   RYKA AOKI   74
Cougar   MARIA ANDERSON   82
After Action Report   PHIL KLAY   95
Windows   SHIVANA SOOKDEO   111
Girls at the Bar   ROXANE GAY   115
Ron   JOY BAGLIO   117
A Place Like Home   MISTER LOKI   129
The Devil's Grip   CASEY ROBB   135
In the Trees   ALICE HOFFMAN   148
Surrounded by Sleep   AKHIL SHARMA   152
The Art of Translation   BENJAMIN ALIRE SÁENZ   166
Movement   NANCY FULDA   182
Moonless   BRYAN HURT   192

About the Authors   197
About the Editor   202
Acknowledgments   203

INTRODUCTION

What is it like to forge your future in twenty-first century America?

These first decades have been defined by cultural reckonings—a time of both deep division and deepening connections. While digital tools have made it easier to dig into our own competing "truths," people have never before had the power to be so collaborative, connected, and aware of each other's lives. We've never been as able to consider how we can be ourselves, together, in this world.

Written by established and rising stars in American fiction and graphic narrative, all published since the year 2000, these stories don't shy away from the rawness and complexity of people's multifaceted lives. As the title states, the protagonists in this anthology are "in the between," finding themselves within a life that was once known but is now unknown. They stand on a precipice, considering how to embrace their true selves in a changing or challenging landscape that can be precarious, absurd, or even life-threatening.

In Rion Amilcar Scott's story, a straight-laced accountant—a young Black man who is mistaken by the police for a drug dealer named Juba—decides to track down his supposed look-alike to learn who this Juba really is. Vanessa Hua's story follows a daughter of immigrants under pressure to meet her parents' expectations. After faking her way into a top university, she finds that the only way out is through revenge. Maria Anderson focuses on a young man questioning his future in a deteriorating town in rural Montana as he struggles with the unexplained disappearance of his father. And in Ryka Aoki's vibrant story, a trans woman considers her femininity and her principles in relation to her activist lesbian friend and her own immigrant grandmother.

There are stories about life in a new country as well, including Robert Anthony Siegel's story of an American man fumbling through a relationship in Japan and Chimamanda Ngozi Adichie's story of a Nigerian woman struggling to date a white American man who doesn't quite get who she is. Phil Klay reveals the plight of an American soldier in Fallujah, who suffers from PTSD after he shields his guilty buddy by taking responsibility for shooting an Iraqi child.

Roxane Gay's flash fiction story embraces the unencumbered bliss of a rowdy girls' night out, while in Shivana Sookdeo's comic, a girl goes outside time and space to find her kindred spirit. Nancy Fulda's story steps into the near future to follow the inner turmoil of a young dancer with autism as she resists the oppression of expectation and disability within a system that wants to "fix" her. In Mister Loki's comic, a young person wanders alone in an aquarium considering correlations to non-binary gender identity, while Alice Hoffman's story portrays the anguish of a girl's choice to have an abortion amidst questions of environmental destruction.

All of these characters navigate the complex cultures and structures that surround them, some more directly than others. Bryan Washington follows a cook of Afro-Latino heritage, who is forced to take a job doing kitchen "grunt work" and soon finds himself in a troubled relationship with an entitled "whiteboy," in gentrifying Houston. In Kali Fajardo-Anstine's story, a young girl in southern Colorado considers her Indigenous and Hispanic heritage as she reconnects with her estranged mother. And in Benjamin Alire Sáenz's story, a teen experiences a violent act of racial hate and struggles to grasp who he can be in the aftermath of such a gruesome act.

The stories that comprise *In the Between* capture hard truths, bringing us into experiences that can open our eyes to lives we might not otherwise see. They can be unsettling, but they are necessary.

Brice Particelli, Ph.D.

IN THE BETWEEN

VANESSA HUA

Accepted

It occurred to me that I'd become too comfortable with breaking and entering. Back from field training, I'd leapt onto the windowsill in a single bound, no awkward scrambling, as though onto a pommel horse, despite my combat boots and my Kevlar. I crouched, resting my hands lightly on the frame. My ponytail bobbed and then went still. In perfect balance, I could have carried a stack of books on my head, a debutante but for the stench of dirt and sweat.

I tiptoed in the dark until realizing my roommates were out. As I set down my ruck, an RA in the lounge shouted an invitation to join a group headed to Flicks. A door slammed, and a basketball thudded down the hallway. From the floor above, reggae blasted, competing with the howl of a blow-dryer. No sign of the dorm settling down Sunday night, not with the last of the weekend to enjoy.

Too tired to shower, I collapsed onto the futon for a nap before my all-nighter. A sudden, strange lull descended, so complete it seemed like I was in one of those sensory deprivation chambers that drive test subjects insane. I couldn't shake the feeling that everyone in the world had disappeared. "Hello?" I called out. "Hello, hello." No one answered, and I fired up Julia's laptop to fill the void with light and noise.

We met fall quarter, after I studied her for a half hour while she sunbathed. Her body long and lean in a black sports bra and board shorts, on the lawn outside her dorm, the new one with spacious lounges and nooks for studying, and where I wanted to live most. Julia seemed like the kind of girl who adopted wounded birds and stray puppies, willing to help a newcomer in need.

I told her I had nowhere to stay because of a mix-up in Housing. Officials said they might find something within a week or two, but until then I'd be sleeping in the 24-hour room at the library. What a way to start freshman year! Julia, a sophomore, invited me to crash in the room she shared with her best friend. One night turned into a week, another and another and then we were at the end of the quarter, Dead Week, finals, and saying our good-byes for the holidays. Without their knowledge, my roommates had aided and abetted me. My classmates considered me no different than them, these student body presidents, valedictorians, salutatorians, National Merit Scholars, Model U.N. reps, Academic Decathletes, All-State swimmers and wrestlers, and other shining exemplars of America's youth.

*   *   *

The rejection from Admissions was a mistake. That's what I told myself after I clicked on the link and logged onto the portal last spring. Stanford had denied another Elaine Park, another in Irvine who'd also applied. I waited for a phone call of apology, along with an e-mail with the correct link.

I hadn't meant to lie, not at first, but when Jack Min donned his Stanford sweatshirt after receiving his acceptance (a senior tradition)—I yanked my Cardinal red hoodie out of my locker. When my AP English teacher, Ms. Banks, stopped to congratulate me, I couldn't bring myself to say, not yet. She'd worked with me on a dozen revisions of my college essay and written a generous letter of rec, and I didn't want to disappoint her.

Another week passed, and I posed with Jack for the school paper. A banner year for the church our families both attended, and for Sparta High, with two students in a single class admitted to Stanford. When I showed my parents the article as proof of my acceptance, Appa held the newspaper with his fingertips, as if it were bridal lace he was preserving on a special order. He reeked of chemicals from the cleaners, the stink of exhaustion and servility.

"Assiduous." His praise for my hard work. My vocab drills, which began nightly when I was in kindergarten, had fallen to him. For years, he'd been reading the dictionary for self-improvement, and the words we'd studied together coded what otherwise might remain unsaid.

"Sagacity." I thanked my father for his wisdom.

In June, with graduation approaching, I politely alerted Admissions of its error.

"You haven't received any notification?" the woman asked on the other end of the line.

"A rejection. For another Elaine Park." Only then did I realize how ridiculous I sounded. Could I appeal the decision, or get on the wait list, I asked.

No, she gently said. She explained that those chosen off the wait-list had been notified two weeks ago, and wished me the best of luck.

All those hours, all that money. The after-school academic cram programs. The cost kept us from moving out of our tiny two-bedroom apartment, whose only amenity was its location in a desirable school district and the stagnant pool where my neighbor taught me to swim. Other sacrifices: Appa put off visiting the doctor until his colds turned into bronchitis and then pneumonia. Umma's eyes going bad, squinting at the alterations she did for extra cash at the dry cleaners where they both worked.

Stanford was the only school to which I'd applied, the only school my parents imagined me attending. Other Korean families aimed for Hah-bah-duh, Harvard, or Yae-il, Yale, but we wanted Suh-ten-por-duh, Ivy of the West. On our sole family vacation, before my junior year, we piled into the car and drove to Stanford and back in a single day, a seven-hour trip each way—enough time to eat our gimbap rolls in the parking lot, snap photos of Hoover Tower, buy a sweatshirt, and pick up a course catalogue and a copy of the *Stanford Daily,* all of which I studied as closely as an archeologist trying to crack ancient runes. I was supposed to become a doctor, and buy my parents a sedan and a house in a gated community. A doctor had a title, respect, and would never be brushed off like them, never berated by customers, and never snubbed by salesclerks. My sister, who sulked the entire ride to campus, wasn't to be counted on. Five years younger than me, a chola in the making, with Cleopatra eye-liner and teased bangs, she'd turned rebellious in junior high. She could take care of herself, and I'd take care of our parents.

When I asked the admissions officer if I could send additional letters of rec, her tone turned icy. "We never reverse a decision officially ren-dered." She hung up.

The problem, I came to understand, was that my story was too typical. My scores, my accomplishments, and my volunteer work were identical to hundreds, maybe thousands of other applicants, and Admissions had reached its quota of hard-luck, hard-working children of immigrants. I'd been too honest, straightforward where I should have embellished, ordi-nary where I should have been fanciful. My classmate Jack had launched his own startup, sending used cell phones to Africa. If only I'd been a homeless teen or knit socks and mittens for orphans in China. If only I'd had cancer.

I couldn't tell my parents the truth, not after my pastor announced my Stanford acceptance at church. If my high school classmates found out, I'd become a joke. But if I spent time on the Farm, I'd discover the secret of how to talk, how to act, how to be. When I became a full-fledged student, no one had to know I had been anything but. I searched Facebook to see what incoming freshman said about forms, housing, tuition, and classes, and told my parents I'd been awarded a government scholarship, and a work-study job to cover the rest.

At the bus station, Umma pressed her papery cheek against mine, and gave me a sack of snacks, puffed rice and dried seaweed. My parents wanted to caravan with Jack's family, but I told them not to waste a day's pay by taking time off. My sister wished me luck, less surly upon realizing she'd get my room after I left. Appa handed me a prepaid cell phone and gruffly reminded me to call on Sundays.

"Cogent," he said. Other words described me more aptly, that I didn't dare say: legerdemain, reprobate.

*   *   *

Early Monday morning, the room phone rang, Julia's mother. I was typing notes for Hum Bio on her laptop, preparing for a test I'd never take. Not strange at all, considering there was a word for it—auditing—learning, but without credit.

Covering for Julia, I told Mrs. Ramirez she was at practice. She had probably spent the night at Scott's, from the men's crew team. They'd been hooking up, but he was also hanging out with other girls.

Scott. He couldn't be trusted. Not after last night, when he'd come looking for Julia. It was late, late for her, usually asleep after dinner, on the water at first light for crew practice. I expected him to leave, but he'd sprawled onto the futon—my bed—and asked about my weekend.

"At the pool." I'd learned how to turn my pants into a personal flotation device. Wriggling out, knotting each leg like a sausage, my fingers cramped and slippery. Jerking the pants overhead in a single motion, to fill the legs with air. How to swim on my side, raising my dummy rifle out of the water. The calm I felt, as splashes ricocheted around me. "Water combat training."

"Bad ass," he said.

He wasn't making fun of me. He was checking me out, his eyes following the line of my legs, up to the powerful curve of my thighs in a pair of running shorts. My body had changed under PT, turned harder, stronger, faster, and the hours I used to devote to studying I now spent jogging on Campus Drive and lifting weights.

I blushed, trying to fasten the buttons of the shirt I'd tossed over my sports bra. Scott had long eyelashes, so lush he could have been wearing mascara. The air between us had thickened. His deodorant had a woodsy, musky smell that made me think of plaid and lumberjacks. His phone had buzzed, a text from Julia. She was waiting for him at his place, he'd said, and loped off.

Although I'd dreamed I would find lifelong friends at Stanford, women who would be my bridesmaids and men to pal around with and maybe date, I remained apart as ever. Except for Julia. Because I was a cul-de-sac, not in her circle of jock friends, she trusted me with her secrets. Her fears about Scott, her complaints about our roommate Tina, so spoiled, so careless with her money.

I pushed Tina's mess away from my corner. She'd begun encroaching, her textbooks, her crumpled jeans, her energy bar wrappers, and hair-balls swirling like the Pacific garbage patch. Tina was Chinese-American, the daughter of immigrants too. From Grosse Pointe, she was used to being the only Asian and had run with a popular crowd in high school.

Before break, I told them that Housing found a spot for me. When the new quarter began, I said it fell through. A few times, I'd walked into the room and the conversation stopped, and I knew they'd been talking about me. Although it might seem strange that they never locked me out, they were too polite, too trusting of a fellow classmate in need.

My stomach growled. Security was lax on campus, but the dining hall at this hour wasn't busy enough to sneak through the exit for breakfast. Freeloading didn't seem like stealing, not exactly, with more than enough food and classroom seats to go around. I only took what would go to waste.

I dug through my ruck, searching for my ROTC assignment due that afternoon. Although the corps had been banned on campus during Vietnam War protests, Stanford students took classes and trained with battalions at other local colleges. I'd slipped through a loophole, easily able to sign up because of the informal communication between the schools about the program.

I hitched a ride three times a week to ROTC with a pair of Stanford seniors, who'd both committed to serving eight years in the Army. Friendly but not looking to make another friend, not with graduation and a likely deployment to the Middle East looming. Still, I was grateful for the

assignments in military history some treated as a joke, and grateful for the
rank of cadet. Grateful for the ruck, and the Kevlar that gave me a look of
purpose, compared to the Stanford students dressed in shorts and sandals
all the time, like they were going to the beach. BDU—battle dress uniform.
LBE—load bearing equipment, harness, canteen, first-aid kit, and ammo
pouch. I was proud to speak the language of ROTC, proud I could navigate
in the dark, armed with a map, compass, and a piece of paper. Finding the
point, finding the code, finding the pirate's buried treasure.

Flipping open my binder, I found a flyer urging Stanford cadets to
apply for the ROTC honor roll with the attached form and an unofficial transcript. A reminder I didn't have grades, and wasn't enrolled, a
reminder I should give up and go home. Surviving day-to-day brought
me no closer to becoming an official student I imagined my father's dis-
appointment, my father's words: ignominious, mendacious.

After re-applying, I was waiting for my acceptance from Stanford.
Sometimes in lecture hall, biking through White Plaza, shuffling through
the dining hall, and at my café job, I sank into the illusion that I belonged
here. No different, common among the uncommon. My fingers moved
over the keyboard, typing out my classes from first quarter and a grade
for each. Three A-s, and a B+ and a B: I wasn't greedy. If only I'd been
given the chance, it would have been my transcript. If—no. The problem
sets were impossible and I probably would have flunked out of pre-med.
I hurled the binder across the room, hitting Julia's dresser, knocking over
a corkboard plastered with photos of her friends and family. Propping it
up, I tried to straighten the crooked picture of us goofing around, wearing
sunglasses and singing into hairbrushes.

Julia burst into the room, back from crew practice. With her broad
teeth, broad smile, and glossy chestnut hair, she'd make a good show
horse. She swept past me, grabbing her birth control pills. As she broke
the foil and tipped one into her mouth, I shoved fallen photos under the
futon with my foot. When she reached for her laptop, I slid it away, snapping the lid shut. She reached again.

"Sorry." I didn't hand it over. I said her mother called, hoping Julia
might thank me for covering for her. She didn't. She hovered as I restarted
her laptop, its hard drive whirring and hanging.

"Never mind." She grabbed her dining hall pass and left.

The day had barely begun, and I'd pissed off the one person who
cared about me here. The laptop woke up, and the file popped open to
my fantasy list of grades. If only those could be my marks. That's when

it hit me: an unofficial transcript was easy to fake, without requiring a watermark or school seal, Courier font in Microsoft Word. With it, I'd apply for the ROTC honor roll. I'd never become Dr. Park, but with a resume listing my honors and awards, I'd get an internship, and later on, a job to support my parents. Weren't tech startups full of dropouts? I hit delete and dropped my A to a B + in Hum Bio. It didn't seem fair to give myself an F for a class I wasn't enrolled in. I decided the grades should reflect my efforts and no one, knowing the lengths I'd gone to, could question mine.

* * *

Over the next few weeks, my luck turned. With my faked transcript, I made the ROTC honor roll, received a ribbon for my uniform, and sent the newsletter listing my award to my parents. It wouldn't be long until I received my acceptance from Admissions, I told myself. Scott was coming around more often, too. Flirting, when he brushed a leaf out of my hair or when he helped himself to dry cereal from a bowl in my lap. His casual touching, as if I were a prized possession. Nothing could happen between us, not if I wanted a roof over my head, and yet I found myself hoping that each knock at the door meant him.

When Julia tried to tell him she loved him, he'd acted weird and left in a hurry, she'd confided. Just before I left for weekend field training, I found the futon folded up into a couch, heaped with dirty laundry, sweat-stained athletic bras and balled-up panties, a move territorial as a dog pissing on a fire hydrant, potent as a radiation symbol not to touch. Julia stood in the doorway, Scott behind her. She drew herself up, and told me I had to be out by next Friday, when their families were visiting for Parents' Weekend.

What if I spent those nights away and returned after the weekend? "From now on, I'll stay out one night a week," I pleaded. She bit her lip. "Two nights. Please. I'll keep out of Tina's way."

Mentioning our roommate seemed to remind her of their arguments against me. Julia straightened. "It's Housing's responsibility. Not ours."

I tried to catch Scott's eye—she'd listen to him—but he was suddenly intent on his texts. Had I imagined his attraction? For him, a game, a reflex.

"I could pay." I had a couple hundred dollars saved from my job at the café. Although their room and board had been covered at the beginning of the quarter, I could give them spending money.

"I have no choice," she said.

"You have more choices than me." I shouldered my ruck and left.

On the drive to field training, my head ached, tender as an overinflated balloon. I stumbled through the mission, to clear an abandoned house on the training course. First the squad leader forced us into a ditch. Soaked, our BDUs clung and chafed, then stiffened in the rising heat of the day.

"Cover me while I'm moving!"

"You got covered!"

"Moving!" I ran flat out for three seconds, my heart pounding in my ears. I cleared my head of everything but the task ahead, hurled myself into the dirt, into the rocks and burrs, a hard landing that stole my breath. When I swiveled my dummy rifle, scanning for enemies, Julia appeared beneath a tree. I aimed. I'd never felt so bright, like ten thousand flashbulbs going off, and then she vanished, quicker than I could have pulled a trigger.

*   *   *

When I returned to campus late Sunday afternoon, red-and-white balloons had sprouted, along with vinyl banners, temporary stages, and areas cordoned off for Parents' Weekend. The window to our room was locked, the shades down. I jogged to the dorm entrance and waited for someone to let me in. I fidgeted in my muddy boots. If I were a cartoon, a grey cloud of stink would have trailed me. At our room, I reached for the doorknob and then dropped my hand. From now on, I had to knock first. Julia told me to come in.

I discovered the futon folded up and my belongings missing. I sank to the floor, everything I'd been carrying these past months crushing me. Julia rushed towards me, her arms out, with the same concern that had welcomed me to campus, a concern that I'd have to kindle if I wanted to remain her charity case. I lied. "There's been a fire." The cleaners burnt down earlier this month, I added. I could almost smell the burnt remnants of the shop, see the collapsed roof and charred timbers and smashed glass, and the melted plastic bags. Taste the sickly-sweet ash floating in the sunshine. My parents were out of work, and sticking them for the bill for room and board would bankrupt them. She hugged me, enveloping me with the scent of laundry detergent and clean-living. I felt guilty for aiming at Julia's mirage during field training, even if I hadn't meant to, even if near heatstroke had put me in a trance.

I became aware of my stench, its density, crowding out the air in the room. Julia said she would take up a collection around the dorm to help my family get back on our feet. Tina hadn't budged from her bunk. *Bullshit,* her expression said.

"We can talk to the RA in your new dorm, too," Julia said. How easily she thought she could get rid of me, how little I mattered. She'd showered me with goodwill until she lost interest in me, as if I were an Easter chick sprouting scraggly feathers.

Stiffening, I drew away from her. She was wearing an over-sized Stanford crew sweatshirt—Scott's. The song ended and in the silence, Julia added that my sister had friended her online. "She wanted directions to our dorm."

My sister and I had never been close. Umma had promised me a baby brother and when Angela arrived sickly and translucent as a tadpole, I had been disappointed.

I jumped up. "What did you tell her? Did you tell her I was moving?"

"For Parents' Weekend," Julia said.

Tina opened the window, breathing through her mouth, making no effort to hide her disgust at my reek. Both their sisters were going to spend the night here, she said. "We'll be on top of each other. But we're used to that."

"I didn't think you'd be psyched to see Tina's family," I said. "Doesn't she get whiny around them?"

Julia opened her mouth, but said nothing, speechless. The secrets she'd whispered to me in the dark were on fire, sticky and searing as napalm. Fighting back, I felt as exhilarated and terrified as I had been on the training mission. As Tina lit into her, I fled outside. My weekly calls home had dwindled to once or twice a month, from a half hour to a few minutes. My sister answered on the first ring.

"Don't do this to them," I said.

"To them?" Angela asked. "You think I want to spend all weekend in the car with them?"

Bedsprings creaked, and I pictured my sister on her back, her narrow feet propped on the wall. "They bragged at church about the honor roll and Jack's parents asked if they were going to Parents' Weekend. Got them excited about visiting their No. 1 daughter."

"I have midterms," I said. Gas prices. The expense. The drive. The hassle of registration.

Each excuse sounded flimsier than the last.

"I get it now," she said. "Why I couldn't find you in the school directory."

I had nothing to negotiate with, nothing but the threat of what would happen if the lies came to an end. "If I move home, you'd be back on the fold-out," I said.

Silence. "Maybe they'll stick you there. Or kick you out." She paused. "It's time they stopped thinking you'll save them."

Time I stopped thinking it too.

* * *

At the dorm, I found my stuff in the lobby. I wouldn't have a chance to apologize. It took a couple hours, dozens of trips with an overstuffed backpack to the library—carrying all my books and clothes at once would make the clerk at the front desk suspicious—but I managed to hide everything deep within the stacks. I was a mess, drenched in sweat, and my hair matted against my scalp, and still filthy from field training. In the restroom, I splashed water onto my face and into my armpits. My shirt was soaked, and after I leaned against the sink, the crotch of my pants too, as though I'd peed myself. When the door swung open, I hid in a stall, trembling. Opprobrium.

My sister had relented and promised to keep quiet, but I had to find another place to live within a few days, before Parents' Weekend started on Friday. When I canvassed dorms in search of roommates, people weren't as friendly to strangers, not like the beginning of the year. Cliques had formed. Eventually, I might find a way in, though not before my family arrived.

My routine saved me. Although I could have stopped going to class and ROTC, I would have had too much time to think about Julia, and how she'd turned her back on me. Blessed with so much, she'd accomplish everything she set out to do. I'd slip into insignificance, a footnote, if anyone remembered me at all.

I saw her once, by an ATM at Tresidder, and debated whether if I should confront her, or convince her to take me back in. When Scott showed up with smoothies, we locked eyes. After he kissed the top of her head, I bolted. Her—his—their rejection felt like Stanford rejecting me all over again. Everything here was sunnier and brighter, with an ease that blinded people, that made them forget about imperfection and turned them heartless.

The day before Parents' Weekend began, the notification arrived from Admissions. I logged onto the portal, feeling as though no time had passed, as if I were again a high school senior on the cusp. The screen flashed. "It is with great regret that we are unable to offer you admission ... you are a fine student ... want to thank you for your interest ... "

Denied. Everything, everything, for nothing. I didn't belong at Stanford, never did and never would, in limbo, not here or anywhere, not of the present and lacking a future. Denied. I must have logged off, must have exited the library but what I remembered next was Jack, my classmate from high school, calling my name. He rolled up on his bike. I hadn't seen him much, except in big pre-med classes, and by mutual unspoken agreement we never sat together. He'd gone preppy, with floppy bangs, khakis and untucked button-downs after joining an Asian frat. He mentioned that our parents were driving up together and would take us to lunch tomorrow at a Korean restaurant.

The news of my deceit would spread through the church, among the only people my parents trusted.

"You can wait a day, can't you?" He grinned.

"I haven't had Korean food since winter break," I said weakly.

After we parted, I narrowly avoided a collision with another cyclist and a wooden bollard. No one loved me like my parents, and I'd returned their love with lies. I collapsed in the grass, watching students and professors zooming by on their bikes, and joggers in sunglasses in tight, shiny workout gear pounding past.

I couldn't stop my parents. But I could stop Parents' Weekend.

Though people here pretended to be laid-back, they couldn't, wouldn't be stopped from reaching their destination. Calling in a bomb threat wouldn't be enough. The situation called for something bigger, something louder, a credible threat, of the kind we'd been studying in ROTC: insurgency.

* * *

Everything fell into place, except for one detail, one that had nothing to do with what I planned but explained everything I'd been driven to do. Minutes before dawn, I crept outside my old dorm, where I found the window cracked open and the room empty. After crawling inside, I searched for the picture on the corkboard of me and Julia lip-syncing, the only hard evidence of my months here.

Gone. Trashed, like she'd trashed me.

The room phone rang and rang, but I didn't answer. Julia's cell phone buzzed, forgotten and left charging on the floor, and when I noticed the caller ID indicating her mother, I answered. I'd been making excuses for

Julia for so long, I couldn't stop. Mrs. Ramirez said they were starting their drive and wanted to know if Julia needed anything. For a second, I almost said she was at Scott's. Mrs. Ramirez didn't know her daughter was hooking up with Scott, who Scott was, or that he wasn't much for relationships, but I said Julia was on the water, and promised to leave a note.

I stared at the background photo on the phone, her and Tina, their heads tilted together, eyes crossed, sticking out their tongues. Friends, best friends. Julia was certain of her love, and her family's, certain about everything, everyone but Scott. The tighter she clung, the more he pulled away, and if she lost him, then she might feel as abandoned as I did.

From her phone, I texted Scott: "I love you." Now we were even.

* * *

The sky was lightening. In the center of campus, nothing stirred but squirrels. At the base of a palm tree outside the Registrar's, I planted a liter bottle of gasoline stuffed with strips of a tee shirt. The golden gasoline sloshed back and forth, a storm in a bottle. Back home, palm trees were common, but not like the ones on campus, which were rumored to cost a year's tuition. The fronds were lush, a country club's, and fallen ones whisked away before they hit the ground.

I heard the whine of an electric cart, I ducked behind a post, and a groundskeeper went by. I'd have to hurry. I set down the letter, sealed in a clear plastic bag and held in place with a brick. Though I'd written it at end of a very long night, the words had rushed out, with the inspiration I wished for in my college entrance essays. I ranted against rich kids and the parents who spoiled them, acting like they owned the world. Like they were the world itself. I taunted them, implying I'd scattered booby traps and bombs around campus.

Dousing the tree with gasoline, I lit the wick, which sputtered with the delicious hiss of a lawn sprinkler. The syrupy fumes made me giddy with the happiness I once thought I might achieve here. In White Plaza, I left another copy of the letter and lit a second firebomb.

I might have predicted the investigation, news stories, the online fan pages—"Elaine Park rocks!" At the jail, my mother in near-collapse, propped up by my sister. Her face, awful and old, marked by grief as all her hard years had never marked her. My father asking why, not in Korean, not in SAT words, but in the plain English he reserved for customers. For strangers. His hope—his hope in me—would do me in. "I can't," I would say, my voice breaking. "I can't lie anymore."

His caved-in expression. "You have to tell everyone the truth. Telling me won't help."

Yet if I had been thinking clearly and stopped, if I had retreated, I would have missed the moment when I became mighty and billowing. The smoke drifted into the stratosphere with the crackle and roar of a wildfire. The dizzying smell of gasoline, of charcoal, of ash come alive. The flaming palm tree the most spectacular of all. An enormous Fourth of July sparkler, a gold-orange celebration burning on and on, a monument, a memory that would far outlast my time here.

CHIMAMANDA NGOZI ADICHIE

The Thing Around Your Neck

You thought everybody in America had a car and a gun; your uncles and aunts and cousins thought so, too. Right after you won the American visa lottery, they told you: In a month, you will have a big car. Soon, a big house. But don't buy a gun like those Americans.

They trooped into the room in Lagos where you lived with your father and mother and three siblings, leaning against the unpainted walls because there weren't enough chairs to go round, to say goodbye in loud voices and tell you with lowered voices what they wanted you to send them. In comparison to the big car and house (and possibly gun), the things they wanted were minor—handbags and shoes and perfumes and clothes. You said okay, no problem.

Your uncle in America, who had put in the names of all your family members for the American visa lottery, said you could live with him until you got on your feet. He picked you up at the airport and bought you a big hot dog with yellow mustard that nauseated you. Introduction to America, he said with a laugh. He lived in a small white town in Maine, in a thirty-year-old house by a lake. He told you that the company he worked for had offered him a few thousand more than the average salary plus stock options because they were desperately trying to look diverse. They included a photo of him in every brochure, even those that had nothing to do with his unit. He laughed and said the job was good, was worth living in an all-white town even though his wife had to drive an hour to find a hair salon that did black hair. The trick was to understand America, to know that America was give-and-take. You gave up a lot but you gained a lot, too.

He showed you how to apply for a cashier job in the gas station on Main Street and he enrolled you in a community college, where the girls had thick thighs and wore bright-red nail polish, and self-tanner that made them look orange. They asked where you learned to speak English and if you had real houses back in Africa and if you'd seen a car before you came to America. They gawped at your hair. Does it stand up or fall down when you take out the braids? They wanted to know. All of it stands up? How? Why? Do you use a comb? You smiled tightly when they asked those questions. Your uncle told you to expect it; a mixture of ignorance and arrogance, he called it. Then he told you how the neighbors said, a few months after he moved into his house, that the squirrels had started to disappear. They had heard that Africans ate all kinds of wild animals.

You laughed with your uncle and you felt at home in his house; his wife called you *nwanne,* sister, and his two school-age children called you Aunty. They spoke Igbo and ate *garri* for lunch and it was like home. Until your uncle came into the cramped basement where you slept with old boxes and cartons and pulled you forcefully to him, squeezing your buttocks, moaning. He wasn't really your uncle; he was actually a brother of your father's sister's husband, not related by blood. After you pushed him away, he sat on your bed—it was his house, after all—and smiled and said you were no longer a child at twenty-two. If you let him, he would do many things for you. Smart women did it all the time. How did you think those women back home in Lagos with well-paying jobs made it? Even women in New York City?

You locked yourself in the bathroom until he went back upstairs, and the next morning, you left, walking the long windy road, smelling the baby fish in the lake. You saw him drive past—he had always dropped you off at Main Street—and he didn't honk. You wondered what he would tell his wife, why you had left. And you remembered what he said, that America was give-and-take.

You ended up in Connecticut, in another little town, because it was the last stop of the Greyhound bus you got on. You walked into the restaurant with the bright, clean awning and said you would work for two dollars less than the other waitresses. The manager, Juan, had inky-black hair and smiled to show a gold tooth. He said he had never had a Nigerian employee but all immigrants worked hard. He knew, he'd been there. He'd pay you a dollar less, but under the table; he didn't like all the taxes they were making him pay.

You could not afford to go to school, because now you paid rent for the tiny room with the stained carpet. Besides, the small Connecticut town didn't have a community college and credits at the state university cost too much. So you went to the public library, you looked up course syllabi on school Web sites and read some of the books. Sometimes you sat on the lumpy mattress of your twin bed and thought about home—your aunts who hawked dried fish and plantains, cajoling customers to buy and then shouting insults when they didn't; your uncles who drank local gin and crammed their families and lives into single rooms; your friends who had come out to say goodbye before you left, to rejoice because you won the American visa lottery, to confess their envy; your parents who often held hands as they walked to church on Sunday mornings, the neighbors from the next room laughing and teasing them; your father who brought back his boss's old newspapers from work and made your brothers read them; your mother whose salary was barely enough to pay your brothers' school fees at the secondary school where teachers gave an A when someone slipped them a brown envelope.

You had never needed to pay for an A, never slipped a brown envelope to a teacher in secondary school. Still, you chose long brown envelopes to send half your month's earnings to your parents at the address of the parastatal where your mother was a cleaner; you always used the dollar notes that Juan gave you because those were crisp, unlike the tips. Every month. You wrapped the money carefully in white paper but you didn't write a letter. There was nothing to write about.

In later weeks, though, you wanted to write because you had stories to tell. You wanted to write about the surprising openness of people in America, how eagerly they told you about their mother fighting cancer, about their sister-in-law's preemie, the kinds of things that one should hide or should reveal only to the family members who wished them well. You wanted to write about the way people left so much food on their plates and crumpled a few dollar bills down, as though it was an offering, expiation for the wasted food. You wanted to write about the child who started to cry and pull at her blond hair and push the menus off the table and instead of the parents making her shut up, they pleaded with her, a child of perhaps five years old, and then they all got up and left. You wanted to write about the rich people who wore shabby clothes and tattered sneakers, who looked like the night watchmen in front of the large compounds in Lagos. You wanted to write that rich Americans were thin and poor Americans were fat and that many did not have a big house and car; you still were not sure about the guns, though, because they might have them inside their pockets.

It wasn't just to your parents you wanted to write, it was also to your friends, and cousins and aunts and uncles. But you could never afford enough perfumes and clothes and handbags and shoes to go around and still pay your rent on what you earned at the waitressing job, so you wrote nobody.

Nobody knew where you were, because you told no one. Sometimes you felt invisible and tried to walk through your room wall into the hallway, and when you bumped into the wall, it left bruises on your arms. Once, Juan asked if you had a man that hit you because he would take care of him and you laughed a mysterious laugh.

At night, something would wrap itself around your neck, something that very nearly choked you before you fell asleep.

Many people at the restaurant asked when you had come from Jamaica, because they thought that every black person with a foreign accent was Jamaican. Or some who guessed that you were African told you that they loved elephants and wanted to go on a safari.

So when he asked you, in the dimness of the restaurant after you recited the daily specials, what African country you were from, you said Nigeria and expected him to say that he had donated money to fight AIDS in Botswana. But he asked if you were Yoruba or Igbo, because you didn't have a Fulani face. You were surprised—you thought he must be a professor of anthropology at the state university, a little young in his late twenties or so, but who was to say? Igbo, you said. He asked your name and said Akunna was pretty. He did not ask what it meant, fortunately, because you were sick of how people said, "'Father's Wealth'? You mean, like, your father will actually sell you to a husband?"

He told you he had been to Ghana and Uganda and Tanzania, loved the poetry of Okot p'Bitek and the novels of Amos Tutuola and had read a lot about sub-Saharan African countries, their histories, their complexities. You wanted to feel disdain, to show it as you brought his order, because white people who liked Africa too much and those who liked Africa too little were the same—condescending. But he didn't shake his head in the superior way that Professor Cobbledick back in the Maine community college did during a class discussion on decolonization in Africa. He didn't have that expression of Professor Cobbledick's, that expression of a person who thought himself better than the people he knew about. He came in the next day and sat at the same table and when you asked if the chicken was okay, he asked if you had grown up in Lagos. He came in the third day and began talking before he ordered, about how he had visited Bombay and now wanted to visit Lagos, to see how real people lived, like in the shantytowns, because he never did any of the silly tourist stuff when he was abroad. He talked and talked and you had to tell him it was against restaurant policy. He brushed your hand when you set the glass of water down. The fourth day, when you saw him arrive, you told Juan you didn't want that table anymore. After your shift that night, he was waiting outside, earphones stuck in his ears, asking you to go out with him because your name rhymed with *hakuna matata* and *The Lion King* was the only maudlin movie he'd ever liked. You didn't know what *The Lion King* was. You looked at him in the bright light and noticed that his eyes were the color of extra-virgin olive oil, a greenish gold. Extra-virgin olive oil was the only thing you loved, truly loved, in America.

He was a senior at the state university. He told you how old he was and you asked why he had not graduated yet. This was America, after all, it was not like back home, where universities closed so often that people added three years to their normal course of study and lecturers went on strike after strike and still were not paid. He said he had taken a couple of years off to discover himself and travel, mostly to Africa and Asia. You asked him where he ended up finding himself and he laughed. You did not laugh. You did not know that people could simply choose not to go to school, that people could dictate to life. You were used to accepting what life gave, writing down what life dictated.

You said no the following four days to going out with him, because you were uncomfortable with the way he looked at your face, that intense, consuming way he looked at your face that made you say goodbye to him but also made you reluctant to walk away. And then, the fifth night, you panicked when he was not standing at the door after your shift. You prayed for the first time in a long time and when he came up behind you and said hey, you said yes, you would go out with him, even before he asked. You were scared he would not ask again.

The next day, he took you to dinner at Chang's and your fortune cookie had two strips of paper. Both of them were blank.

You knew you had become comfortable when you told him that you watched *Jeopardy* on the restaurant TV and that you rooted for the following, in this order: women of color, black men, and white women, before, finally, white men—which meant you never rooted for white men. He laughed and told you he was used to not being rooted for, his mother taught women's studies.

And you knew you had become close when you told him that your father was really not a schoolteacher in Lagos, that he was a junior driver for a construction company. And you told him about that day in Lagos traffic in the rickety Peugeot 504 your father drove; it was raining and your seat was wet because of the rust-eaten hole in the roof. The traffic was heavy, the traffic was always heavy in Lagos, and when it rained it was chaos. The roads became muddy ponds and cars got stuck and some of your cousins went out and made some money pushing the cars out. The rain, the swampiness, you thought, made your father step on the brakes too late that day. You heard the bump before you felt it. The car your father rammed into was wide, foreign, and dark green, with golden headlights like the eyes of a leopard. Your father started to cry and beg even before he got out of the car and laid himself flat on the road, causing much blowing of horns. Sorry sir, sorry sir, he chanted. If you sell me and my family, you cannot buy even one tire on your car. Sorry sir.

The Big Man seated at the back did not come out, but his driver did, examining the damage, looking at your father's sprawled form from the corner of his eye as though the pleading was like pornography, a performance he was ashamed to admit he enjoyed. At last he let your father go. Waved him away. The other cars' horns blew and drivers cursed. When your father came back into the car, you refused to look at him because he was just like the pigs that wallowed in the marshes around the market. Your father looked like *nsi*. Shit.

After you told him this, he pursed his lips and held your hand and said he understood how you felt. You shook your hand free, suddenly annoyed, because he thought the world was, or ought to be, full of people like him. You told him there was nothing to understand, it was just the way it was.

He found the African store in the Hartford yellow pages and drove you there. Because of the way he walked around with familiarity, tilting the bottle of palm wine, to see how much sediment it had, the Ghanaian store owner asked him if he was African, like the white Kenyans or South Africans, and he said yes, but he'd been in America for a long time. He looked pleased that the store owner had believed him. You cooked that evening with the things you had bought, and after he ate *garri* and *onugbu* soup, he threw up in your sink. You didn't mind, though, because now you would be able to cook *onugbu* soup with meat.

He didn't eat meat because he thought it was wrong the way they killed animals; he said they released fear toxins into the animals and the fear toxins made people paranoid. Back home, the meat pieces you ate, when there was meat, were the size of half your finger. But you did not tell him that. You did not tell him either that the *dawadawa* cubes your mother cooked everything with, because curry and thyme were too expensive, had MSG, *were* MSG. He said MSG caused cancer, it was the reason he liked Chang's; Chang didn't cook with MSG.

Once, at Chang's, he told the waiter he had recently visited Shanghai, that he spoke some Mandarin. The waiter warmed up and told him what soup was best and then asked him, "You have girlfriend in Shanghai now?" And he smiled and said nothing.

You lost your appetite, the region deep in your chest felt clogged. That night, you didn't moan when he was inside you, you bit your lips and pretended that you didn't come because you knew he would worry. Later you told him why you were upset, that even though you went to Chang's so often together, even though you had kissed just before the menus came, the Chinese man had assumed you could not possibly be his girlfriend, and he had smiled and said nothing. Before he apologized, he gazed at you blankly and you knew that he did not understand.

He bought you presents and when you objected about the cost, he said his grandfather in Boston had been wealthy but hastily added that the old man had given a lot away and so the trust fund he had wasn't huge. His presents mystified you. A fist-size glass ball that you shook to watch a tiny, shapely doll in pink spin around. A shiny rock whose surface took on the color of whatever touched it. An expensive scarf hand-painted in Mexico. Finally you told him, your voice stretched in irony, that in your life presents were always useful. The rock, for instance, would work if you could grind things with it. He laughed long and hard but you did not laugh. You realized that in his life, he could buy presents that were just presents and nothing else, nothing useful. When he started to buy you shoes and clothes and books, you asked him not to, you didn't want any presents at all. He bought them anyway and you kept them for your cousins and uncles and aunts, for when you would one day be able to visit home, even though you did not know how you could ever afford a ticket *and* your rent. He said he really wanted to see Nigeria and he could pay for you both to go. You did not want him to pay for you to visit home. You did not want him to go to Nigeria, to add it to the list of countries where he went to gawk at the lives of poor people who could never gawk back at *his* life. You told him this on a sunny day, when he took you to see Long Island Sound, and the two of you argued, your voices raised as you walked along the calm water. He said you were wrong to call him self-righteous. You said he was wrong to call only the poor Indians in Bombay the real Indians. Did it mean he wasn't a real American, since he was not like the poor fat people you and he had seen in Hartford? He hurried ahead of you, his upper body bare and pale, his flip-flops raising bits of sand, but then he came back and held out his hand for yours. You made up and made love and ran your hands through each other's hair, his soft and yellow like the swinging tassels of growing corn, yours dark and bouncy like the filling of a pillow. He had got too much sun and his skin turned the color of a ripe watermelon and you kissed his back before you rubbed lotion on it.

The thing that wrapped itself around your neck, that nearly choked you before you fell asleep, started to loosen, to let go.

You knew by people's reactions that you two were abnormal—the way the nasty ones were too nasty and the nice ones too nice. The old white men and women who muttered and glared at him, the black men who shook their heads at you, the black women whose pitying eyes bemoaned your lack of self-esteem, your self-loathing. Or the black women who smiled swift solidarity smiles; the black men who tried too hard to forgive you, saying a too-obvious hi to him; the white men and women who said "What a good-looking pair" too brightly, too loudly, as though to prove their own open-mindedness to themselves.

But his parents were different; they almost made you think it was all normal. His mother told you that he had never brought a girl to meet them, except for his high school prom date, and he grinned stiffly and held your hand. The tablecloth shielded your clasped hands. He squeezed your hand and you squeezed back and wondered why he was so stiff, why his extra-virgin-olive-oil-colored eyes darkened as he spoke to his parents. His mother was delighted when she asked if you'd read Nawal el Saadawi and you said yes. His father asked how similar Indian food was to Nigerian food and teased you about paying when the check came. You looked at them and felt grateful that they did not examine you like an exotic trophy, an ivory tusk.

Afterwards, he told you about his issues with his parents, how they portioned out love like a birthday cake, how they would give him a bigger slice if only he'd agree to go to law school. You wanted to sympathize. But instead you were angry.

You were angrier when he told you he had refused to go up to Canada with them for a week or two, to their summer cottage in the Quebec countryside. They had even asked him to bring you. He showed you pictures of the cottage and you wondered why it was called a cottage because the buildings that big around your neighborhood back home were banks and churches. You dropped a glass and it shattered on the hardwood of his apartment floor and he asked what was wrong and you said nothing, although you thought a lot was wrong. Later, in the shower, you started to cry. You watched the water dilute your tears and you didn't know why you were crying.

You wrote home finally. A short letter to your parents, slipped in between the crisp dollar bills, and you included your address. You got a reply only days later, by courier. Your mother wrote he letter herself; you knew from the spidery penmanship, from the misspelled words.

Your father was dead; he had slumped over the steering wheel of his company car. Five months now, she wrote. They had used some of the money you sent to give him a good funeral: They killed a goat for the guests and buried him in a good coffin. You curled up in bed, pressed your knees to your chest, and tried to remember what you had been doing when your father died, what you had been doing for all the months when he was already dead. Perhaps your father died on the day your whole body had been covered in goosebumps, hard as uncooked rice, that you could not explain, Juan teasing you about taking over from the chef so that the heat in the kitchen would warm you up. Perhaps your father died on one of the days you took a drive to Mystic or watched a play in Manchester or had dinner at Chang's.

He held you while you cried, smoothed your hair, and offered to buy your ticket, to go with you to see your family. You said no, you needed to go alone. He asked if you would come back and you reminded him that you had a green card and you would lose it if you did not come back in one year. He said you knew what he meant, would you come back, come back?

You turned away and said nothing, and when he drove you to the airport, you hugged him tight for a long, long moment, and then you let go.

ROBERT ANTHONY SIEGEL

The Right Imaginary Person

We were part of a large group of people at a *yakitoriya* in Shinjuku, celebrating somebody or other's birthday, but we'd both gotten stuck at the wrong end of the long table, cut off from the main conversation, which was drunken and flirty. "I bet everyone tells you how great your Japanese is," she said, lighting a cigarette.

"They do," I acknowledged.

"Then let's talk about something else."

It was 1985, almost the end of summer. Sumiko told me she was nearing the end of a long, boring adolescent period in which she was trying to become the opposite of her mother. She didn't want to become a good cook, or keep the house clean, or be loved by children—or be nice to anyone, for that matter—or cultivate any of the traditional arts expected of a young lady of marriageable age from a good family. "Calligraphy?" she said. "Can you think of anything more boring? And flower arranging? It makes me want to throw up." Instead she drank a sort of white lightning called *shōchō* and smoked Golden Bat cigarettes and wrote science fiction stories in which androids took on unplanned human emotions, slept with each other, had imaginary pregnancies, and gave birth to children that were strings of computer code.

"But what about you?" she asked. "It's not fair if you don't tell me anything."

I looked at her hand, the delicate fingers smudged with ink. There were nights when I rode the Yamanote Line in a circle, jammed against the other passengers, just to feel someone else's pressure on my skin.

But what I told her about was my trip to Shikoku, how I went alone with a backpack over the vacation, taking old buses from village to village, and how in one of those villages a group of kids had formed a circle around me and asked to touch my hair. I had kneeled down on the grass beside the road, closed my eyes, and felt their hands running over my head. Small, gentle hands reading my otherness like braille.

"Was that creepy?" she asked.

"No, it felt deep."

Later, after the party broke up, I walked her to the train station, and in the shadows by the entrance where I was going to ask for her phone number she unexpectedly reached up and brushed my bangs from my face. "It does feel a little different," she said. "Softer than Japanese hair."

We went to her place, a six-mat *tatami* room with a little kitchen she never used and a single window that looked out on the courtyard in back. We stood in the middle of the tiny space and kissed, bodies slowly softening like candles. Her mouth tasted like *shōchō* and smoke. She pulled off her shirt and her breasts were in my palms, the nipples long and thick, the color of chocolate. And then she was melting to the *tatami,* pulling me down on top of her. With each touch of her hand I felt like I was being sewn back together.

Afterward, we bathed in her tub, which was square and deep, the water so hot that her hand on my thigh felt like a bruise. Then we stretched out naked on top of her futon, and I watched the steam rise from her body into the air. She had a mole in the hollow at the base of her neck, a small half-moon scar on her calf, and silver polish on her toes. "Do you ever get homesick?" she asked.

"Never," I said, though of course I did. A part of my mind was stuck roaming the big Victorian my parents had so painstakingly restored and now left only when they had to, for the pharmacy or the liquor store.

"I don't think I could live in a foreign country," said Sumiko. "I get lonely too easily, and then I end up doing things like this."

Resting her head on my chest, she read me a story she'd written about a group of children who live in a colony on another planet and are taken care of by parents who are nothing but computer-generated holograms. The story wasn't science fiction at all, or not what I thought of as science fiction; it felt honest and emotional, full of the yearning to touch and the sadness of not being real. "That's just so beautiful," I said, thinking of the letters I wrote to my parents, packed with fabrications about my life in Tokyo: how I had discovered an ancient scroll with the work of a lost poet; how I had an audience with the emperor and he handed me a silver tray of bonbons with his own hands, scandalizing the officials around us... I never actually mailed those letters, just collected them in a box in the closet.

"The secret is to pretend you're someone else," said Sumiko, taking my fingers from her hair and holding them in her hand, kissing them one by one. "You can't be the person who worries what other people think."

"Who's left then?"

"The imaginary person who tells the truth."

The next day, I left the library early, went to the market, and carried the groceries to her place, where I made dinner using the one pan that she owned. While I cooked she read me a story about an alien race that is being destroyed by a plague of dreams so beautiful that the sleeper refuses to wake. The cure for this plague can only be made from the hearts of human children who have never known love, so a scientist is sent to Earth to collect as many sad orphan hearts as she can. Wearing the body of a teenage girl like a space suit, she goes from orphanage to orphanage, killing children and extracting their hearts, even as spring comes to Tokyo, the cherry trees bloom, people get drunk in the park, and the last signal from her planet dies away forever.

Sumiko didn't have a table, so we ate at the lovely Japanese-style desk where she did her writing—sitting side by side and looking out the window at the evening light blueing the courtyard. "Do you ever feel like the alien in your story?" I asked.

"Sometimes," she said.

I thought of the children in Shikoku, how they had touched my hair and run off, leaving me at a bus stop that was nothing but a patch of grass by the roadside. "I never realized Japanese people got lonely in that way."

"You speak the language, but you don't know anything about real Japanese."

"You're a real Japanese, and I know you."

"That's what I like about you, that you need me so badly. You're a being from another planet, and I'm your human guide, like in a sci-fi movie." She rested her hand on my knee, very lightly. "I want to be the only one on Earth who understands you," she said.

"It's not like there's a lot of competition." But I could feel something happening inside me, a slowing down, like when the kids touched my hair.

"And I want *you* to be the only one who understands *me*," she said.

"I would like that."

She gave a little laugh. "No, you wouldn't, not really. If you did, you'd realize this is all just playacting."

"What is?"

"All of this—dinner, my stories, you and me. In less than a year I'll graduate from school and get a job teaching kindergarten in some suburb or other while looking for an eligible man to marry."

"You don't have to do what everyone else is doing."

"Resistance is futile in a country like this, because the thing you reject isn't just out there, it's in here." She tapped her head. "Obedience is encoded in us through two thousand years of inbreeding."

"Are you saying that you are genetically unable to stop yourself from becoming a kindergarten teacher?"

"Can a sunflower refuse to follow the sun? Can a girl refuse to grow breasts?" She got up and placed the notebook with her story back in the bookcase: four shelves of cheap notebooks dating back to grade school, their covers imprinted with red hearts or Hello Kitty cartoons. "You'll never understand," she said, running her finger over the spines. "You don't want to."

Sumiko wasn't completely wrong; deep down I couldn't understand. That made her furious and she broke up with me often, usually late at night, when the trains had stopped running and I had to walk two hours back to my place. I'd call and leave messages, and we'd meet the next day, or the day after that, to argue and then kiss so that we could see how exactly we fit together, her body pressed to mine.

But one night in February I looked up from my book and found her observing me with a hard, clinical expression, as if I were a beetle and she were going to pin me to a board. "I know what the problem is," she said.

"What problem?" I asked.

"You think I'm ugly."

Sumiko looked like she'd come off a scroll from the Heian period, the era of aristocratic women in flowing robes and long hair: a pale round face, full lips, and eyebrows so elegant I would sometimes trace them with my finger. "That's ridiculous," I said.

"I've been teased all my life about my fat face."

I had no idea that her looks weren't the general ideal anymore, that they hadn't been the ideal for about a thousand years. "I think you're beautiful," I told her.

I could see that she knew I meant it, and that she despised me for it. "That's because you're a foreigner and don't really know what Japanese women are supposed to look like."

"So you think you're ugly too?"

"Obviously."

"And what does that make me?" I asked, not sure I had a right to be hurt when the subject was her looks.

"Blind."

The walk home was so cold that it felt like ice crystals were forming inside my heart. I couldn't erase the look of contempt Sumiko had given me. Back in my tiny four-mat room, I lay shivering under the quilts, unable to sleep, and then in the empty space before dawn I began thinking about my sister, Daisy, remembering how I'd stood in our backyard in New Jersey and watched her climb out of her bedroom window onto the roof of the house to scream at her boyfriend. *That's right, you better run,* she yelled down at him as he jogged across the grass toward the gate. *You better fucking run.* She stood at the very edge of the roof, giving him the finger with both hands, and when he was gone she lay down on the black shingles, her arms and legs spread as if claiming space.

"Hey," I yelled up.

"Leave me alone."

She was vice president of the drama club at school, and still bitter about losing the presidency. She wrapped scarves around her neck and played dress up and made faces in the mirror: her Marilyn Monroe face, her Jean-Paul Belmondo face, with a cigarette drooping from the corner of her mouth. She had a maddening way of narrowing her eyes at me, as if she knew something about adulthood that she wasn't telling. She wrote messages to herself in felt-tip pen on her arms—*Only 10 miles to Broadway, you can walk if you have to.* She was seventeen, and I was fourteen, and we'd just found out that she would need another round of chemo.

I got up and called Sumiko and left a long, rambling message—left messages every day for a week till she finally picked up the phone. "I'm angry at you because you left," she said to me.

"You told me to leave."

"If you really loved me, you would have found a way to convince me to let you stay."

I was sitting with my legs in my *kotatsu*, a little table with an electric heat lamp on the bottom, surrounded by a quilted skirt to hold in the warmth. A half-finished letter was spread on the Formica tabletop, destined, like all the others, for the pile in the box. I'd taken Sumiko's advice and pretended someone else was writing it, one of my professors, an elderly man with a vague manner and white chalk dust on his baggy suit. *Dear Mr. and Mrs. Nussbaum,* it ran, *I regret to inform you that your*

son, Benjamin, seems to have fallen ill. He sits in the library with a book in
front of him, but he never turns the page . . .

I'd picked that professor because he always seemed so serene, sipping
tea in his little office, which was lined with novels in three languages. But
I'd clearly made some kind of mistake. He could tell you the plot of every
story by Balzac or Chekhov or Tanizaki, but he couldn't explain why I'd
suddenly begun remembering my sister, particularly the last few months
of her illness. I'd tried to make him write to my parents about her, about
the way she looked sitting in the big armchair in her hospital room, her
head tilted to the side, her eyes closed, resting in the sun coming through
the window. Her face was all eyes by then. I got up to go for a walk—anything to get out of that room. "Stay," she said, and I sat back down.

I'd wanted the professor to tell my parents all of that, everything, but
each time he lifted his pen, the words disappeared.

"Remember what you said to me about an imaginary person writing
your stories?" I asked Sumiko.

"Why are you asking me this when we have serious things to discuss
about you and me and this relationship?"

"How do you know it's the right imaginary person?"

I heard her light a cigarette, as if considering the question, but what
she finally said was, "My parents want to meet you."

She'd told me once that if she ever brought a foreigner home her father
would probably force her to leave school and move back to Kamakura.
"Do you think meeting them is a good idea?" I asked.

"Don't you think it's time?"

I'd heard her talk to them over the phone at night: conversations
about relatives and school and her internship at the kindergarten. I'd
stop whatever I was doing and watch her press the receiver to her ear
with her shoulder. She'd be in nothing but a towel, shaving her legs or
rubbing in moisturizer or brushing her hair as she talked, her face slowly
changing back to some earlier version of herself: placid and contented,
the face of a girl.

"Your parents aren't going to like me," I said.

"They need to know who *I* like."

We took the train out to Kamakura that Saturday afternoon, carrying overnight bags. I'd cut myself shaving—a long, stinging cut too big
for a Band-Aid. It had occurred to me that meeting the parents must
mean something more than it did in New Jersey, but I didn't want to
think about that. Instead, as the endless suburbs rolled by the window,

I practiced with the flash cards I'd made, each one containing a polite phrase I'd found in an old grammar book, the sort of phrase so arcane, so excessively, self-abasingly polite that it was almost never used anymore, even by the most punctilious of native speakers.

"You don't have to worry," said Sumiko. "Just be yourself and everything will be fine." She was dressed in a prim outfit I'd never seen before: wool tights, a gray flannel skirt and cashmere sweater, a string of pearls, a headband. She lit the end of one cigarette with another all the way to Kamakura, and then threw out the remainder of the pack as we pulled into the station. "Just don't say anything about me smoking or drinking or you staying over at my place," she told me.

"I'm not an idiot."

"And don't say anything about my writing, either."

"They don't know about that?"

"Of course not."

Sumiko's parents were bigger, bulkier versions of her, with the same round faces and elegant eyebrows. They ushered us into the family car and took us to an ancient Buddhist monastery, where we walked the grounds, pretending to sightsee, our breath making steam in the air. Gravel paths, delicate wooden temples that seemed to sit weightlessly, like birds ready to take flight: the place was so beautiful that it felt otherworldly, and that aura transferred to Sumiko's parents, who looked as if it all belonged to them, as surely as their camel-hair coats and kid-leather gloves. I walked beside them with a mixture of anxiety and hunger, waiting for a chance to use one of the phrases from my flash cards, waiting for the chance to be loved. Sumiko kept close, pitching in with the small talk, but after a while she drifted off with her mother, the two of them talking together in low, conspiratorial voices. Her father turned to me, smiling. "They've left us alone for a man-to-man talk, haven't they?" His tone was bemused, but I could see that it was put on for my sake, a form of delicacy.

"You are far too kind to an undeserving wretch like myself," I said, finally using one of the flash-card phrases.

"What marvelous Japanese," he said, giving an embarrassed little laugh. "I understand you plan to become a professor?"

"Yes, that's my intention." But as soon as I heard the words out loud I knew that I wouldn't, that I would never be able to follow through. I didn't want to do anything but watch the late movie with Sumiko, and listen to her stories, and run out and buy roast potatoes from the cart pushed by the old man with the plaintive call.

"And will you seek a post here, or in America?"

"Here, definitely."

He fell silent, and I listened to the gravel crunch underfoot as we walked, waiting for him to tell me that I was full of shit and he knew it. But he just kept smiling his troubled smile, and a moment later we had rejoined the women. They were examining a line of stone Buddhas, heartbreakingly beautiful things worn smooth by the years, stippled with yellow lichen. "Lovely, aren't they?" said Sumiko's mother.

"So peaceful," I said, looking at their bald heads and serene baby faces, their eyes closed against the world. They were images of the Buddha called Jizō, guardian of children and travelers. I'd seen smaller versions of them now and then at the side of the road, marking the spot of a traffic fatality, or in temple cemeteries, pinwheels and plastic toys left by their feet as offerings.

"It's getting late," said Sumiko's father, looking at his watch.

"We should probably head home for dinner," said Sumiko's mother, and the four of us started up the path, walking slowly in the falling light. After a little way, I veered off to examine a stone marker, pretending to read the characters running down the side but really watching the others as they continued on: Sumiko between her mother and father, her father with his hands behind his back, her mother gripping her pocketbook. They had that aura families have, of existing in a self-enclosed world, tucked inside this one but separate. At the big front gate, they turned back to view the grounds, looking as if they'd momentarily forgotten my presence.

Sumiko's parents fussed over me during dinner, her mother picking out the best things and putting them on my plate, her father filling and refilling my glass with beer, both of them asking questions about my family back home. I had no choice but to tell them about my father, the math professor; my mother, the cruciverbalist, meaning a designer of crossword puzzles. But I didn't tell them that my sister had died when I was sixteen, and that the remainder of the Nussbaums had never quite recovered the ability to speak to each other. I didn't mention the antidepressants and the anti-anxiety meds and the sleeping pills and the time my mother took too many by accident and we had to call an ambulance.

"And do you have any brothers or sisters?" asked Sumiko's father, finally, smiling his patient smile.

"No, I'm an only child."

"It must be hard for your parents, having you so far away," said Sumiko's mother, choosing yet more things for me with the long chopsticks used for serving.

"I write to them all the time."

Her face was like Sumiko's, but with deep creases around the eyes, which were humorous and kind and disappointed all at once. "I don't think we could stand Sumiko being so far. I'd worry too much."

"Even Tokyo's too far," said Sumiko's father, pouring me more beer. "But then a girl's different from a boy."

I glanced over at Sumiko to see how she was taking this. She sat by her mother, a glass of tea cupped in her hands, nothing showing on her face.

I excused myself to go to the bathroom, but really just wandered the house, trying to breathe. Down a long polished hall, I came across Sumiko's old bedroom, a Japanese version of my sister's: anime posters on the walls, shelves with dolls and stuffed animals, a shoe box full of mix tapes.

That night, Sumiko slept in her old bedroom, seemingly a world away. I slept in the guest room, which, like the rest of the house, expensive and elegant, smelled of new *tatami* and varnished wood. But I couldn't really sleep, and I kept imagining that I heard Sumiko's footsteps coming down the hall, forbidden and dangerous. Eventually I got up and went to the window to look at the moon, which was just a cold sliver.

In the last year of her life, my sister and I used to sneak out onto the roof of our house at night to smoke weed. This was in Leonia, New Jersey, right across the George Washington Bridge from Manhattan, in a neighborhood of big oaks and old Victorians restored by a generation in search of cheap real estate—our parents and their friends. Daisy and I made a big show of turning up our noses at their hand-painted Italian kitchen tile, their charcoal water filters and basement radon detectors, their inexpensive but highly drinkable wines—everything they used to convince themselves that they were exempt from the dangers outside. We would climb out the bay window and sit on the rough black shingles, looking up at the spray of stars above our heads, feeling the rush of the river beyond the black silhouettes of the trees, and beyond that the dense presence of the city, where life really happened. We never talked much; we had already picked up the habit of silence. We would pass the joint between us, a little star traveling from her hand to mine and back, and the house would seem to float beneath our weight like a ship on the water, traveling with the current, faster and faster into the darkness.

* * *

Back in Tokyo on Sunday, we went straight to Sumiko's apartment and flopped onto her futon, too tired to take off our coats. We hadn't touched all weekend, had hardly spoken, and now we lay inches apart, staring up at the ceiling. "Your parents aren't so bad," I said, unable to lift my head, which was still full of polite Japanese conversation, spinning around and around. I'd played go with her father, had allowed her mother to teach me calligraphy in a studio full of morning light at the back of the house. Before we left for the station, her mother had given me a scroll with an example of her own writing, surprisingly thick and muscular, full of sharp angles and mad splatter. I'd felt like she was declaring something about herself, something that secretly linked us together. "I think they liked me," I said, wanting to believe it, testing the sound of it.

Sumiko turned to look at me. "In Japan, politeness is a wall. The more polite, the higher the wall."

"And how high was their wall?"

"It was electrified, with barbed wire on top."

I thought of Sumiko's mother serving me at dinner before anyone else, thought of Sumiko's father refilling my glass with beer over and over, though etiquette required the reverse, that I pour for him. I had tried once, but he had grabbed the bottle from me. "At least they weren't rude," I said.

"In the kitchen, my mother turned to me and said, 'Don't give me blue-eyed grandchildren.'"

Everything inside me got very quiet; I could feel the blood moving through my heart. "You're not pregnant, are you?"

"Don't be stupid."

"You don't think that they know that we—"

"I don't care what they know, and anyway, they're not idiots."

And then I felt the delayed sting of her mother's comment. "My eyes are brown, not blue," I said, remembering Sumiko's mother handing me the brush, guiding my hand over the paper, showing me how to write the long dripping letters that looked like rain on the window. I had thought she liked me, maybe she even had, but the more important thing was that I had liked her: her gentleness, which was akin to melancholy, her ability to instruct without saying a word. "I don't think anyone in my entire family has blue eyes."

Sumiko sat up. "You don't want to marry me. You would never even consider marrying me."

"What are you talking about?" We had never used the word together, and it seemed startling, naked.

"You won't marry me," she said.

"I would marry you," I said, phrasing it as a hypothetical.

"No, you wouldn't."

So frightened it almost seemed to be happening in a dream, I asked her to marry me. She burst into tears and asked why I hadn't proposed sooner. "Because I didn't know you'd say yes," I lied.

"I'm not *saying* yes." She put her head down on my lap, hiding her wet face with her hands. "Poor sweet boy, I feel sorry for you."

Sumiko went to her first job interview dressed in a blue suit and cream blouse and carrying a leather portfolio tucked under her arm, like all the other soon-to-be-graduated job seekers I saw on the subway. Afterward, she came back and lay on the tatami with her eyes shut while I kissed her face and neck and shoulders. "Why don't you write something?" I suggested. "Writing always makes you feel better."

"There's no point," she said, her eyes still closed.

"Write something gory, about aliens who hollow people out and lay eggs inside their skulls."

"It would only make me sad."

"I'll do dinner and the dishes, and you can work till we go to bed."

"That me is gone. I have to be the other me now, the one who pretends to like children."

The job interviews became routine. Sumiko would iron the cream-colored blouse and the blue suit, then spend a long time in front of the mirror, painting her face into a heavy mask. Back at home, she would wash it all off and change into jeans and we would go out for ramen, then watch TV till late at night, as if waiting for some undefined miracle to happen, something that would put a stop to graduation forever. Sitting in the blue glow of her little TV, I wanted to close my eyes against the world, like the beautiful statues of Jizō in the monastery, and imagine us back at the beginning, when she had laid her head on my chest, reading me a story.

And then one night, she shook me awake in that dead space before morning, saying that there was something we had to do. I got dressed in the dark, feeling lucid but not really awake, as if I were just a guest inside her dream. She gave me a big black garbage bag to carry, then grabbed a bottle of *shōchō* from the kitchen counter and opened the front door. I followed her out onto the open-air veranda, dragging the bag, which was surprisingly heavy.

The street was motionless, like an artifact contained in a museum case. The only thing alive was the thrumming of the cicadas, a metallic sound like the whirring of an engine deep inside the world. I followed her around back to the courtyard, a square of concrete on which sat a row of garbage cans, frosted by the light of a single streetlamp.

"Dump the stuff in there," she said, pointing to a big metal tub used for burning leaves.

I carried the bag over and undid the twist tie. Inside were her notebooks, their covers decorated with hearts and Hello Kitties. "Hey, wait a second," I said.

"We're celebrating." She reached into the pocket of her sweatpants and pulled out a very official-looking piece of correspondence. "I got a job. I'm now a kindergarten teacher." She opened the bottle of *shōchō* took a swig, and handed it to me.

"You can't burn your work," I said.

"Kafka did."

"He asked Brod to do it, knowing full well that he wouldn't. And Kafka was dying, not graduating."

She lit a Golden Bat. "You know what, you're not my husband, so you don't tell me what to do."

"You're going to regret this."

"What do you know about me, anyway?"

Maybe she was right. Was this a test? Did she want me to stop her? I watched her use two hands to dump the notebooks into the metal tub, scooping them out of the trash bag in heaps, as if they were fallen leaves. Her cigarette bobbed between her lips as she worked. When she was done, she lifted the bottle of *shōchō* from the ground and took another swallow.

"Writing was just a stupid fantasy, anyway," she said.

"I love your stories."

"But you don't love me."

"I wish you'd stop saying that."

I watched Sumiko pour *shōchō* onto the notebooks in the tub and then use her lighter to set the acceptance letter ablaze. For a second, it was like a little handkerchief of fire between her fingers. She held it aloft as if waving goodbye to someone leaving on an invisible cruise ship, and then dropped it into the tub to light the rest.

There were some loose pages that caught and curled first. The flames burnt green and then orange. I could see Sumiko's handwriting twisting, turning brown. Bits and pieces of paper flew off into the darkness. The cardboard covers burnt, curving like smiles. I passed the bottle back and forth with Sumiko, feeling the heat from the fire on my face and hands.

In that moment, I knew that I would pack in the morning and go back to my place, and that I would quit grad school and get on an airplane and fly back to America. I knew that my parents would meet me at the airport, looking boozy and frail. I knew that I would go with them for the very first time since the funeral to visit my sister's grave in the big cemetery next to the highway, where the headstones were lined up like millions of chessmen. I knew that I would have to do something to start my life.

Till then, I was just watching.

About a year later, living in New York, I got a letter from Sumiko. It was our first communication since I'd left Japan, and my chest tightened as I opened the envelope and saw the handwriting I knew from her notebooks, that swift native speaker's hand that I could never imitate:

Dear Poor Sweet Boy,

The cherry blossoms are falling, and for some reason I think of you.

The school where I teach looks exactly like the one I went to as a child: the concrete building, the playground with the metal climbing set and swings. On the first day, I got there very early, and as I walked the empty hall I had the feeling that I had gone back in time to become a kindergartener again—worse, that I had somehow fallen asleep in the middle of class and dreamed that I was an adult. Though the dream had seemed to take twenty-two years, it was really only a few minutes long, and in a second I was going to wake up in my little girl body, and my mother would be waiting outside at the end of the day to take me home. I got so confused that I had to sit in my chair at the front of the empty classroom and put my head between my knees and breathe, wondering when I would wake up and be my real self again in the real world, not the dream world.

But I've grown used to teaching since then, and I find that I now take a great deal of comfort in the daily routine. There is a

*working agreement here that makes life reassuring: I pretend to
be a teacher and the children pretend to be my students. Parents
and teachers agree to forget that children are in fact lunatics,
and that what we call growing up is just learning to hide it better so nobody will lock us away.*

*Oh, did I mention that I'm engaged to be married? He works
at the same insurance company as my father, which is convenient. The only problem is that he has a good heart, so we have
some trouble communicating—just like I had with you. But I'm
trying to learn how good people talk, so I can fake it.*

I don't miss you at all.

My first thought was to tell her that she should leave her fiancé and come
join me in New York. In America we would switch roles: she would be the
space alien and I would be the human guide, the one whose job it was to
explain the world. But I knew she would never listen to me.

I sat with the letter in my hand, remembering the sound of her voice
as she read me a story for the first time. We were naked, her head resting
on my chest. The story was about children whose parents are nothing
but holograms, beams of light, and the words were so full of sadness that
I knew then and there that I could love her if she let me—if I let myself.

The story was long, and it wasn't till I realized that I could hear every
word of it that I grabbed a notebook and a pen and began to write. My
fingers ached as they chased her voice, the voice that had made me feel
free and alive and frightened all at once, whether we were hiding in the
shadows outside the train station or soaking in her deep tub, the water
so hot I couldn't breathe. I was going to save her story from the fire, save
it and send it back to her as a wedding gift, save all the stories in all the
notebooks. But when I came to the end, what I had written was about the
night my sister and I sat on the roof of my parents' house in Leonia, right
before she went into the hospital for the last time: Daisy and me staring
at the stars, those tiny points of light, and feeling as if we were falling
upward into the sky.

BRYAN WASHINGTON

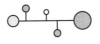

Navigation

1.

It started how you'd think, with this whiteboy throwing up in an alley. I'd pulled a job at a taqueria dumping pig guts out back. The cooks gave me grunt work, the way they do when you're starting out, like when my father had Javi and me pinching the shells off shrimp back in the restaurant as kids. It didn't matter that I'd been fixing mole in Ma's kitchen for years; I was short on money.

My managers looked like gauchos. Porno mustaches, bloated frames. They read my name and they saw my face and they pointed to the dishes. One of them told me I looked like a pinche negrito, y probablemente ni siquiera hablaba español, and I wanted to snatch his ears off but then I'd be out of a check.

So I should've left the whiteboy outside alone. I had enough on my plate.

But I stayed. Watched him heave. When he finished I came back with a glass of water.

He took me home. Dude had these little hairs climbing his belly. His eyes got wide at how furry my legs are. When we finished he gulped at the air in the room, he asked for my name as we were sliding down the futon, and when he couldn't pronounce it the whiteboy gave me a new one.

He lived in a condo on Navigation. Said he stayed there because *this* was the *real* Houston. This Houston came with needles in the grass, but he said I was lucky, lucky to have it all in front of me. I told him if somebody gave me an out, they wouldn't have time to finish their sentence.

His bedroom was nice and the building was nicer. Wood flooring. Green walls. Like the inside of an avocado. I remembered when the lot had been cleared for the building's construction, when it was just a busted Mattress Center I went to once with Ma, but then the whiteboy started asking me what was wrong, and I said it was nothing, I was gassed, he should be proud of himself.

I grabbed my kicks and left is what should've happened next. That was my thing. And I did dip out, eventually.

But the whiteboy told me he had a job; he needed help with his Spanish because he was gunning for some promotion. He temped at some nonprofit over on Pease, a house for battered refugees. One of those places where everyone's lived through everything. They needed help getting papers, with reaching their people back home, but if he couldn't understand them then he couldn't do much about it. What he really wanted was this position upstate, way out in Dallas, but they'd stuck him in the Second Ward.

The whiteboy told me I could expedite the process. Give him some lessons. Help him help the rest of the world.

I gave him this look like maybe I'd just beat his ass instead. Case his place for fun. It would be so easy.

He asked how much I made dumping napkins. He said he could double it. We'd keep it up as long as we had to. I asked why he didn't just find someone else, someone official, and he said I was already in his bed.

It's one of those moments where I could've done the good thing. Apropos of nothing. Hooked him up, just for the sake of doing it.

I told him for fifty a session I'd think on it.

2.

Meanwhile the taqueria was eating me alive. It was an ultra-retro dive, the kind with barbacoa roasting at dawn. A line of construction types looped the building every morning just to walk like twelve plates home to their kids. We had a guy whose job was sweeping people off of the sidewalk, waving them onto Leeland when the crowd shot through the doors. But somehow the gabachos knew about us too, and by mid-afternoon we looked a lot less like el D.F. and more like the U.N.

One day nobody was manning the counter, and some blondie yelled to the back for chilaquiles, and when no one else looked up I told the guy we didn't do that. He was a snake in a suit. Glasses tucked in his pocket and everything. He gave this slow nod, like, Well, okay, we'll see.

I was sweeping under the fryers when one of the managers asked for a minute. Something'd come up. Could we touch on it outside. I thought that he'd ask me some bunk about my hours, but when we made it to the back he grabbed me by the throat.

Next time a customer asks for something, he said, you find it. Claro?

I felt like a bobblehead.

I needed the money.

I picked up the phone at Ma's that night, told the whiteboy I was free after ten.

3.

Long story short, this guy was hopeless. Doomed. It took four, five days to stuff the *o* into his *hola*.

We started with greetings. He had so many questions. He wanted to know why he couldn't use *usted* with everyone. He wanted to know why the *x* had to be silent. He wanted to know why every morning had to be bueno.

Some days are just bad, he said. Some people live their whole lives and not a single good thing happens to them.

I told him those were just the rules. He should follow them unless he had something new to say.

I thought he'd bow out, because it really wasn't worth it, but what he did was take notes. He wrote it all down.

Vámonos, I said.

Bamanos, said the whiteboy.

Vámonos. *V.* Think *volcano.*

Bamanos.

No. *Vulcan. Velociraptor.*

Right. Bamanos.

That's how we did it. Had us a full-stop barrier.

And the people at his shelter—on the trains from Tapachula? San Pedro Sula?

Forget about it. They wouldn't be talking to him anytime soon.

I told him this. I told him not to get his hopes up. He rubbed my earlobe with his fingers, said that was where I came in.

Hey, I said, don't get too comfortable.

Cómodo, said the whiteboy. Cómodo?

Correcto.

So we kept it up.

And the whiteboy always paid me afterwards.

And we'd always, always, always, always end up in bed.

Lo siento.

Las siento.

Negative. Lo. Lo.

Las siento.

Weeks passed, then months. We moved from greetings to goodbyes. We brushed by commands. We jumped back to directions. I told him about my father living who the fuck knew where. About my brother in the ground. About Ma and I, stuck in East End, scrambling to keep everything together in a home we no longer owned. The whiteboy told me about his sisters, about his parents in Alamo Heights, and when I asked how many guys he'd been with before me he told me about an ex, some genius over at Rice.

He asked if I was out. I told him I didn't know what that meant. He asked if I'd thought about abandoning Houston, and I said if I had I'd have done it by now.

I kept my head down at the job. Did what I was asked to do. The kitchen was sloppy, utterly inefficient, but every now and again one of the cooks asked for a hand—with temping the oil, with keeping the cow heads intact, or some other no-brainer thing they should've known how to do.

They'd laugh afterwards, pat me with their gloves. Smear all that grease on the back of my tee.

Mostly I wiped benches. My bosses spat on the tile I mopped, asked how my day was going.

I kept my mouth shut about it, kept my eyes on the ground. Because if someone else put their hands on me, I didn't know what I'd do.

Creo que sí.

Creole.

Creo, creo.

Creole, creole.

I started spending my nights with the whiteboy. Dropped whatever scraps I stole from the job over at Ma's. Then took the sidewalk lining Milby on the way to his condo, just before the neighborhood dips into the bayou, and most nights the whiteboy met me at the door; he'd reheat a bowl of whatever he'd ordered for dinner.

We continued our education.

At some point I stopped jumping when he touched me. At some point the whiteboy started rolling his *r*'s.

At some point I decided I'd make him fluent, however long that took. We would see that through.

4.

Then one night, after a long day, we were rehashing phrases. Things he'd been hearing on his day-to-day. He'd started having piecemeal conversations at work, putting names and addresses together.

The whiteboy told me about the woman who came to Texas in the trunk of a Chrysler, who worked off her debt by dancing in the Galleria.

He told me about the man who'd sold his oldest daughter to traffickers to get his youngest into Brownsville, and how, months later, he still hadn't found either of them.

He told me about the little girl who hadn't said anything, just touched his cheek, rubbing the skin between her fingers, and how after she'd done that he knew no matter how much money he brought in or where he put her family up or how much relief they signed off for, he couldn't do anything to help her at all.

One night, we had a six-pack between us, and his legs on my stomach, which should've been awkward for us. We weren't even fooling with English by then. I was filling in his blanks.

Te amo, I said.

Te amo.

Nice. Good. Te amo.

Te amo.

Right.

Sí.

I laughed in his face, told him to say it again.

I dumped garbage all day, taught my whiteboy at night.

This is how things happen. Even for us.

5.

A few weeks later, he got the promotion.

His supervisor said it wasn't like he was a natural. But out of all the whiteboys they had on hand, he was the closest to whatever they needed.

A position had opened up out in Dallas, if he wanted it. He had a few days to decide.

Of course we had to celebrate. We sat at his table, sober for once, and I told him that was great. He'd probably enjoy himself.

He made this face like that was the wrong response.

I knew what he'd ask, and I answered before he said it.

The whiteboy said I knew I could come too, come with him, and I told him I did.

The whiteboy said this was it, what we'd been working toward, and I told him it may have been.

The whiteboy said there was nothing left for me in Houston, he said that I didn't have to punish myself, and he said my name, my actual name, and I didn't have the words for that.

I stretched my cheeks as far as they'd go. Put a hand on his thigh.

I grabbed my socks and my cap and my belt and I left and he did not put up a fight.

This is how easy it is to walk out of a life. I'd always wondered, and now I knew.

I didn't see him before he took off.

Who knows what he's doing now.

6.

But a week or two later, I was working the night shift, scrubbing blood off the floor, when one of my managers asked for a word.

I'd already decided to put him in the dirt if he touched me. Someone, somewhere in Houston needed a fry cook. I'd twirl signs on the street. Dance on the curb in a phone suit.

He put his hand on my shoulder, and I clinched for the punch.

He told me they'd fired a couple of fatheads for pocketing tips. He called them idiot cabrones, as if he weren't one himself.

But we need a guy who has experience, he said.

We'd start you slow, he said. Behind the stove. Work you up from the bottom.

You're asking me to cook for you, I said, and he shrugged, said, If that's what you want to call it.

I'm asking you to do yourself a solid, he said.

And if this were a different story, a story about something else, a story where we did the things we know we need to do, I'd have smiled real wide, the same as with the whiteboy, and with a little more feeling, or maybe a different one entirely. But I just put my hand on his shoulder, and I squeezed around the edges, and I loudly, gracefully, told him to go fuck his mother.

RION AMILCAR SCOTT

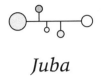

Juba

The man walking toward me stretched his hand out as we crossed the street. I shook it and kept walking, as I had never seen him before.

Juba, he said. Boy, Juba, I ain't seen you in a long time. Juba woo-wee.

Because my name is not Juba, I was content to keep moving. The man stopped right in the middle of busy Carroll Street, still gripping my hand. A money green Acura turned sharply in front of us. I dipped and jerked to avoid being struck.

Are you crazy? I asked as we made it to the sidewalk.

Sorry, Juba, man. It's just that I ain't seen you in so long. It's good to see you, man. You still up to your old tricks?

I had an idea what sort of tricks he might be talking about. The man looked old, but it was an artificial old. The kind of old that seizes a person who abuses himself. That sort of old comes from too many late nights. The old of hard liquor and worse. He was scarred in the face and on the arms, but also on his wrinkled hands. He wasn't the sort of man you saw around here very often.

I'm sorry, buddy, I said, but I'm not Juba.

Stop messing around, Juba. You always was a trickster. Stop playing games, man. You still hustling?

Sir, I'm hustling to catch this bus. Other than that I don't hustle, and I really have to go.

I really did have to go. I had a job interview at an accounting firm downtown in an hour, and I had timed everything perfectly. If I caught the 12:45 p.m. B58, I would make it there exactly fifteen minutes early. I had performed a test run the day before and another one a day before that. This was my second interview, and I could tell the woman who ran the office liked me. All I had to do was show up. Since the layoff I had been out of work for several months. In another couple weeks my unemployment checks would be at an end.

There was something odd in this man's smile, perhaps something in the webs of wrinkles at his cheeks.

Juba, you something else, boy. The man let out a wheezy, whining squeal. Man, I'm trying to buy a dub. Can you help me out with that?

A dub?

Yeah, a dub. Remember when you used to be selling nicks down by Riverhall? But then one day you said since times is hard it's dubs or better.

I have no idea what you're talking about, I said. I think you have the wrong person.

I reached into my pocket and pulled out a $5 bill. Here, buddy, I said. Go get yourself a sandwich or coffee.

The man stared at my hand, curling his lip in disgust. Man, I don't need your money, he said. I'm tryna buy some green.

I turned and started to walk when the man grabbed at my elbow.

Hey, Juba, man, he said. Stop playing games, all right?

I thought I heard his voice change. I snatched my arm from him and nearly tumbled backward, but I caught myself. I hadn't been in a fist-fight since I was a young man at District Central mixing it up with guys from the Southside who thought I was a punk because I lived on the Northside. I wondered if I even remembered how to fight. I balled my fists and stepped backward a bit. He was big guy, and his hands seemed built for strangulation. I used to be so skinny back then, nearly frail. In college I lifted weights to give myself some definition, but it didn't work, so I stopped. It was important not to get wrapped in his massive arms, because then I'd never break free. I had to strike first, and then strike again and keep moving if I had any chance. All that was jumping the gun, though. I had no intention of getting into a fight.

He appeared to be looking over my shoulder. I glanced back to see three men approaching me with guns drawn. Confused, I raised my hands over my head. They wore badges around their necks and light black jackets. There was one to my left with a puffy pink face and a brown mustache. He appeared tense. I looked from man to man quickly, disoriented by their shouting. I put my hands out in front of me, but I wasn't sure if that's what I was supposed to do. They kept calling me Juba. All I had to do was explain that I didn't know this man and that our very conversation was a simple misunderstanding. If only they would stop shouting.

Juba, get down on your knees and put your hands to your head, the man with the puffy pink face said.

I . . . Am . . . Not . . . Juba! I screamed it as loudly as I could. You can check my ID. My name is not Juba.

I became aware of each and every one of my movements, each individual heartbeat and blink. I slowly moved my arms to reach for my pocket where my IDs were, but that seemed to make them more agitated. They screamed at me, and I could barely understand them. I looked over at the man who had started all this confusion. They didn't seem to be troubling him. It dawned on me that he was with them, perhaps an undercover or a neighborhood snitch.

I fell to my knees as they asked. The officer with the brown mustache shoved me face down so that my cheek pressed flat against the sidewalk. One of them wrenched my arms together behind my back and pinched cuffs tightly around my wrists.

For some reason, even with all my attention on my movements—both involuntary and otherwise—I didn't realize that I had been yelling, screaming all along: *I am not Juba! I am not Juba! I am not Juba!* They had been telling me to shut up, but I kept screaming, *I am not Juba!* as I lay there on the ground. I suppose I had said it so much that it lost all meaning. It was the truth, though. I am not Juba.

They didn't release me from the police station until after midnight. All I got was a halfhearted apology from some detective who remained unconvinced that I wasn't Juba. They showed me photographs of myself leaving my condo, driving, going to catch the bus, and meeting with family members on the Southside. One officer slid me a cup of coffee after it was established that I wasn't Juba. He told me to watch my back because Juba is still out there. I had only a vague sense of what he meant. But they had to let me go, as there was no evidence that I was Juba.

Still, no one told me who Juba was or what Juba was supposed to have done. For all I knew, I was uncomfortably close to lying strapped to a gurney with chemicals streaming into my veins.

I called the accounting firm in the morning to explain my absence. The office manager told me she was sorry, but they filled the position when I didn't show. She asked why I didn't call, and I couldn't make up something fast enough. I turned off the telephone and threw it across the living room of my condo. It slapped against the wall and nicked it.

I thought about suing. I invited my cousin over for a drink that night.

He was a few years older than me and ran a private law firm downtown. I would have offered to go to dinner, or at the very least a happy hour or something, but thanks to the CRPD I was still unemployed.

My cousin always made an impression. He stood tall as a professional basketball player and had the sturdy build of one. Women seemed to like him. Guys wanted to hang around him. I wanted to hang around him, but I was always too broke to keep up. When he came to my door, he wore a sports jacket over a white shirt with thin brown vertical lines and a stiff, stiff collar.

He slapped my hand and held it firmly, pulling me into him and embracing me tightly. My cousin often went overboard with his handshakes and hugs. It was like something out of the seventies.

Cousin, he said sitting on my couch. I haven't been here in such a long time. I been meaning to come see you.

Yeah, I replied. Man, you look like you're here for a job interview.

Just trying to look as fly as my cousin. Speaking of job interviews, what happened to the one you were supposed to have by the place near my office?

Man, I said, and paused briefly. We'll get to that one.

He nodded, peering down at me quizzically. I didn't want to seem as if I'd just called him to do me a favor, so I led the discussion to any number of things from politics to his cases to family—the normal topics people usually talked round and round.

Listen, jack, I said. You'll never guess what happened to me. I got arrested, man.

What? I told you to stop going to those grimy Southside Row clubs, man. Don't nobody go to The Garden no more, anyway. I got some clients trying to get some of them dirty buildings torn down so we can get some condos up—

These fools cost me a job, I said, cutting off my cousin's ramble. Kept me locked up all day. I missed my damn interview.

That's terrible, my cousin said.

I wasn't doing anything.

You know how often I hear people say that? You had to be doing something.

I was walking down the street and then I get accused of being someone named Juba.

Juba? I heard a hint of fear in my cousin's voice. They actually called you Juba?

Yes.

Did you have any marijuana on you?

What?

Weed, cousin. When they busted you, did you have any weed on you?

Of course not. What are you getting at?

Did they charge you with anything?

No. But I'm thinking about suing. They cost me a great job. This damn condo's not cheap.

Look, I think you should drop this whole thing. You're free. No one thinks you're Juba, thank God. Let it go.

I'm not letting shit go.

I didn't realize it, but I had raised my voice. My cousin jerked back, somewhat rattled, I think. I softened a bit.

I had everything planned to the second, I said. I was going to arrive early and make small talk with the secretary, so I could look all witty and charming and shit. Then I was going to spend my wait time reading, so I could look sophisticated when the executives passed. After that I was going to sail right into the position. Now all that is ruined, man.

Blame Juba.

Who's Juba, anyway?

You sounded like him for a minute, yelling like a crazy man, my cousin said. Juba is bad news. Bad news.

Yeah, he has been for me.

Well, cuz, he's a phantom. A convenient explanation. Juba may not exist, but the cops in Cross River are convinced he does, and they plan on locking his ass up. They been prowling the city for a while looking for this dude. I'm starting to think he's an underworld myth. An urban legend. Juba.

What did he do?

He's sold enough weed to keep half the country high. The war on drugs is just a war on Juba. My cousin slapped his knee when he said this. He's Tony Montana, my cousin continued. The Medellin Cartel, John Gotti, and Black Caesar in one. It's hell up in Cross River, boy. Juba is one bad nigga. He supplies the Washington, Johnson, and Jackson crime families, and he got them all going to war over his product. You know how many folks are dead behind Juba?

And they think I'm this dude?

They've thought a lot of people were Juba. One of my clients, they initially thought he was Juba. Turns out he was a little punk from the

Northside who went to Cross River Community College and sold a little herb to look cool. He's at Freedman's University now. Probably pretending he's tough and slinging nicks. One of my dummy clients. Clown.

I've never even smoked a joint before.

Not even in college?

Nope.

What the hell have you been doing with your life, cousin?

I didn't respond to that, just shook my head, thinking of Juba.

We talked for a few hours, had some more drinks, and then my cousin left. Before leaving, though, he told me again to forget about Juba. I hadn't made up my mind whether or not I would leave it alone, but I told him I would. There was so much on my mind, and most of it involved Juba.

Every day I sat at home without a job I thought about what had happened. I awoke from nightmares where winged beasts with guns swooped in and slammed me to the ground. I felt so weak and powerless and foolish, and still so unemployed.

I kept hearing the name, folks mentioning him in idle conversation. Juba's name seemed to pass from every lip. I wondered if people bad alway talked about Juba this much or if something new had seized the consciousness of the town.

In between submitting job applications, I went from person to person telling them about my ordeal. To a man, all knew of Juba. Some said I was lucky I still had a life. Others tied Juba to a police slaying so many months ago. A good number of people described Juba as a happy-go-lucky guy, the Santa Claus of marijuana peddlers, a grandfatherly guy with good advice and a sack of chronic. Only I, it seemed, had never heard of Juba. One cousin, one I rarely spoke to, said: Juba ain't shit. That nigga sells nicks and dimes, but he smokes most of it himself. I used to buy weed from him. High off his own supply every damn time I seen him. He ain't no throat-slitter. He a joke.

Where can I find Juba? I asked.

Fuck if I know. I ain't seen him in a long, long time.

And that was what most people said. No one knew where Juba stayed. Most had never even seen him. I couldn't be sure he even existed.

My cousin the attorney checked up on me from time to time. He kept telling me to drop it. I grew sick of hearing from him, so eventually when his number flashed across my phone, I didn't answer. One time he called, I let it ring, and when it finished ringing, I thought to call a reporter friend of mine. I figured if anyone had the resources to find out more about Juba, it was him. He sounded rushed. Told me he had never heard of Juba and apologized about what had happened to me. Before I could say anything more, he said he had to go and hung up abruptly. I sat in my living room smoking a cigarette right down to the filter, hoping to forget about Juba.

I decided I wouldn't obsess about Juba anymore or think about that day the police shoved me to the ground. But two things happened to make it impossible to forget.

Each week, I volunteered at K.I.D.S. Community Center in the McCoy neighborhood on the Southside. I forget what the letters stood for, but it could have been Khaotic, Ineffective, and Detrimental Supervision. I taught math skills to children who were behind in school, but mostly I told them to shut up, as the brats were forever talking out of turn and fighting with each other.

Before class one week, an adorable girl with big eyes, brown skin, and hair plaited into one thick braid hugged me as I came in the door. I smiled at her embrace. Most times she was the loudest, most unruly of the bunch, forever threatening to punch one of the other kids, including boys older than her.

Are you going to be boring today? she asked.

I felt my smile wither, and immediately I wanted to go home. I watched the kids scurrying about, finding places to hide from me. I looked down.

Are *you* going to be boring today? I said, and she jumped back as if I had burned her. Even I was surprised by the heat of my words.

I got through about half of the lesson before I became frustrated with their interruptions and walked off to talk to a pretty counselor with reddish brown eyes and long hair that I later learned was a weave. In the past she had seemed unimpressed with my condo and my watch. I kept telling her about them, hoping to wear her down.

The counselors ignored the children who now ran through the place tossing things about. Occasionally a counselor would shout at a student, but for the most part the adults and the children didn't at all interact. To make conversation, I told the pretty counselor the story of my confrontation with the police. When I said the name Juba, her eyes widened. She pointed to the cute little girl who had accosted me. The girl, the counselor said, was Juba's niece.

The little girl raised her head when she heard her uncle's name and looked over at us, meeting our gazes and the counselor's pointing finger.

You guys talking about my Uncle Juba? she asked.

No, no, sweetie, the counselor said. No. We're not talking about your Uncle Juba. No.

Sweetie, I said. Tell me about your Uncle Juba.

My Uncle Juba is tall and his hair is black and gray. And he's smart. Smarter than you. I bet he knows more about math than you.

I bet he does.

He taught me how to count and he taught me how to spell. And he's always reading the Bible. His eyes are big like my mother's, but they're always red.

Red like a sunset?

Red like when I get cut. My mother said that's 'cause Uncle Juba never sleeps. He stays up all night and all day long. I seen Uncle Juba asleep before, but mostly he don't sleep.

Where's your Uncle Juba now, sweetie?

She shrugged. I haven't seen Uncle Juba in a long, long, long, long time, she said. He calls me. Sends me e-mails too. Says I'm the prettiest little girl he has ever seen, and Uncle Juba is right. I'm the prettiest little girl in all of Cross River and the whole world.

Juba Franklin. That was his name. That's what the little girl told me. I didn't ask any more questions because I didn't want to let on that I was looking for Juba.

The second thing that happened to keep Juba on my mind was that my reporter friend called back that night. He was just as brusque as he had been the day before, but he had found something from talking to his sources. There was a Juba Franklin who hung out in a bar in Port Yooga, Virginia. He was there every night. Why the police didn't know, my friend wasn't sure. Juba had moved his shady business from Cross River to Port Yooga, hiding in plain sight, and the fools couldn't figure out how to find him. Get me a nickel bag, he said before hanging up.

I've never been a religious man. My mother says that's why I had such a hard time finding a job. Still, I took the turn of events as a sign. Maybe to find a job, I needed to track Juba down. I needed to see his face to understand all that had happened to me. Perhaps I could even say a word or two to him.

I brushed that idea out of my head. There were so many incarnations of him. He could have easily been a cold-blooded killer, but it was just as likely that he was a friendly neighborhood pot peddler. I figured the truth of him rested somewhere in the middle. I called a few people to ask their advice, but I only called those who shared my curiosity and thought Juba was probably not a dangerous guy. Sitting at home all alone, watching daytime television, I had a lot of time to think about things. Such a man, one who knew everyone at all levels from the dirtiest dealer on Angela Street to the well-heeled people on the Hilltop, could explain so much that I, with my limited experience, had never understood. In all honesty, I had made up my mind after I got off the phone with my reporter friend, but it took me a few days to realize it.

I sat in a bar in Port Yooga in the middle of the day drinking a beer called Purple Haze in honor of my potential meeting with the weed dealer, Juba Franklin. I felt preposterous, but less preposterous than I had felt with my cheek to the pavement and my hands cuffed behind my back.

I glanced around, trying to figure which of these men was Juba. It was an easy question to answer, as I was the only black man in the bar. I chomped on peanuts to pass the time and at one point ordered chicken wings. I felt foolish with the grease from the wings on my fingers and asked for a knife and fork. The bartender looked at me strangely and then handed me the utensils. Eating the wings with a knife and fork made me feel like more of a fool, and I stopped, letting the wings grow cold. At about six I realized the ridiculousness of the whole enterprise and planned to leave, but before I could summon the will to walk away, two men strode into the bar. The shorter man had an ashy bald head shaped like the peanut I ate. The other was tall and dark with black, lightly salted hair. His eye were blood red, nearly glowing in his face. Juba. There was a part of me that said just turn and go home, but I could still feel those metal bracelets pinching at my wrists. I walked over to the man's table. Nearly called the man Uncle Juba when I opened my mouth, but I caught myself.

I'm new in town, I said. I don't trust these crackers. They don't seem too cool. You know where I can get some pot?

Uh-uh, Juba replied. I really don't know nothing about that.

You Juba?

Sorry, jackson, don't know nobody by that name.

I twisted my brow, giving him a puzzled look. He blinked a lot, so I wondered if that had some sort of meaning. He shook peanuts from their shell and crunched them in his teeth. It seemed like he was making fun of me.

The other man tried his hand at looking menacing. He gave me a flat look of irritation. It said he was unafraid and would destroy me if I bothered him for too long. His intimidation was a moderate success. I could see myself turning and running, but I held firm.

Well, I said. I guess it's for the best that you're not Juba, because I was going to tell that guy that his weed isn't shit. He's trying to pass off dirt as the chronic.

The bald man cracked a smirk, his head a flaky white under the dull glow from above. Juba's face remained flat and expressionless, but he bowed his head and shook it side to side as if lost in prayer.

Boy, why you want to mess around with your life, huh? Juba asked. Don't even ride yourself like that, my nig-nig. Everybody from Cross River to Port Yooga and all spots in the middle know that Juba got them fire tea leaves, chief.

So you do know Juba?

You police?

If I was, you know I could lie if I wanted to, I said. It's a myth that I legally have to tell you the truth if I'm a cop. And I'm not a cop. But if I was one, I'd just lie.

Ain't you a reg duboishead? he replied.

A what?

A regular genius, jack. Keep up, my nig-nig.

You speak fast. It's hard to follow sometimes.

The bald man's eyes danced in disbelief.

I'm not rapping fast, Juba said. I'm just talking a different language than you. When two niggas from El Salvador get together and talk, neither one of them complain that the other is all flashy speaking or whatever. Its just the squares, the outsiders like you—not me, I know Spanish—like you that complain. You a Riverbaby?

I prefer Cross Riverian.

Course you do, he said. Bougie niggas always prefer Cross Riverian.

It's better than being a baby, I replied. The problem is we always infantilize our people. Folks don't want to grow up and be men and women. The world would finally respect us if we'd just be men.

Blah, blah, blah; right and sure. Tell me, if y'all niggas got money and houses and things over there on the Northside, and I can already tell you a Northside nigga, then why y'all so cross? Cross Riverian literally means angry river person, you know that, right?

Looks to me like Southside folks are more angry. That's where people get robbed and shot and stuff like that.

Checkmate. I tell you what. You look like a true. I'll griff you some of that Starr Product if you give me a fumi.

Huh?

Juba sighed. The bald man grunted and crunched peanuts between his teeth.

Riverbabies don't even own their own tongue no more. Nigga, give me a cigarette and I'll sell you some weed. Shit, may even have a story to tell you too.

I handed him a cigarette and he asked me to follow him. Juba and I left the bar; the bald man stayed behind.

Juba took me into a basement apartment so small it seemed like a cell—a spacious cell, but still a cell. A few beams of natural light came in from the streets above. Juba's bed took up most of the space. He had a bookshelf filled with holy books and books about the holy books. In the corner sat a little desk and atop it a thick raggedy Bible with torn pages and Post-It notes sticking out from the edges. It was opened to the first page of the Book of Revelation. Juba had several sentences underlined and notes running up and down the margins in a graphomaniacal frenzy.

Juba rolled a joint, lit it, and offered it to me, but I passed. He sat it at the right corner of his mouth and blew smoke out of the left. Then he spoke rapidly about the flow of the Cross River for minutes on end, the way a man might speak about a lover he missed.

I got a sale on that Starr Product, he said. Chronic's always a crowd pleaser. I got 'Dro Purple Haze, but I recommend the Starr Product. Cross Riv's finest. They don't grow that shit nowhere else. Only find that shit in and around Cross River. I'm smoking it now for your sampling pleasure.

I looked around at his cramped apartment.

You don't make a lot off of this, do you? I asked.

Enough to afford this mansion and to keep me in these fancy Armani linens, he said, running his hand along his jeans and long-sleeved T-shirt, both torn and faded from frequent washing. Naw, my man, it's all shorty-cool. Don't need to make a lot. Just enough for rent and books.

I—I heard you were a kingpin.

Yeah, there are competing versions of me out in the world. Damn near heard I popped a Kennedy one day in November.

His words were slightly amusing, but as I watched him, something shocked me so much that my skin tingled. I noticed that he and I did share a slight resemblance. He too had drawn cheeks and big eyes that looked as if they were floating in his head.

Hear the police tell it, I got tons flying in on planes every afternoon. They scared of me 'cause they think I'm getting their little daughters hooked on my jungle weed. He paused. I guess I am. I sell dubs and half-centuries and centuries and sometimes I might sell an LB, but that's as much as I griff. I ain't trying to be their monkey in a cage. That's why I had to come down here until things ain't so radioactive. I found out they were after me. Accused me of doing some apocalyptic shit, of being behind all the tea in Cross River, jackson. You know how many niggas be selling grass? They looking for me back home, they can't even imagine I'm over here. They know how much I love Cross River. They figure I'd never leave my home. Shit, I never thought I'd leave The Riv, myself. Things'll calm down eventually and I'll be back. I don't even like this job.

You don't?

Fuck no, my nig-nig. Been doing this too long. You look cool, so I'll tell you this.

Juba walked over to his desk and picked up a notebook. He flipped through the pages before putting it into my hands. See that? That's my real job. I'm just doing this weed dealer biz until I can finish up this project.

There were strange markings on each page, words I didn't understand, beautiful sketches that had an unfinished quality.

What is this?

Man, can't you read? See, Cross River folks so busy talking like white people, they done lost their tongue. Every strange word you hear in Cross River, every little piece of slang, probably sprang from me. Like seventy-five to eighty-seven percent. I come from a long line ...

Of weed dealers?

Don't get smart, my nig-nig. You knew I wasn't gonna say that. My dad was an engineer, but that wasn't his main thing. I capture and create the language we speak in Cross River. Just like my daddy before me and my grandfather before that and my great-grandfather who was in the Great Insurrection before there even was a town called Cross River in Maryland. We done lost our tongue. Some shit I got to say to you, I won't even try to say 'cause there ain't no words for it. I got to use more words than I would have to use if we had our language back. I got to speak slowly so you understand me, even though we from the same place. Ridiculous, but it ain't your fault. I'm trying to complete the Cross River tongue.

I flipped through the book. The words started to make sense a little, but there were huge canyons of language I couldn't understand. It's probably the way, with my high school Spanish, I'd look at a book written in that language.

So what is this, a dictionary? I asked.

A dictionary? You niggas in Cross River are more lost than I ever thought. Shit. He stopped speaking for a moment. Naw... naw... hell naw, this ain't no damn dictionary. The people ain't ready for that. For like twenty years, I been translating the Bible into Cross Riverian, as you bougie niggas like to say. Naw, y'all wouldn't even call it that. Y'all don't think the way we talk is nothing special. At least not special enough to have a name. Y'all spend a lot of time translating from English to Cross Riverian and back in y'all heads. Y'all just don't know it. Niggas ain't slow, they just translating.

I'm gonna do the Koran next, and then the Bhagavad Gita. I already did the Heart Sutra. Did that shit to warm me up. I got a rack of other sutras to do, but that's a ways off. I got a lot of books to translate. It's gonna take a while, though. Once I finish the Bible, everything else should move quickly. I need to capture the language first. It's triply hard now that I ain't in Cross River no more. Got folks mailing me new words in exchange for 'Dro. The police might catch up to me before I'm done.

As he spoke, it was like a spirit moved over the void of the words on the pages, and I started to understand completely what Juba had written. I came to the end of the story of the Great Flood and it was like one of my cousins from the Southside had whispered it into my ear.

I tell you what, brotherman. I've enjoyed this convo with you, Juba said. Take a dub of that Starr Product for the road.

I shook my head. I-I-I can't—

Naw man, you don't know how good this has been for me. I like meeting Riverbabies. I don't hardly get a chance no more since I'm in Port Yooga. Not that I don't like Port Yooga in its own way, but it ain't Cross River.

I pocketed the bag of weed. It was nearly black, and it smelled like all outdoors. One whiff was enough to intoxicate me for precisely fifteen seconds, at least that's what Juba said. I never did smoke it, though. I put it in my basement in a briefcase where I kept things I wanted no one to find. After a while I forgot the code and couldn't even get back into the briefcase if I wanted to. Juba and I stayed in touch, but I never saw him again. I offered him words, phrases, and critiques on his translation of the Bible by mail. Sometimes he'd send me weed as payment, and I always threw it away. As I walked from his house that evening, I had no idea what to make of the afternoon.

When I got onto the bus to Cross River, I sat next to a man from the Southside who spoke to me about his life. His accent was thick, so at times I got lost, but when I was engaged I felt transported to his childhood. As the bus crossed the bridge from Port Yooga into Cross River he said, I know who you are.

Who am I?

He leaned in and whispered, You that dude they call Juba.

I shook my head and smirked a bit. I'm not Juba, I said. I'm not him at all.

It's okay, he said. I ain't a yauper. I can keep it to myself, my nig-nig.

The man pulled out a piece of paper and wrote down some words and phrases. They were things a Cross Riverian might say. He nodded and crinkled the paper into my palm and I accepted it, folding it away in my left breast pocket.

KALI FAJARDO-ANSTINE

Sugar Babies

Though the southern Colorado soil was normally hard and cakey, it had snowed and then rained an unusual amount that spring. Some of the boys in my eighth-grade class decided it was the perfect ground for playing army. They borrowed shovels and picks from their fathers' sheds, placing the tools on their bicycle handlebars and riding out to the western edge of our town, Saguarita, a place where the land with its silken fibers of swaying grass resembled a sleeping woman with her face pressed firmly to the pillow, a golden blonde by day, a raven-haired beauty by night.

The first boy to hit bone was Robbie Martinez. He did so with the blunt edge of a rusted shovel. Out of the recently drenched earth, he lifted a piece of brittle faded whiteness and tossed it downwind like nothing more than a scrap of paper. "Look," he said, kneeling as if he was praying. "Everybody come look."

The other boys gathered around. There in the ground lay broken pieces of bowls with black zigzagging designs. Next to those broken bowls were human teeth, scattered like dried kernels of yellow corn. Above them the sun had begun to fade behind the tallest peak of the Sangre de Cristo Mountains. The sky was pale and bleak, like the bloated belly of a lizard passing above.

"Don't touch it," Robbie said. "None of it. We need to tell somebody."

And tell they did. The entire town. Everyone, it seemed, was a witness.

Days after their discovery, our final eighth-grade project was announced. We gathered in the gym for an assembly. The teachers brought together the boys from technical education class and the girls from home economics. We sat Indian style in ten rows beneath dangling ropes and resting basketball hoops. The room smelled like a tennis ball dipped in old socks and the cement walls were padded in purple vinyl—supposedly to minimize dodgeball injuries. I thought it looked like a loony bin.

Mrs. Sharply, a bug-eyed woman with a neck like a giraffe's but a torso like a rhino's, stood before us on a wooden box. "For the remaining two weeks of your junior high career," she said, "you will care for another life." She then reached behind her into a paper grocery bag, revealing a sack of C & H pure cane sugar. "Sugar babies. We will be raising our very own sugar babies."

Older kids had gossiped about notorious school projects. We had heard stories of piglet dissections, the infamous "growing and changing" unit, rocket launches with carbon dioxide canisters, and a cow's lung blackened and doused in cigarette smoke, but no one had warned us about this.

"Sugar babies are a lot of responsibility," Mrs. Sharply said as she stepped down from her box and paced with the sugar sack. She explained we were to be graded on skills like feeding, bonding, budgeting, and more. She then passed around diaper directions.

"We do it all alone?" It was Solana Segura. She was behind me, her perpetual whimper causing every sentence to end like a little howl. "Like single moms and stuff?"

Somewhere, down the rows, a boy croaked, "But the DNA shows I am *not* the father."

We chirped with laughter until Mrs. Sharply held up two fingers, signaling silence. "Of course not. You'll be in committed partnerships. We're drawing names."

A teacher's aide in Payless flats scurried like a magician's assistant toward Mrs. Sharply. She carried two Folgers cans decorated in pink and blue glitter. Mrs. Sharply set down her sugar, taking the cans from the aide and giving each a good shake. From the pink can, the first name she pulled was Mimi Yazzie, who stood and slinked forward, burying her face into her arms as Mrs. Sharply called out her partner, Mike Ramos. This cycle of humiliation lasted for several more rounds before I was partnered with Roberto Martinez, the bone boy.

After school, Robbie and I sat outside on the swings. He was a scrawny kid with frequently chapped lips and a light dusting of freckles across his low nose. He played soccer and always wore a beat-up blue windbreaker and knockoff Adidas sneakers, with four stripes instead of three. The sugar baby was planted snug in his lap, balanced ever so gently between his two stick-arms. His dark eyes were so big and wide they resembled two brown pigeon eggs and he spoke with a quavering, squeaky voice. "They said we have to name it. Do you want to pick it out, Sierra?"

"No, you name it." I swung up. "And you take it home tonight." I swung down. "I'll watch it tomorrow, but only if I have to."

"That's cool," he said. "What about Miranda? That's my grandma's name."

"Whatever," I sighed, leaning back on the swing. "Name it after your grandmother. Name it after your entire family. I don't care." I pumped until the rusted chain pulled taut. Then I jumped, landing in the mushy gravel with both feet. I took off for home.

"Ain't that something," my father said as he and I ate breakfast the next morning. On our small black-and-white TV above the microwave, aerial shots of the dig site were being shown on the news. The land appeared as an enormous shadow box with scraps of ancient people instead of thimbles and porcelain knickknacks.

"Can we go see it?" I asked, spooning my last bit of corn flakes into my mouth.

"I suspect they don't want us to do that," he said, keeping his eyes to the TV. There were deep lines around his eyelids, his hair was purely sliver, and his hands were spotted from years of working as a roofer beneath the Colorado sun. People had begun to mistake him for my grandfather.

"Why not? We should be allowed to." I walked to the sink and tossed my dirty dish inside. "It's where we're from. It's *our* people."

My father scratched his chin. There was a thin turquoise ring on his finger where there had once been a gold wedding band. "Don't leave a dish in the sink," he said. "How many times I got to tell you that, Sierra?"

I turned back and soaped up my bowl. "I mean it. I want to go."

"Things like this have always happened around here. It's nothing special."

I told him it was new to me as I scrubbed my dish with a green and yellow sponge, the milky water gargling loudly down the drain's black rubber lips. As I rinsed the bowl once more, I peered through the window above the sink. The morning was clear and in the distance the mountains were crystal blue like an enormous wave. As if sailing across those waters, a small white pickup truck with a front-end bra pulled down our street and rumbled over the gravel in our driveway. Long dark hair clouded the truck's windshield and very red and very long fingernails were coiled around the steering wheel. A silver rosary dangled above the dash.

"Papa," I called over my shoulder, drying my hands on my jeans.

My father rose and stood tall behind me, smelling of leather and dirt. "Looks like she's back again." He grunted some, swishing spit around inside his mouth before shooting a stream of yolky bile into the sink. "Go outside, Sierra. Say hello to your mother."

My mother first left three years earlier. It happened one morning after she cooked breakfast. I watched as she gathered her keys and coat and walked into our wintry yard without any shoes. She left footprints as slight as bird tracks in the snow. When I asked my father later why she had left, he simply said, "Sometimes a person's unhappiness can make them forget they are a part of something bigger, something like a family, a people, even a tribe."

My mother occasionally would come home for a day or two to gather forgotten necklaces or purses, though over time my father moved her things from the bedroom to a box in the crawl space. Her visits were infrequent enough that I learned to live without her. It wasn't easy at first. Sometimes I'd hear a funny story at school or church and my first thought would be, *You have to tell Mama.* But over time that urge to be with her, to tell her things, to be a part of her, it went away. Just like she always did.

On my mother's first night back, she couldn't find an apron so she made dinner in one of my father's old T-shirts. With the kitchen TV up loud on *Entertainment Tonight,* she cooked pork chops sizzled in their own fat and smothered in green chili. Whenever I'd glance up from my math homework on the coffee table, I'd catch glimpses of her in the kitchen rummaging through junk drawers and cabinets. I wondered what she was searching for and thought to offer my help, but I realized I didn't care if my mother found anything in our home again.

When she finally called my father and me to the big table, I pulled my sugar sack—Miranda Martinez-Cordova—from my backpack. "Dinner-time," I whispered, admiring the face I had given her with a Sharpie. Her eyes were big and wide with short lines for lashes. Her mouth was a bliss-fully flat smirk.

"Your favorite," my mother said, handing a plate to my father. He casually spun it above his head and eased into his seat at the table. The two of them were acting as if nothing had happened, as if my mother had always been there cooking in the kitchen. I felt like my father was a liar, someone who could pretend everything was fine when, really, how could he be anything but sad?

"Do you want something to drink, Sierra?" asked my mother.

"No," I said, covering Miranda's mouth. "I don't want anything."

"Nonsense," said my mother. "You're becoming a woman. Women need vitamins and nutrients. You'll have some milk."

My mother opened a cupboard, the small one beside the stove where the glasses had once been, but my father corrected her with a flick of his knife. "Left of the sink."

My mother tilted her head and steadied her mouth into a tight smile. After pouring the milk, she placed the glass in front of me and quickly glanced at Miranda. Robbie had dressed her in one of his little sister's old striped pink onesies. "Does your doll want a plate?"

"She's not a doll. And she's way too young for solids."

My mother laughed and took her seat, closing her eyes while my father led us in prayer. Miranda and I kept our eyes open. My mother had taken off the old T-shirt and wore a blue dress with white-embroidered flowers that had many loose threads. Her lips were thinner and her black hair was shorter than I remembered. She used to only wear silver, but she had on a gold necklace, the thin braided chain glowing against her bronze skin.

After we said amen, my parents made the sign of the cross and my mother opened her reddish-brown eyes. Her eye makeup appeared as a buildup of silt. "You know," she said, turning to me, "I thought we were out of salt. I was going to have you run next door to ask Mrs. Kelly if we could borrow some."

"She's dead." I hunched down and rested my chin on Miranda's head.

"What?"

"She's not alive anymore."

My father gently said, "Old Mrs. Kelly passed away last winter, Josie."

My mother mouthed an "Oh" and looked at her plate. She briskly apologized and we continued dinner in silence. Above us the ceiling fan spun in rapid circles, slicing the air, sending waves of coolness over each of us. My mother and father kept glancing at one another—smiling, chewing, smiling, sipping, and smiling some more. After some time, I got sick of their cheeriness and gulped the last of my milk. Then, as loud as possible, I slammed my empty glass on the table.

"So, *Josie*," I said, "what brings you down from Denver? Or do you normally drive around cooking pork chops for people?"

"Sierra," my father barked. "Don't you call your mother by her first name." He shook his head and I avoided his strict gaze.

My mother smiled sweetly. "Tell me about all those Indian graves the boys from your school found out west."

My stomach suddenly lurched with the sounds of digestive failure. "I don't know anything about it," I said, stroking Miranda.

"Sure you do," my father interjected. "That Roberto Martinez, the boy who found the bones, he's your partner for that sugar thing. Your school project."

"To think," my mother said. "This whole time those bones were right in Saguarita beneath our feet."

"That's not true," I said. "They weren't beneath *your* feet."

She giggled a bit. "I was here for a long while, Sierra. I think I know a thing or two about Saguarita."

Though I wanted to tell her she didn't know about anything, I turned my face to my lap and went quiet. After dinner, I sat in my room, where I pressed my ear against the cool white door. Muffled and low, I could hear my father in the living room ask my mother about her drive—road conditions, springtime flurries, if the mountain goats hobbled along the pass. He didn't ask why she was back or if she missed us—questions that hurt me to think about. I moved away from the door and tossed Miranda into the corner.

"She cried all night. I didn't get any sleep," I told Robbie the next morning as I shoved Miranda into his arms. We met outside thirty minutes before school in our usual spot by the swings. It was chilly and the air smelled like pancake breakfast and frost.

"How could she cry?" he asked. "She's only sugar."

The sun was coming up. The light leaked over the land in velvety streaks of pinks and golds. My mother once told me this meant the angels were baking cookies. "Isn't that what babies do? Cry and crap themselves and cry some more?"

"Hey," Robbie said, his chapped mouth bunched to the side. "Where's her outfit?"

"Lost it."

Robbie sighed and bent down to his backpack. He pulled a diaper from the front mesh pocket. "Give her here. We'll lose points if she's wearing the same diaper from last night." He lay Miranda on the loose gravel and frowned at the new sad, sleepy face I had given her that morning. Her eyelashes were tarantula-like and her mouth was down-turned. Robbie fumbled with the diaper, applying and reapplying the adhesive sides.

"So," I said, standing above him, "what was it like?"

"What was what like, Sierra?"

"Finding those dead people. Was it scary?"

Robbie got the diaper to stick. He patted Miranda's black marker face and stood up with a bounce. "Not scary," he said. "But it was weird, you know? We've lived here our whole lives and no one knew about all this old stuff in the ground."

"I guess," I said, thinking of the piñon trees where my father had hung a bluish hammock in our yard. Their roots, he said, had undoubtedly grazed the dead bodies of our ancestors, both Spanish and Indian. I used to play in the shade of those piñons, cracking their nuts with two rocks held firmly in my hands. After pulling away the hard shells, I'd toss the spongy insides into my mouth. I didn't swallow them, though. I was afraid of letting any amount of death, from the soil or elsewhere, work its way into me. "Everything is old here. I mean *everything*."

Robbie nodded. He was rocking Miranda back and forth in such a way I'd only seen small girls do with dolls. "I heard your mom's back again. My grandma saw her buying pork chops at Rainbow Market."

I kicked at the gravel, scuffing my Mary Janes. Dust flew between us. "The bitch is back."

Robbie pretended to cover Miranda's ears. "Dude," he said, "don't call your mom a bitch. What if Miranda called you a bitch?"

"Guess it's a good thing babies can't talk," I said. "Especially ones made of sugar."

Robbie was smiling and had lifted Miranda into the air. He briefly held her against the sky before bringing her back down. "Remember when your mom was our group leader for Day on the Prairie?"

"Yeah," I said, lowering my voice.

"And we all got lost looking for that old barn she said was haunted? Then she let us eat three packs of Oreos? And you had to go to the bathroom in the bushes." Robbie laughed, but I frowned and he quickly turned serious. "Why is she back this time?"

The school bell sounded. Class was starting in ten minutes. We reached for our backpacks and walked toward the front doors. I lifted Miranda from Robbie's arms. "Who knows with that woman? Maybe she wants to see the dig site. Or maybe she likes taking vacations to her old life."

Within a week, my mother blended into our home as well as Miranda did. Which is to say, not very well at all. When it was just my father, he worked late and usually only had time to heat up a frozen pizza or fix a box of macaroni. Our small purple house was often messy, though we each had a chore list that was conquered by Sunday. With my mother back, the home took on a new order, a different rhythm. She cooked unhealthy but comforting foods, the house constantly emitting a pungent odor of bacon grease and red chili powder. Other times she cleaned. She'd twirl around with a broom, swaying her hips to the music on the radio—an oldies station or some honky-tonk crap. Most evenings, after my father came home from work, he'd unlace his boots in the foyer and then move his arm along my mother's slight waist. Together they'd rock back and forth to the music. It was nauseating.

Each day after school, I'd come home to discover that my mother had made my bed and placed my stuffed animals in a dog pile above my pillows. I'd immediately throw them to the floor. With a detergent that reeked of artificial springtime and cottony clouds, she also did my laundry, taking the time to match my socks, a luxury I hadn't experienced in years. One afternoon, as I sat on the couch, my feet covered in those matching socks and kicked up on the armrest, my mother walked by and swiped them down like she was swatting a fly. "What're you doing inside? It's a beautiful day." Her arms were planted firmly at her sides. She wore a brightly colored tunic and black leggings, making her appear like a 1960s glamour model. She was young still, only in her mid-thirties.

"It's hotter than a pig's armpit out there." I craned my neck, looking past her at the television. An Herbal Essence shampoo commercial was on and long-haired women were moaning under waterfalls.

"You have such a foul mouth," my mother said. "And pigs don't have armpits, genius." She began lifting sofa pillows as though searching for something. "Hey, where's that sugar bag you carry around? Your little baby for school."

"She's with her father. He has her until the weekend."

"Oh," my mother said. "Well, get up off this sofa. We're going for a drive."

I couldn't remember the last time I had been alone with my mother in a car. "What? Where to?"

She smiled, the seams of her mouth running with red lipstick. "You'll see."

We parked on a steep hill overlooking the dig site. Below us archaeologists in white hats and khaki shorts swarmed the gutted earth like invasive ants. The plot was as long and wide as a shallow public swimming pool and was divvied up into human-size squares. The sky was cloudless and blue, except for the sun's golden orb. At the horizon, there was a crashing display of earth and air. My mother stood before me and held her arms out, flapping them as if they were useless wings. Wind blew her hair, twirling the strands around her face, hiding her eyes behind sections of black. For the first time since she'd come home, I remembered how beautiful I once found her to be. As a little girl, I'd play dress-up in her satin nightdresses and lacy bras, admiring their slight weight and wondering if I'd ever own clothes like that.

"What do you think?" she asked. "Isn't it pretty?"

I shrugged and stood beside her. The wind carried her jasmine scent.

"Ever feel like the land is swallowing you whole, Sierra? That all of this beauty is wrapped around you so tight it's like being in a rattlesnake's mouth?"

"I see this all the time," I said. "And I don't feel like I'm being eaten alive by anything."

My mother gave me a sideways glance. "You will someday. Maybe it'll come later for you than it did for me. Children tend to do that. Marriage. Life. All these things." Moving behind me, she hunched down and slipped her cold hands over my eyes. "Try it. Close your eyes and hold your arms against the wind. You'll feel it."

I allowed my arms to float up and coast. A kaleidoscope of images spun against my closed lids. I saw the day when I was ten years old, right before my mother left for the first time. She took me to the pueblo where her grandmother was born in New Mexico. Holding my hand, my mother walked us through a small adobe church. She touched the pews with the tips of her red nails as we moved closer to the altar. We stepped into a side room where we lit white candles with long, slim sticks. My mother sent prayers for all those she loved into the sky with smoke, but I sent only one. *Please,* I pleaded to the Virgin, *don't let my mother cry anymore.* I was sick of finding her silently weeping, the sobs bobbing in her throat— at the stove, in the bathtub, kneeling in the dead garden beside our house.

When I opened my eyes, my mother was beside me, a strange blank expression on her face. "Did you feel it?" she asked.

"No," I said. "I didn't feel anything." Goose pimples rose on my neck and arms. "It's just windy and cold."

"All right, Sierra. Then let's get home. I'll start dinner."

As she headed for her pickup, I looked over the hill's edge and down into the dig site once more. The archaeologists were huddled in small groups. The rich odor of disrupted earth blew into me. Everything was terrifyingly silent. I thought about how quiet the world could sound and how when I stood there beside my mother, for a moment, I was afraid she had left me on the hillside, stranded forever.

"Xerophthalmia," Mrs. Sharply said, "is one of many childhood diseases your babies could get." It was the following Monday, the final week of sugar babies. Another assembly was being held in the gym. Two kids in front of me had swaddled their baby in a blanket, while others around us had glued on googly eyes and red yarn mouths. Robbie sat beside me with Miranda. She looked exceptionally fashionable. That morning I had wrapped a quilted pillowcase around her like a muumuu dress.

"Among other things," Mrs. Sharply continued, "xerophthalmia is a vitamin A deficiency which makes it so a person can't produce tears."

I leaned over to Robbie. "I wish you had that disease. Then you'd stop whining about me drawing on Miranda." I had recently drawn crucifixes and anchors across her back. Tattoos, I called them, but Robbie said she looked like a bathroom wall.

"She's a baby," he whispered with closed eyes. "Babies don't need tattoos."

"Sugar," I said. "She is a bag of sugar."

"Now think for a moment," Mrs. Sharply said, waving both arms into the air. "Think of all the times you cry. Sometimes they are happy, and, sometimes, they are sad. But crying is natural. Take a moment to remember the last time *you* cried."

The gymnasium went silent. Only the hiss of the fluorescent lights above us could be heard. Students hung their heads, as if possessed by their darkest, most sorrowful memories. I waited for the other students to finish reminiscing about their dear old dead grandparents and broken bones.

"Now, parents," said Mrs. Sharply, "you can see that not being able to cry would be an awful condition. For homework, we will each need to research a childhood disease. Tomorrow we will draw diseases from a hat. Some babies will get a disease, but—just like in life—some will not. It's the luck of the draw."

* * *

Later that day, Robbie hurried after me as I walked home. His backpack seemed comically wider than he did. "You have to take Miranda," he said. "I have soccer tonight." From the giant backpack, he scooped Miranda out, slowly handing her over. She was somehow heavier than usual.

"What the heck have you been feeding her?" I asked.

Robbie petted her belly. "That was weird, Mrs. Sharply asking about crying."

"She's a real wacko," I said, hoisting Miranda on my hip. The sky was endlessly blue with paper wisps of clouds. I caught myself tilting Miranda up to see. "So, when was it, Robbie? The last time you cried?"

"That's sort of personal, Sierra."

"Roberto Martinez, I'm your child's mother. I deserve to know these things."

"All right." Robbie took a deep breath. "After I found the bones, that night I woke up and thought I saw a skeleton woman at the foot of my bed. I didn't know who she was, but later my grandma told me it was Doña Sebastiana, the lady version of the grim reaper. Death."

"You cried from a bad dream?"

"No, Sierra. It was more than that." Robbie scratched his head and his scalp sounded sandy. "What about you? When's the last time you cried?"

I peered down the block at my little purple house. My mother's pickup wasn't in the driveway and I figured she had gone to Rainbow Market for more pork chops, but for a moment something in my chest ached, a gnawing worry that she was gone again, this time for good. I broke into a sprint and ran toward home. "I don't cry," I called over my shoulder. "Only little girls and babies do that."

"I have some new tattoo ideas," I said to Miranda, who sat on the kitchen table, stiffly leaning to the left in a column of sunlight. I was sifting through the junk drawer looking for markers. I had opened every window and for the first time in days the house didn't smell like pork. It reeked with the richness of the mountains and desert, rain and sage and cedar pulled together as one. When I realized the drawer only had rubber bands and dead batteries, I said, "Don't worry, you little sack of cavities. I have some markers in my room."

I crawled beneath my bed, over the uncrushed carpet, surrounded by gobs of lint and balled hair. I was looking for a shoe box filled with art supplies, but I ended up fishing out my PRIVATE PROPERTY box instead, the place where I kept movie ticket stubs, old diaries, and birthday cards from my mother. She made the cards herself and I imagined her in some sunny apartment in downtown Denver. Houseplants and cacti lined the windows while filtered city light fell upon her at the sofa licking stamps and writing out her old address.

Sitting on my floor, my legs spread and the birthday cards dumped around me like confetti, I ran my fingers over their sharp edges and smooth ribbons. I came upon one from my eleventh birthday, the first card my mother sent after she left. I held the purple and gold paper in my palm, then opened the card as if it were the warm, beating heart of an animal. My mother had placed three marigolds inside and they nearly crumbled in my hands.

> *To my baby, Sierra. Today is your birthday, and when you were born, I knew everything would change, that every day would be your day, that nothing would be the same.*

I climbed onto my bed, where I nestled into Miranda. "See this," I said. "This is from *my* mom." I looked at her sad face, and, for a split second, I imagined Miranda as a real infant, a baby who breathed and cried. I rolled her to my lips and dryly kissed her forehead. "I don't know if I'm very nice to you," I whispered.

I then caught a glimpse of my mother standing in the doorway. She was leaning into the wall, limp and fragile. Her reddish-brown eyes were without makeup and her hair was stacked in a sloppy pile on top of her head. "You're good with her."

"She isn't real," I said.

My mother stepped toward me, moving gracefully in her skin. She at on the foot of my bed with very straight posture and stiff arms. She seemed nervous—the way cats stiffen their backs before danger strikes. "It's sort of strange they make you kids do this. You're only thirteen, but I can understand how they think it prepares you, I suppose. Not that having a sack of sugar for two weeks would prepare anyone for a new life."

I pulled Miranda closer and wiggled my thumb over her quilted midsection.

"I'm not sure if anyone is prepared for raising a child. It doesn't seem to be something we can practice before it actually happens."

I shrugged and rolled Miranda onto my belly. "Where did you go today?"

My mother stared straight ahead, her eyes glassy. "For a drive through the canyon. Would you believe it? I saw two hawks. They were playing in the wind."

Hawks were common in Saguarita. We had an entire unit in sixth grade about them. They danced before mating, could dive 150 miles per hour, stayed with one partner all their lives. I was surprised that my mother paid them any attention. "What kinds of birds do you see in the city?" I asked.

"Crows," said my mother. "Just a bunch of crows." She paused, tracing Miranda's eyelashes with her long red nails. "How long do you have her?"

"A few more days," I said, rubbing Miranda's back slowly. "I can't wait to get rid of this thing. She's so annoying."

"Imagine someday when it's a real baby. It will be much harder."

"That's the point," I said. "Miranda isn't real. If she was, I'd be a lot nicer to her, like Robbie is. He's better at taking care of her."

My mother folded her hands neatly in her lap. She kneaded her fingers back and forth and a trickle of sadness moved between us like a static shock. "Can you believe that when you were born I was only three years older than you are now?" She forced a laugh, dropped her gaze to the carpet. "I had to stop going to school."

"Did you miss it?" I asked.

My mother sighed and considered my question for a long time. "I didn't know I could miss school. I thought I was just sad, but I take classes now. At a community college. You could go there someday."

My mother went quiet. She pulled the rubber band from her head, allowing her hair to unravel around her shoulders and neck. She looked gloriously dark and light at the same time. There was a shining glint in her brown eyes. She looked younger. She looked happy. "I bet you'll be an artist someday, Sierra." My mother pointed to the tattoos across Miranda's back. "That's what I wanted to be." She smiled and we both laughed.

"Here," she said. "Let me braid your hair. I can do a tight one that will last for a few days."

I pulled away at first but soon moved back toward my mother. I was ashamed of myself that I still wanted her close to me, even after everything she had done. I eventually rested my head in her chilly hands and tried to forget how bad my mother had hurt me. Her fingers wove through my hair like she was sewing a quilt. I nearly fell asleep in her arms as I held Miranda in my own. Lying there with my mother in the afternoon light of my bedroom, I imagined her far into the future, driving day and night, her little white truck sliding from mountain peak to valley, through snow and heat waves, windstorms and lightning. Her headlights beam bright and warm, shining into town, the place where I'll live when I'm finally a grown-up and my mother's black hair is silver and her face is well lined. In the distance, I see her arriving, joyously waving to me, her last stop.

When I woke up the next morning, my father was alone at the kitchen table eating oatmeal and reading the newspaper. Part of me wanted to ask where my mother was, but I knew she was already heading north over the pass, back to that sunny apartment of hers in Denver. Even her chair was gone from the table. My father scooted a bowl of cereal toward me. He then smacked the paper with his hand. "I'll be damned," he said. "Those Indians on the ridge, they got some formal petition going. They're closing up the dig site." His eyes met mine over the top of the paper. "Sorry I didn't take you to see it, Sierra. There will be another one someday."

"I did see it," I said. "Mama took me."

My father swallowed hard and shook out the paper. It sounded like rain. "Want some orange juice with your breakfast? I got the kind without pulp that you like."

"No, Papa," I said, "I'm not feeling too good. Would it be okay if I stayed home from school?"

He raised his white eyebrows. They reflected the low sunlight pouring into the kitchen through the sheer curtains above the sink. "If you feel that bad, then of course you can."

I spent most of the day in bed with Miranda cupped in my arms. We listened to the radio perched on my windowsill. The country songs my mother liked filled the small bedroom and every now and then I'd lean over with Miranda close to my chest and feel like crying. Then, at three o'clock, there was a quick knock on the door.

Robbie stood on my stoop covered in a mist of sweat around his temples and beneath his mouth.

"What're you doing here?" I asked. "And why are you out of breath? Did you skip or something?"

He wagged his head back and forth. "It's awful, Sierra. Just awful."

"I'm sure you're a wonderful skipper. Don't be so hard on yourself."

"No, not that. It's Miranda." He hunched over and took a huge breath. "She's dead."

"Miranda can't die, moron."

Robbie peered at me, a deep sadness in his gaze. "We pulled diseases out of a hat today. Most kids didn't get anything bad. Some got chicken pox. But Miranda, she got SIDS. If you don't know what that is because you didn't do your homework, it means sudden infant death syndrome."

"I know what SIDS is," I said. "What are we supposed to do now? Throw her away?"

"But we can't," Robbie whined. "It's Miranda."

I stared at him for a long while, counting how many times he blinked without tears rolling out of his eyes. Then I said, "I have an idea."

Robbie and I parked our bikes near the edge of the hill overlooking the dig site. I had wrapped Miranda in a black pillowcase. She resembled a baby nun. I pulled her from my handlebar basket and one last time arched her face to the heavens. There was a mass of gray clouds. They spread evenly over the land like a patchwork of fog. "Look," I whispered. "Even the sky is sad for you."

Robbie stood beside me at the border between the hill and the dig site. He reached out with a thin chicken wing of an arm and patted Miranda softly on the head. We stood at the edge of the hill for some time, listening to the grumbling moans of the clouds and the far-off crackling of thunder. I picked out a spot easy to aim for in the middle of the pit. Then, tipping back, I readied myself to launch Miranda above my head with both arms, but Robbie stopped me. "You're going to throw Miranda in there?"

"What else can we do?"

With those big sad eyes, he looked into the dig site. Then he looked at me. "I can kick her farther."

"You're going to kick our baby into her grave?" The wind carried my voice away from me as if it wasn't my own to begin with.

"I play soccer, Sierra."

Taking her from my arms, he delicately set Miranda on the edge of the hill, her limp body leaning mostly to the left. He backed up a few steps, and then pushed himself forward with huge strides, his arms flying. When his tennis shoe made contact with Miranda, her body lifted from the earth as though she was nothing more than a helium balloon. She twirled in the air as her sugar insides spiraled out of her body from a hole Robbie's foot had torn in the bag. The sugar blew with the wind, sprinkling the dirt with bits of white. How pretty, I thought, and she landed with a thud.

RYKA AOKI

To the New World

D*ammit—I thought Asian hair was supposed to be easy!* Millie Wong was on the verge of tears. She yanked her brush through her hair. *Tangled and frizzy... shouldn't it be long and straight?* Maybe there was some hidden, female thing: her sister had perfect hair and her mother, too. *You're so stupid! You don't even pass to your own hair! You clumsy, tranny freak....*

As strands of her hair snapped, a sharp pain brought her back to reality. *Okay, okay, calm down. Come on, Millie, deep breaths. You slept with wet hair, that's all. Deep breaths. No yelling today. Breathe. Think of Grandma.*

Millie steadied herself, took small handfuls of hair and brushed them gently down to the ends. When she was done, she repeated the process with her straightening iron. Feathers of steam floated off the iron, leaving her hair like shimmering ribbons. *Thank goodness.*

She peeked at the clock and shook her head. Getting ready was bad enough on any Sunday morning, but this was her grandmother's birthday.

For Millie, her grandmother's birthday was not just about remembering her passing. It was her most important family gathering, even if it was just between herself and the photograph of her grandmother on the kitchen table. Back when she was Victor, Millie had been her favorite grandson. Of course, Millie had no idea how her grandmother would have reacted to her transition—she probably would have been horrified. But one could always imagine otherwise, and besides, since her death two years ago, she was the only person in her family Millie could love without fear of getting disowned.

And today, Millie was going to the farmers market. She wanted to cook something to offer her grandmother—nothing fancy—just some simple food, like they used to share so many years ago.

She peeked outside and frowned. It was another stupid L.A. winter day—not enough drizzle to call rain, but enough to spoil all the work she had put into her hair. But so it was. She sighed, grabbed her purse, and trudged past the greasy Thai restaurant to the crosswalk. A tow truck stopped to let her pass—and the driver nodded as she hurried across the street.

Millie Wong smiled for the first time all day.

You see, that truck—that driver—would *never* have stopped for Victor. It's not easy, almost getting run over by the cars and trucks pretending not to see you, not even trying to disguise that they don't care. That's how it was for Victor Wong. A nondescript Asian boy, he was an afterthought. A non-thought. It wasn't so much being hated—it was being invisible. It was going to the mall and having the salespeople help the customer who came in after you or waiting too long to get a table at a restaurant. But for Millie? Cars would stop. Doors would open. People would smile—even flirt sometimes.

Millie knew about objectification. She knew about racism and oppression. She knew how ugly anti-Asian violence could be. And she knew most people could barely tell the difference between Chinese and Japanese, let alone discern the identities of ethnic Chinese from Thailand, Malaysia, or Vietnam.

But after a life of being ignored, was it wrong to like people being *nice* to you?

By the time Millie wandered down Sunset to Ivar and turned into the farmers market, the skies had cleared and a clean offshore wind mixed the familiar smell of car exhaust with the aromas of fruits, vegetables, and sweaty patchouli. Almost instinctively, Millie studied other women—how they were walking and speaking. Her parents had lost their accents by mimicking the TV and radio. One of Millie's main reasons for listening to KPFK was to practice saying "Nina Totenberg, NPR News, Washington." But nothing was better than watching people live, catching snippets of conversation that conveyed gender, ethnicity, even social standing:

"I'd *like* a mocha *latte* with *soy* milk."

"What's a *good* recipe for Hun-*garian* peppers?"

While listening to conversations swirl around her, Millie purchased two heirloom tomatoes, which were strangely available even though out-of-season. However, it wasn't a great day at the market; much of the produce was pretty sketchy, and she tried not to judge the sorry excuse for fresh basil. *We're not in an Asian market in San Gabriel. We're with the white people in L.A., in Hollywood, and the basil is organic. It's organic.*

And then she saw it: a poofy loaf of sweet bread, made with milk and sugar and butter. It was soft, like a steamed bun. Her grandmother had loved that sort of bread, especially toward the end, when she couldn't chew very well. Putting the loaf into her bag and preparing to pay, Millie remembered the hospital room. She remembered pulling off small bits of steamed bun and feeding them to her grandmother with fragrant, luke-warm tea.

Suddenly a loud voice brought her back to Hollywood.

"Yo, Millie, what up?"

Her name was Sierra, and to Millie, she looked the part. She seemed as tall and solid as a mountain, with sky-blue eyes that rarely blinked. She was one of those dykes who didn't just want to take back the night—she wanted to grab and throttle it. When Millie had first met Sierra at this very market, a little over a year ago, as a loud voice from above complain-ing about the excessive sweetness of Fuji apples, she had been awestruck. How could Sierra be so loud and yet so completely female? When Millie first asked this, Sierra had laughed. She said, "You Asian women are like those little *beep beep* horns on a Prius. Sure, it sounds cute, but the big truck crowding your lane ain't gonna move. You gotta sound like you *mean* it!" Sierra had said. And whatever "it" was, Sierra meant it.

Millie had never been exactly comfortable with Sierra's blanket take on Asians—she knew some loud and obnoxious Asian women—but she had been happy to make a new friend. Sierra warmed to Millie quickly over afternoons of homemade scones and political protests, and she infused Millie with opinions on nuclear power, on meat, and on the patriarchy. Then, during a conversation about "Why penises?" Millie responded, "Sierra, I'm trans."

Just like that. She had no idea why it slipped out like that.

Mille remembered being frozen, horrified, half-expecting Sierra to get up and walk away. But instead, Sierra busted out laughing.

"I *knew* there was something about you. I mean I couldn't tell, real-ly—I mean you're beautiful, but something was different . . . *shit!*" Millie started laughing, too, and then came all the usual Trans 101 questions, which Millie tried her best to answer. Sierra listened, and then pro-nounced Millie to be okay, because she didn't feel that male energy come off her. This made Millie feel happy and safe, especially since Sierra was pretty buff: not someone she wanted to see mad.

But from then on, it wasn't the same. Oh, Sierra was still just as friendly as ever, but Millie could sense the difference. Sierra started treating Millie less like possible dating material and more like a younger brother-sister. She was happy to tell Millie what it meant to be a socially and politically responsible woman, but also made it clear that, with trannies, there was always male privilege to root out. "You can't go out alone at night or walk into any old sports bar without fear anymore, you know!" she told Millie. Coming from Asian parents who taught her to avoid large groups of drunken white men, Millie had actually never been to a sports bar, but she nodded and listened, careful not to interrupt her friend.

Today, Sierra focused on the bread in Millie's bag. "So you're still supporting the dairy industry, eh?"

Millie trembled. She had been caught with the non-vegan bread. Of course it wasn't vegan. It was her grandmother's favorite type of American bread. If it wasn't for her grandmother, she probably wouldn't have chosen it, because Millie was thinking about becoming vegan. She really *was* sad that she had been born with male privilege and thought that maybe by being vegan in some way she could be closer to the woman she wanted to be. A caring woman. A strong woman. A *vegan* woman.

"It's my grandmother's birthday, and it was her favorite bread," she finally ventured.

But Sierra continued, "Patriarchy is patriarchy. It's not just animal flesh. Do you know that dairy cows end up in McDonald's hamburgers? They're genetically engineered to produce milk, but once their production falls, they're just killed. It's worse than what happens to beef cattle, in some ways. I mean, it's like the Tibetan women—they have nothing but their stories and weaving, but the men in the Chinese government want to take those away from them, too."

Millie wondered what Tibetan women had to do with dairy cattle and the loaf of bread, but she knew better than to interrupt. She knew that Sierra was an activist on so many fronts that sometimes she made connections that might seem convoluted to others. Plus, any argument Millie might make would surely trigger accusations of male privilege and, in this case, of possible connections with the Chinese government.

Millie nodded at Sierra and put the sweet loaf back.

As they walked away, Sierra gushed about this great spa just outside Palm Springs with an authentic Japanese Zen garden. Millie mentioned she might like to go, but Sierra said no, it's a women-only space. "You know,*women* women—but I thought you might appreciate the Zen part, being Asian and all. Very feng shui."

Again, Millie nodded. She tried not to dwell on "women-only" spaces, or why someone would mention a Japanese Zen garden in the same breath as feng shui. She remembered that she had made the mistake of talking about Asian issues to Sierra before. Sierra had told her that "men are men: Chinese men and Japanese men both abused women, like those women in World War Two.... Oh, that was the Korean war? Whatever. It's all the same oppression."

Millie wondered if all men and Asians and wars really were the same. Whatever?

Millie thought about her grandmother as one particular girl escaping Vietnam in one particular rusty, rotting boat.

And today was her birthday.

"Hey, you okay?" Sierra's words shook her out of her thoughts. "That women-only stuff didn't bug you, did it?"

"Uh-uh."

"You can tell me. I know all about tranny issues. I'm still friends with you, right?"

Millie tried to smile, but this time the smile wouldn't come. Sierra noticed and put her arm around her. "Listen doll: I've been there. I know what it's like. One of my girlfriends went and transitioned on me once," she said.

Millie looked up at her, surprised.

"Yeah, it was rough. One day she was she, then the next day—I don't know. I was confused, I'll tell you what. Of course I made sure that everyone knew that James had been Rebecca, and that she—I mean he—I mean I—was still a dyke. I didn't want people thinking I went straight. No way am I going to be straight..." Sierra's voice seemed to tremble before she caught herself. "James was so mad! But what could I do? I mean, hey, it's okay if she wants to go be a guy or something, but don't push that on me."

"Maybe you just weren't meant for each other," Millie offered.

"Yeah, no shit. James was great, though," Sierra blinked, coughed, and tried to turn it into a chuckle. "Trans women. What's up with that?"

Millie didn't know what to say. She didn't even think of correcting her on trans men. Instead, before she could stop herself, she blurted, "Well I think *you're* great." Then, wondering why she said that, she fidgeted and added, "I have to go home now. Get back to my grandmother."

Sierra didn't seem to notice Millie's distress. "Cool beans! I'd like to meet her one day—she sounds like a great woman. I gotta run anyway. Call me later, okay? Ciao!"

Sierra winked and turned away, then stopped. Suddenly she spun around and hugged Millie very lightly, as if she were made of clouds. She gave an awkward half-smile, a little wave, and was off.

Millie stood there waiting for the city to stop spinning. She considered going back to get the bread, but she wasn't sure if this would be male privilege and about what to do if Sierra came back. So she took her heirloom tomatoes, along with some rather nice parsnips, and walked home. As she walked, Millie again noticed the politeness of the drivers. She didn't need Sierra to tell her about fetishizing Asian women, but all Victor had ever gotten were sneers and indifference. It never seemed like much of a privilege. Was it wrong to feel good about being nodded at? About having a door opened? About having a car stop? Didn't they also stop for her grandmother? The same grandmother who would have been killed, or worse, by soldiers in Vietnam?

In the kitchen, Millie took off her shoes and studied the photograph of Grandma. She retrieved the vegetables from her shopping bag, noticing that they looked a little smaller and tougher than they had at the market. Tomatoes . . . parsnips.

Parsnips? Gazing at them, Millie suddenly started to cry.

You stupid! It's Grandma's birthday, and you didn't even bring home the sweet bread! She had bought tomatoes and parsnips—Grandma didn't even know what parsnips *were*.

Oh Grandma! Only three years ago, they were strolling through San Gabriel looking for cheap groceries and steamed pork buns. Grandma would tell stories about coming to this wonderful country, how they fled Saigon, endured pirates from Thailand, about being so crowded aboard the boat that she could only sit because there wasn't enough space to lie down.

Millie looked at the parsnips. She tried to imagine what Grandma would say, not just about her transition, but about this whole vegan business and how it somehow related to womanhood. Heck, what would she say about the organic vegetables at the farmers market, when at Ranch 99, they were half the price and twice as fresh?

And then Millie stopped. In a daze, she opened her freezer and dug around. The two pork buns she found there weren't from providence. They were from being Asian and having a freezer full of ethnic food. She paused, full of trepidation about backsliding to meat, about oppression and male privilege and Sierra. Nevertheless, with Grandma's photograph looking right at her, she put the buns in the microwave.

Of course, the buns weren't from her grandmother—*that* would have been weird—but from her last visit to her parents. "Victor, why is your hair so long?" they had asked. "Who's going to marry you like that?" She had been waiting for the right time to tell them, knowing that it might never come. She was still waiting.

The microwave beeped, and Millie hesitated before opening it. She put a bun in front of Grandma's photograph, then took the other one and bit into it. The scalding pork filling burned her tongue, but instead of bringing tears, the pain brought memories. There was a rush of spices and aromas and tastes, a rush of family and faces and sounds. She remembered moon cakes and pork buns and screaming kids and beating her cousins at poker late into the night. Violin from Suzuki and math from Kumon. Smuggling bags of dried cuttlefish into the movie theater and Costco beef jerky into Disneyland. She remembered all these things, and so much more.

If I come out to the family, I'll lose everything. But it's more than that. I don't want my family to be laughed at, for all my mother's friends to see her and say, "Look, there's the one with the freak for a son." Yet, I can never go back to living a lie.

Suddenly, Millie realized something in a new way.

Once, when Grandma was in the hospital, Millie had told her that she was very brave to have left home for America. To her surprise, Grandma had started laughing.

"Brave? No, not brave. You do because you have to. Oh, you give things up, but maybe you find new things, too. I left so much family behind," Grandma had said. "They called me crazy. But they couldn't leave, and I couldn't stay. Of course I miss home, but look at my life here! We didn't have Ranch 99 Supermarket in Vietnam, you know!"

As Millie remembered Grandma's laugh, she started to cry again, but it wasn't from sorrow. She felt new, a new connection with her grandmother and with the rest of her family as she saw her own life and identity, for the first time, as an immigrant. It didn't matter whether the distance was measured in miles or communities, whether you were going to a new country or to a new gender—it was still a long and violent journey. It was still full of people who would call you brave, people who would call you crazy, and people who would never call you again.

"Brave? No, not brave. You do because you have to."

Millie looked at the parsnips, seeming sad and out-of-place on the countertop. She thought about Sierra and about her other friends, too: gay, queer, trans, Goths, poets—friends who sometimes just didn't understand, but who really meant well. *"Oh, you give things up, but maybe you find new things, too."*

She held up her bun, flipped her hair from her eyes, nodded at Grandma, and said, as if she were making a toast: *"To the New World!"*

She chuckled as she imagined Sierra's reaction to her and her pork buns. Then she took another bite and stopped thinking altogether. When she was done eating, she smiled, sighed, and decided that she might call Sierra in a while, maybe to grab some coffee. Yes, she'd like that. Sierra seemed like she needed to talk—besides, maybe Millie could tell her the difference between trans women and trans men. Maybe one day she might even ask Sierra out to have lunch with her in San Gabriel, go shopping at Ranch 99—who was to say?

With a practicality that would have made Grandma smile, Millie covered the other bun and put it on the kitchen counter, not in the freezer. The pork bun had been frozen all this time—but once it was warm and steaming, its spices and flavors were to be experienced as soon as possible, like a life now ready to be real.

MARIA ANDERSON

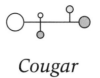

Cougar

Our trailer sat on cinder blocks in a half-acre lot a four-cigarette drive outside of town. There wasn't much else around except Jenny's trailer and forest that started at the end of the lot and went on for as far as you could see, dim and impenetrable. Dad kept pink healing quartz on the porch steps, rocks he'd found in the deepest parts of forests, back when there was still old-growth forest to be logged. He was a sad, quiet guy. Never argued with me or knocked me around like dads of guys I used to know. We played cards with his old logging friends when they came through town. Summers we shot coyotes in the Rattlesnakes. Slept outside without tents or bear spray. I never felt safer. We hunted elk and deer. I loved having my hands deep inside something just barely dead, seeing what organs and muscles and fat looked like from the inside. Better than any science class. We had a decent, quiet life in that trailer.

Dad's logging operation went under. He got even quieter. When he wasn't sleeping, he would drink Heinekens and sit in the living room, which was really just a wide hallway between the bedrooms and kitchen, and watch the forest through the window. Most dads I knew drank Bud, but mine liked Heineken and was okay with paying more for it. Koda would sit protectively next to him. She was a mute Pyrenees, who like my father was parted from her natural vocation—her ancestral duties were keeping livestock alive—and so cared for us instead, herding our trucks out of the driveway and guiding them back in whenever we returned, that kind of thing.

What was Dad thinking about when he sat like this? Just going over things in his head? All the trees he'd run chainsaws through with crews of guys from all over, the few women he'd slept with, wobbly nights driving back from Bonner bars with old logging buddies. Dad loved the woods, and, I think, for him, felling the oldest trees in the oldest forests didn't mean he loved them any less. Maybe he was thinking about my mother, who left when I was two. Maybe he was just watching the trees and not thinking about anything at all. Maybe he was hoping to spot the cougar I'd seen a few times now, the one folks were saying killed Shively's new colt and came back for the rest of him before they could get him buried.

Dad disappeared the day I got my senior pictures back. Late April. His wallet on the table with everything still in it, empty Heinekens in the sink. I checked the closet and was relieved to see the rifle and shotgun. His truck was still there, key in the ignition, old Copenhagen cans on the floor, orange juice bottles half-full of his spit, SunChip bags crammed into the seats. I touched the chewed passenger's-side seat belt where Koda had worked on it all the way home from the pound. I pulled out my senior pictures. I was eighteen, but in them I looked like a kid. A dumb, smiling kid, because when people asked me to smile, that's what I'd do.

Search and rescue never found a body. One member of the search committee, a homeless asshole there for the free lunch, pulled me aside and told me it was "them aliens" who took my father, the ones who doodled on all the trees. He pointed at a larch.

"That's Dutch elm," I said.

He nodded. Licked a yellow stain at the corner of his mouth and wiped the area dry with his sleeve. "Nope," he said. Before he took off, he pressed fifteen dollars and the Snickers bar from his sack lunch into my hands.

The rifle was a gentle-looking black .22 semiautomatic. Polymer plastic blend. I associated it with the peaceful feeling of completing a hunt, the comfort of fresh meat. I carried it into the living room and pointed it out the window, hoping the cougar would choose this moment to stroll through. I peeled off a sock and clicked off the safety and aimed at my big toe. I stood there for what felt like hours, wondering what kind of hurt could come from something small as a toe. I tried to think about all the places Dad could have gone and might still be. Tried not to think about how he might have offed himself, if that's what he'd done. I shot a few holes into the ceiling above where Dad used to sit, and when that didn't make me feel better, I kicked the wall until I hit a stud and cut my foot so bad I couldn't make myself keep going.

The pain felt like something else in the dark room, dim and sweet.

I searched the woods for weeks, ignoring the throbbing cut in my foot. Hoping to find what search and rescue couldn't. I never fixead the ceiling or the wall and tried not to look at them. Koda started sleeping in my bed at night instead of Dad's, arranging herself in the center of the mattress at crotch level, so I'd have to lie on one side around her or else sleep with my legs spread. She'd close her eyes but was awake in a way and watching me. Any time I got up during the night, she'd snap open her eyes and follow me to the bathroom or kitchen, making sure I returned to bed. There her ribcage rose and fell slower than I thought possible. Watching her breathe reminded me of the one girl I'd slept with. I used to watch that girl's belly go up and down and press my hand into it. Her stomach went concave when she inhaled, and my hand was sucked into her by her breathing. It was strange, pressing my hand into Koda's long white fur and feeling the same thing. That girl now sold eight-dollar coffee in Williston to creepy oil-field guys.

A hawk or something that sounded like one made a long, ugly noise in the distance.

In June I went full-time washing dishes at one of Bonner's worst restaurants, a Chinese place by the interstate. Bonner was an old logging town, population 1,600 and shrinking. Business was usually slow. Even when we were busy it felt slow. And the food was rough. Real rough. Greasy piles of chicken or beef probably slaughtered years ago, thawed and slopped with sauce that left orange residue on the plates. I'd turn down a free ticket to China if anybody ever offered me one. They'd go, "Here, Cal. Round-trip to Beijing. On me." Thanks, but no fucking thanks. The only places Dad ever traveled were logging camps in Washington and Oregon. Except one time he'd gone to California, where a kid tried to grab his wallet. Hit him in the face with a busted lightbulb when Dad wouldn't give it up. The bulb nicked the artery in his cheek.

Washing dishes wasn't bad. You could go the whole day without talking to anyone if you didn't feel like it. A lot of jobs weren't like that— you had to bullshit with customers or coworkers whether you liked it or not. Here you just stuck in your headphones and everything disappeared. Some days, though, I was happy to have company. I'd smoke a cigarette with the old grandma whose son and daughter-in-law owned the place. She chain-lit stale Montanas she got cheap off the Rez, squinching her eyes shut and breathing the smoke in deep.

Slow days the owners had me drive trash to the Clark Fork and throw it in. They didn't want to pay for a dumpster. This got me out of the restaurant, but I hated leaving garbage in such a beautiful place. The river was so blue and clear I didn't have words for it. Dry heat wagged the horizon. I'd smoke on the muddy bank and stare at the water. Once a moose and her calf were drinking from the far shore. I wanted to shoot them, thinking of the nice, oily meat. The calf walked underneath its mom to get to the other side of her, then looked up at her to see if she'd noticed, but the mom was watching me. Other times I'd see what I thought were probably their heart-shaped tracks on my side of the shore, their toes splayed in the mud. After that day with the moose, I started leaving the trash in the back of my truck to ditch on my way home from work. I'd toss it in an abandoned sawmill instead, where the flies and bees buzzed so loud in the heat that I could hear them before getting out of the truck.

The owners of the Chinese restaurant, who were actually Korean, kept a quiet shrine on the floor in the corner of the dining room. The shrine had a picture of a sad-looking man with a dented head, a bowl of bruised clementines, and a plastic cat that waved its paw at you. An up-and-down wave. Maybe that was how Korean people waved. The cat waved at you like it was waving away all the stuff you thought about. Like it was urging you not to think, not to worry about being able to buy food or pay rent or feel like you should try to make some friends or have sex again because that was what eighteen-year-olds did. I sometimes stole clementines from the shrine. At home I peeled them and gave half to Koda. She'd accept them and gravely spit out the pulpy mess.

After Dad disappeared, Jenny would come over to pick up the rent. He'd trip on the quartz in the dark and cuss his way up the porch steps. The old Indian had a fat, gray rattail that looked like it was feeding on his brain. He lived across the lot in a trailer that was out of earshot but close enough for me to see the shape of him moving around, trimming the bushes around his property, dragging long, limp branches inside for his stove, pounding some skinned animal into the side of his shed. I'd heard Jenny had some kind of cancer, or some other disease. Something eating him from the inside.

"Met these women on the internet," he told me once, a few months after Dad left. We were on my porch again. He tucked the rent into the pocket of a grimy, striped T-shirt. His armpit skin was tanned and saggy, but the skin on his face was pale and smooth. I didn't know about meeting women online. Seemed desperate. If I met a girl, I'd want it to be in person. But then again I wasn't meeting anyone at all.

From the restaurant parking lot, I'd sometimes see Jenny pull into the

Super 8 across from the Chinese restaurant and sit at the lobby's guest computer. What kind of picture was he showing these ladies?

I'd hear music blasting. See the shapes of Jenny and a woman playing a game of naked tag outside like kids. The whitish glow of a woman's ass in the porch light. Some nights I wondered if they weren't playing at all, and the woman was trying to get away from him, or if play had tipped into something else. When the campers took off, Jenny would usually come over, tripping on the steps, red-cheeked and reeking of sex. He was usually drunk and happy and had a joint he wanted us to smoke. This happened a couple times a month.

"Cal, you got to try it. Young guy like you, you need to get your dick wet," he said one evening. Koda was lying in the dirt but kept getting up and going inside and coming out again, wanting to go to bed. If she could speak, she'd whine, but instead she hovered, moving from one side of us to the other, trying to herd us inside.

"My dick's just fine," I said.

"Cal, I'm serious," he said. "You got to get out of Bonner. You got to start figuring out what you want to do next."

I was quiet. Koda gave up and lay down next to me.

"You're not living in this trailer for good, are you?" said Jenny. "You can't wash dishes forever." He sat on the porch steps and stuck the unlit joint all the way inside his mouth, pulled it slowly out to coat it with spit, and passed the lighter back and forth as he rotated it, drying out the paper before applying the flame.

"Your dad was a weird duck—never knew what that guy was thinking. But guys like him, they're so nice they sometimes can't say what it is they want. I think wherever he is, it hurt him bad to leave you. That's all you need to know."

I took a big drag of the joint and coughed. We passed it back and forth, pressing our lips to the same soggy end, and sat there awhile after we finished.

"Man, I'm flipped outta my rig," said Jenny. "Flipped outta my fucking rig!" He hauled himself up by the porch railing, took a last coughing drag, and stumbled down the steps. He tripped on a piece of quartz on the last one, picked it up, cussed, and chucked it toward the forest. It bounced off something and came rolling back into view.

I was still living with Koda in that trailer over a year after Dad left, working at the Chinese restaurant. I'd been alive nineteen years and had no idea what to do with myself. I finally cleaned out Dad's old wallet and threw it away. After staring into his face for a long time, I threw out his driver's license and old ID cards too.

I saw my friend Blake outside the gas station, holding a cup of shit coffee in a fancy portable mug. It was summer. The asphalt was starting to radiate heat. Blake had heard about Dad, and he didn't like that I was still living in the trailer.

"It's not so bad," I said.

He told me about Williston, where he worked on an oil rig. He was here to see his folks. "Hard living, but a couple years of this and I'll be doing anything I want." I didn't understand exactly what it was he did. "Two weeks on, one off, bud. Fifty thou a year. Pretty good for a Bonner High School grad, huh bud."

"It's not bad here," I said.

"Cal, you want to end up like these people?" He looked around the empty parking lot. Across the street, guys piled into a truck loaded with construction supplies, and we heard one give a loud, girlish giggle. They seemed all right to me.

"Williston's the kind of place that can change your luck," said Blake. "Make enough money to do whatever you want. Hell, you could live in my basement. Bring Koda. Think about it. We could get beach houses in Florida, bud. Watch ladies in bikinis walk through our yard every day. Track caribou up in Canada. You could finally teach me how to hunt."

I'd heard about guys losing a finger or arm at those jobs, or getting hooked on pills or whatever else they had down there. But a beach house sounded nice.

Jenny and I hunted together all fall. Mulies, mostly. Once in a while an elk. He didn't need my help and I didn't need his, but I think we both liked the company.

Jenny's legs had gotten so thin his pants hung off them. Whatever disease he had seemed to be getting worse. His face wasn't smooth and puffy anymore. His cheekskin hung on two cheekbones. Oily skin under his eyes the color of chow mein. Looking at it made me hungry, even though I hated chow mein. The rattail was the only thing that looked healthy about him. It looked fatter than before. It reminded me somehow of the waving cat at the restaurant, this long piece of hair rooted into his skull, wagging at me as I followed it through the woods. Slowly sucking the fat out of him, but also saying, don't worry, don't worry. I wondered where his meat was going, since we split whatever we got. He was so skinny. I figured he gave some of it as presents when women visited.

We had to walk farther than usual to find game, and the animals we did find looked hungry. On our longest hike, I shot a porcupine. Jenny showed me how to skin it. We roasted it over a fire, and he explained you have to cook it a long time because of tapeworms. The meat was greasy and crisp and tasted like pine.

"You think my dad killed himself?" I asked. That's what I'd come to believe. It was easiest thinking he'd made a choice and acted on it. That he hadn't left me to go live somewhere else, or died by accident in some far-off ravine in the woods. Even if I didn't believe it, it seemed like the best way to stop wondering.

"I don't think he would," said Jenny. "But you never know."

We never saw the cougar that killed Shively's colt. The Korean grandma told me she'd seen it on one of her nighttime walks around town. "My son thinks mountain lions are the most beautiful animal in Montana," she said. Her son was tracking him. Wanted to stuff him, mount him on the restaurant wall like he was about to jump. "Like a display he saw in a museum in San Francisco," she said. "It would bring business in. People like to see." I pictured a cougar crammed with stuffing, bigger than he'd ever been alive. Stuck crouching sadly above diners. Eyes made in a factory by children. Wanting to maim these Chinese-food-eating cretins. The gross orange sauce and greasy chicken smells seeping into his corpse.

A postcard came from Blake. A well spit up black oil on the front. On the back, in smashed-together handwriting, like maybe his hands were tired, it said, *Basemnt still free. Talked to my boss abt a job for you. Come out, bud.* I stuck it on the fridge.

At the restaurant, I came to look forward to talking to the grandma. There was never anything to report on her son's cougar hunt, so she'd tell me about the sad-looking man in the shrine photo and how he and her dad had sampled LSD and eaten gas-station steak and eggs every morning for a month. He'd also smuggled a lemon the size of a football from California to Korea in the '70s. This all seemed unappealing to me, stuff I'd never want to do. The lemon, her dad said, was from a famous lemon farm and would bring his family luck. She said she came from a place called Soul.

I started smoking Rez cigarettes too. Mostly quit buying beer. Drove slower to save gas, so that the trailer was now a six-cigarette drive from town.

Stole more than usual from the Missoula Walmart, filling a trash can in the self-checkout line with Koda's food and other junk and just ringing up the heavy can, which I'd later return. I'd save as much cash as I could every month, rolling the twenties and sticking them in a cigarette carton.

After work I'd sit with my back to the living room window and the forest, watching the shapes the light and the trees made on the wall. I stared for once at the six holes in the ceiling which formed a loose circle and at the kicked-in part of the wall I'd ended up nailing a piece of plywood over. I made a beer last a long time, closing my eyes and sipping and looking at the colors the sun made through the skin of my eyelids.

Blake called to tell me he'd spoken to his boss about me, but I needed to pass a test first. Over the next weeks he helped me study over the phone. I drove to Missoula for the exam. Most questions I had to just guess. At least, that's what I thought. A few weeks later a letter came. I'd passed.

When Jenny smoked a cigarette I'd go out and smoke one too, so I could wave at him and see him wave back. I'd wave up and down, like the cat in the shrine. I'd go inside, sit on the couch, and think about how many moments like this a man could have in a day, a week, a year. A year felt like an unbearably long time.

When Jenny didn't want to hunt, Koda and I roamed even farther from the trailer, and I guided us back. The Clark was muddy from runoff and no longer as blue. I was still leaving trash at the sawmill, where the growing pile was drawing more and more flies and bees.

One day I was sitting on the porch hoping Jenny would come over after he was finished with the woman whose camper was parked in his yard. I hoped he'd bring another joint.

I heard a strange, muffled wheeze, the kind Koda would make if she had to make a noise. At first I just saw her running. A ways behind her was the cougar. The air smelled sour. The cougar was moving fast but with a limp. In front of the cougar was Koda, running along the side of the ravine. She was heading for the brush where the forest started. I needed to run inside for the rifle, but I couldn't move. I wanted to throw up. She was going fast for an old dog, but not as fast as I knew she could run. As she neared the forest, she became a white blur.

He got her before she could reach the brush. I went inside for the rifle. When I went outside they were one big shape, like a cartoon of the Tasmanian Devil I'd watched as a kid, churning up dust. He had her by the neck. I got a bead on the shape and shot. The cougar dropped her and loped away.

I'd hit Koda in the leg. I carried her back to the trailer and tried to pry the bullet out with a knife while I hugged her body to keep her still. She panted but otherwise made no sound. She grinned in pain. All I could do was move the bullet around. Finally I carried her inside and laid her on my bed.

The next morning when I woke up, Koda was gone. I got the rifle and ran outside. I ran along the ravine, thinking she maybe went for water. There was one spot with a lot of blood that looked shiny in the sun. It might not have been hers.

I looked for her until it got too dark to see.

That night I sat outside until I couldn't feel my hands or face. I thought of how the cougar had returned to eat the rest of Shively's colt. For the next few days I kept looking for Koda, barely taking time to eat, ditching work. I saw what I thought was cougar shit, which looks like cat shit, only bigger. There was no sign of Koda.

At work the son told me to start collecting uneaten meat from peoples' plates for his dogs, but I was pretty sure he didn't have any dogs. I turned the water to the hottest setting and sprayed my hands until they turned red, until I couldn't stand it anymore. When the cook warned me a pan was hot, I'd pick it up anyway. Soon my hands were covered with burns. I couldn't stop looking for Koda. I couldn't sleep. I'd lie awake looking at the friendly burns on my hands. In the dark they looked like leeches.

After a week, I found her. There were big cat prints around her body. Smaller prints that looked like little hands—raccoon, probably—had been patting the ground around her, as though trying to comfort the tail and paws that still looked like paws and the matted and reeking outsides of her. None of this looked like it had ever been part of the dog that used to watch me while I slept. Her eyes were closed and her lips were pulled back into a snarl, or a grimace. Her front paws were bent, as if trying to protect her stomach; this part of her that I'd watched rise and fall was gone. The middle of her had been eaten, everything inside her rib cage and some of the bones too, and the ground where her stomach used to be was dark. The fur around her back paws was pink. I hugged her head, stroked her big smooth teeth. I buried her under the living room window, inside one of Dad's old sleeping bags.

I threw out her bowls and blanket. I wouldn't need them in Williston. After a few years, I'd go to California to see the lemon farms, if those still existed. I'd go to Florida and buy a house with a pool and pay someone to clean it.

For a while I would wake up and find Koda's white hair everywhere. The hair both depressed and comforted me. I tried to pick it off my clothes, but it kept reappearing on stuff I'd already washed. I missed sleeping with her in my bed, letting her eat fried rice out of my hand, dumping out her water bowl, shouting her name to call her back inside, an excuse to yell as loud as I could. Later I removed her water bowl from the trash, running a finger along the rough white crust. At breakfast I'd read the calcification rings like a cereal box, looking for something I could use.

A postcard arrived from Blake with the same oil well. Maybe they sold only one kind of postcard in Williston. It said in this same smashed handwriting: *Florida. Beach. Caribou. Come out, brother. Boss has ben asking abt you.* I put it next to the other one on the fridge. I took out the cigarette carton and counted the cash I'd saved so far. Not much.

The grandma was unhappy I missed work. She cut my hours. I tried not to worry. I quit putting twenties in the carton. Sometimes I needed to borrow a few, and I could never pay myself back.

One morning I walked to Jenny's. He'd installed a Cherokee Nation sticker on the mailbox: a man's face inside a red square. Above him, a star and some kind of branch. The man looked tired, stuck to that mailbox, like he was sick of seeing the mailman's hand crammed inside his little metal establishment every day, stuffing circulars and impersonal letters, never a fat check or a *Penthouse* or a wedding invitation.

Jenny emerged from his trailer. He was wearing clothes that struck me as not being his, though of course they could be no one else's. I asked him if he'd seen the cougar.

"The thing killed Koda," I said.

"Dammit. Dammit, Cal, I'm sure as hell sorry to hear that." Jenny scratched his knee through a hole in his jeans, moving the hole around to reach more skin. He coughed and wiped his chin. "Sometimes those big cats, they come down from the mountains when they can't get enough to eat."

"Jenny." I'd never asked him for help since my dad went away, tried never to be late on rent. I asked if he'd help me find the cougar.

"Why? You thinking of killing him?" said Jenny.

I wasn't sure why. Maybe I was. I wanted to at least get a good look.

"I'm not sure an animal deserves getting shot for being hungry," said Jenny. "Nope, I'm not sure it does at all."

I resolved to go out on my own but lost my nerve.

* * *

The grandma fired me from the restaurant. Her son's son had aged out of his paper route. "My grandson tried to find a job everywhere else in town, you know. He did not want to work here. But no one would hire him. You're a good worker, but he's family, you know? You know we are the only Korean people in Bonner?" She lit her cigarette on the third try and tucked my lighter into my sweatshirt pocket.

"We had a Korean restaurant but no one came. People here only want shit Chinese food. No *kalguksu*, no *gimbap*, no *bibimbap*. Nothing crazy. Nothing they wouldn't like. But they didn't want it. They wanted shit. They wanted a very cheap, big portion of shit." She closed her eyes. "What I decide is, people want shit, you give them shit," she said.

I finished my shift even though she implied I wouldn't get paid for it. I wondered if my trailer was shit, if my way of living was shit. If Dad's life had been shit. As I was leaving—I later regretted this—I kicked the shrine. Clementines rolled across the floor, and the grandma's dad, the lemon smuggler, tipped face-first onto the ground. The cat fell on its side but kept waving.

"Bibimbap! Bibimbap! Bibimbap!" I said. I shot the place up with guns I made with my hands. I didn't shoot any people, just the walls. Even this felt wrong to me. But something had clenched inside me when I got fired, Williston and beach houses and chicks in bikinis all shriveling up, and so I shot. I looked back before running out, and the grandma was standing there, looking tired and old.

I'd already sold Dad's truck, and the money from that was gone. The two oil wells slid lower and lower on my fridge. It was almost winter. I daydreamed about jumping into a Florida swimming pool, my body cold all over and weightless. I'd keep a waving cat in the window where I could see it from the pool, reminding me that the times I worried about money were over for good.

When Jenny didn't come by to pick up rent a few days later, I went to check on him. He answered the door with his rattail in his hand. Its fat body curled over his shoulder like a snake. The planter of cigarette butts had been tipped onto the ground next to the porch. Someone had tried to peel the Cherokee man off the mailbox and failed, or the weather was slowly undoing whatever made him stick.

"Jenny," I started. I was going to tell him they'd fired me.

"You call your mom? Bet she'd like to hear from you." He was slurring.

He seemed to be having trouble walking and took my arm. With his free hand, he put his rattail in his mouth and chewed. He chewed and stared at me and opened his mouth, using his lip to flap the end of the braid. He removed the rattail and held it in his hand, and we both looked at it. Up close, the hairs were all squiggly, like he'd been electrified.

"I don't talk to my mom," I said. "Never have. You know that."

He wanted me to come inside. He went into the back room where it was dark. He kept sheets nailed over his windows to keep out the light. I heard him take a big huff of something, moving around. I found him in his bathroom, pants down, lying on the floor. I decided for his pride to leave him there.

The next day I went again to tell him about getting fired. I wouldn't be able to pay rent that month or maybe ever. I brought the last twenties I'd saved to give him, but before knocking I tucked two or three back in my pocket.

We were standing on his porch. That morning I'd found a white, worry-doll-shaped mummy of hair the size of my thumb. One of Koda's hairballs. No matter how much I cleaned, parts of her remained.

"You know, maybe your dad did kill himself. Maybe it's best to think that. Man, I think about going that way, taking a rifle and going out back into the forest here, maybe on the river. I've lived a good life, you know. I'm about ready to give up." Jenny spit into the planter. "I think Koda maybe went that way too."

"I don't believe you," I said. "She ran. She was trying to get away from the thing. I saw it." But I did believe him.

Jenny looked in his mailbox. There was nothing inside but a few crumpled papers. Someone miles away was burning trash.

He pulled his rattail over his shoulder and arranged it in the middle of his chest. "I've been feeding him," he said. "The cougar."

He told me he'd been setting out meat for a while now. "I know he killed Koda, and I'm sorry, but being hungry's no one's fault. Everyone's hungry, everyone's got to eat."

I could taste the burning garbage on my tongue.

"I'd like you to keep feeding him for me, when I'm not around," Jenny continued. "That's one thing I need you to do for me."

He got me a cold beer with a soggy label, which I took but did not drink.

Jenny told me I reminded him of a son he once dreamed he had. He squeezed my armpit. It was horrible, standing there, listening to him. I remembered an old man I'd seen in the restaurant trying to get the plastic wrapper off his straw. You could tell it was important to him to get the wrapper off, and he kept trying. Finally, he set the straw down, and the waitress came over and undid it for him.

Jenny pulled open his mailbox again, and still nothing was there but those crumpled papers.

A few nights later I saw the cougar again. He was walking about twenty feet from my living room toward Jenny's trailer. His eyes were the size of clementines—big, black clementines. He was moving slowly, swinging his head low to the ground, looking toward my trailer and away and back again. I didn't want the cougar to have killed Koda, to have given my dog a scary, painful death. But there it was. I could not believe the way this lone thing walked, placing each foot heavily down, shifting one shoulder bone, then the other. His fur was gray in the dark. His tail was as big around as a bull snake. I could make out a pink smear on his flank where a wound might have healed. He made his way to Jenny's trailer, paused outside, and continued on into the trees.

After Action Report

In any other vehicle we'd have died. The MRAP jumped, thirty-two thousand pounds of steel lifting and buckling in the air, moving under me as though gravity was shifting. The world pivoted and crashed while the explosion popped my ears and shuddered through my bones.

Gravity settled. There'd been buildings before. Now headlights in the dust. Somewhere beyond, Iraqi civilians startling awake. The triggerman, if there even was one, slipping away. My ears were ringing and my vision was a pinpoint. I crawled my eyes up the length of the barrel of the .50-cal. The end was warped and blasted.

The vehicle commander, Corporal Garza, was yelling at me.

"The fifty's fucked," I screamed. I couldn't hear what he was saying.

I got down and climbed through the body of the MRAP. I went on my hands and knees across the seats and opened the back hatch. Then I stepped out.

Timhead and Garza were out already, Timhead posted on the right side of the vehicle while Garza checked the damage. Vehicle Three came up with Harvey in the turret to provide security. It was a tight street, just getting into Fallujah, and they parked off to the left of the MRAP, which was slumped down in the front like a wounded animal.

The mine rollers weren't even attached anymore. Their wheels were spread out everywhere, surrounded by bits of metal and other debris. One of the vehicle's tires was sitting a few feet out, cloaked in dust, looking like the big granddaddy of all the little baby mine roller wheels around it.

I wasn't quite steady on my feet, but training kicked in. I put my rifle in front, scanning the dark, trying to do my fives and twenty-fives, but the dust would have to settle before I could see more than five feet in front of me.

A light in one house glowed through the haze. It flickered, quickly dimming and brightening. My head rang and my back hurt. I must have slammed into the side of the turret.

Timhead and I stood on the right side of the MRAP, oriented outboard. When the dust settled I saw Iraqi faces in a few shitty one-stories, looking out at us. One of them was the bomber, probably, waiting to see if there was gonna be a CASEVAC. They get paid extra for that.

The civilians were probably watching for it, too. You can't plant a bomb that big without the neighborhood knowing.

Since my heart was pumping fast, the pain throbbed in my back in superquick spurts.

Corporal Garza circled to the other side of the MRAP, assessing the damage. We stayed where we were.

"Fuck," I said.

"Fuck," said Timhead.

"You all right?" I said.

"Yeah."

"Me too."

"I feel fuckin . . ."

"Yeah?"

"I don't know."

"Yeah. Me too."

There was a crack of rounds, like someone repeatedly snapping a bullwhip through the air. AK fire, close, and we were exposed. I had no turret to crouch down in, and only my rifle, not the .50. I couldn't see where the rounds were coming from, but I dropped back behind the side of the MRAP to get cover. I snapped back to training, but there was nothing to see as I scanned over my sights.

Timhead fired from the front of the MRAP. I fired where he was firing, at the side of the building with the flickering light, and I saw my rounds impact in the wall. Timhead stopped. So did I. He was still standing, so I figured he was okay.

A woman screamed. Maybe she'd been screaming the whole time. I stepped out from behind the MRAP and felt my balls tighten up close to my body.

As I approached Timhead, I could see more and more around the wall of the building. Timhead had his rifle at the ready, and that's where I kept mine. On the other side there was a woman in black, no veil, and maybe a thirteen- or fourteen-year-old kid lying on the ground and bleeding out.

"Holy shit," I said. I saw an AK lying in the dust.

Timhead didn't say anything.

"You got him," I said.

Timhead said, "No. No, man, no."

But he did.

We figured that the kid had grabbed his dad's AK when he saw us standing there and thought he'd be a hero and take a potshot at the Americans. If he'd succeeded, I guess he'd have been the coolest kid on the block. But apparently he didn't know how to aim, otherwise me and Timhead would have been fucked. He was firing from under fifty meters, a spray and pray with the bullets mostly going into the air.

Timhead, like the rest of us, had actually been trained to fire a rifle, and he'd been trained on man-shaped targets. Only difference between those and the kid's silhouette would have been the kid was smaller. Instinct took over. He shot the kid three times before he hit the ground. Can't miss at that range. The kid's mother ran out to try to pull her son back into the house. She came just in time to see bits of him blow out of his shoulders.

That was enough for Timhead to take a big step back from reality. He told Garza it wasn't him, so Garza figured I shot the kid, who everybody was calling "the insurgent" or "the hajji" or "the dumbshit hajji," as in, "You are one lucky motherfucker, getting fired on by the dumbest dumbshit hajji in the whole fucking country."

When we finished the convoy, Timhead helped me out of the gunner's suit. As we peeled it off my body, the smell of the sweat trapped underneath hit us, thick and sour. Normally, he'd make jokes or complain about that, but I guess he wasn't in the mood. He hardly said anything until we got it off, and then he said, "I shot that kid."

"Yeah," I said. "You did."

"Ozzie," he said, "you think people are gonna ask me about it?"

"Probably," I said. "You're the first guy in MP platoon to..." I stumbled. I was gonna say "kill somebody," but the way Timhead was talking let me know that was wrong. So I said, "To do that. They'll want to know what it's like."

He nodded. I wanted to know what it was like, too. I thought about Staff Sergeant Black. He was a DI I'd had in boot camp, and the rumor was he'd beat an Iraqi soldier to death with a radio. He'd turned a corner and run smack into a hajji so close he couldn't bring his rifle around and he'd freaked, grabbed his Motorola, and bashed the guy's head in until it was pulp. We all thought that was badass. Staff Sergeant Black used to chew us out and say crazy shit like, "What you gonna do when you're taking fire and you call in arty and it blows that fucking building to fuck and you walk through and find pieces of little kids, tiny arms and legs and heads everywhere?" Or he'd ask, "What you gonna tell a nine-year-old girl who don't know her daddy's dead 'cause his legs is still twitching, but you know 'cause his brains is leaking out his head?" We'd say, "This recruit does not know, sir." Or, "This recruit does not speak Iraqi, sir."

Crazy shit. And crazy cool, if you're getting ready to face what you think will be real-deal no-shit war. I'd always wanted to get hold of Staff Sergeant Black after boot camp and ask him what had been bullshit and what was really in his head, but I never got a chance.

Timhead said, "I don't want to talk about it."

"So don't," I said.

"Garza thinks you did it."

"Yeah."

"Can we keep it that way?"

Timhead looked serious. I didn't know what to say. So I said, "Sure. I'll tell everyone I did it." Who could say I didn't?

That made me the only sure killer in MP platoon. Before the debrief, a couple guys came by. Jobrani, the only Muslim in the platoon, said, "Good job, man."

Harvey said, "I'd have got that motherfucker if fucking Garza and Timhead hadn't been in the way."

Mac said, "You okay, man?"

Sergeant Major came over to the MP area while we were debriefing. I guess she'd heard we had contact. She's the sort of sergeant major that always calls everybody "killer." Like, "How's it going, killer?" "Oo-rah, killer." "Another day in paradise, right, killer?" That day, when she walked up, she said, "How's it going, Lance Corporal Suba?"

I told her I was great.

"Good work today, Lance Corporal. All of you, good work. Oo-rah?"

Oo-rah.

When we were done, Staff Sergeant pulled me, Timhead, and Corporal Garza aside. He said, "Outstanding. You did your job. Exactly what you had to do. You good?"

Corporal Garza said, "Yeah, Staff Sergeant, we good," and I thought, Fuck you, Garza, on the other side of the fucking MRAP.

The lieutenant said, "You need to talk, let me know."

Staff Sergeant said, "Oo-rah. Be ready to do it tomorrow. We got another convoy. Check?"

Check.

Me and Timhead went right back to the can we shared. We didn't want to talk to anybody else. I got on my PSP, played *Grand Theft Auto,* and Timhead pulled out his Nintendo DS and played *Pokémon Diamond.*

The next day. I had to tell the story.

"Then it was like, crack crack crack"—which it was—"and rounds off the fucking blown-up fucking mine rollers and me and Timhead see hajji with an AK and that was it. Box drill. Like training."

I kept telling the story. Everybody asked. There were follow-up questions, too. Yeah, I was like here, and Timhead was here ... let me draw it in the sand. See that, that's the MRAP. And hajji's here. Yeah, I could just see him, poking around the side of the building. Dumbass.

Timhead nodded along. It was bullshit, but every time I told the story, it felt better. Like I owned it a little more. When I told the story, everything was clear. I made diagrams. Explained the angles of bullet trajectories. Even saying it was dark and dusty and fucking scary made it less dark and dusty and fucking scary. So when I thought back on it, there were the memories I had, and the stories I told, and they sort of sat together in my mind, the stories becoming stronger every time I retold them, feeling more and more true.

Eventually, Staff Sergeant would roll up and say, "Shut the fuck up, Suba. Hajji shot at us. Lance Corporal Suba shot back. Dead hajji. That's the happiest ending you can get outside a Thai massage parlor. Now it's over. Gunners, be alert, get positive ID, you'll get your chance."

A week later. Mac died. MacClelland.

Triggerman waited for the MRAP to go past. Blew in the middle of the convoy.

Big Man and Jobrani were injured. Big Man enough to go to TQ and then out of Iraq. They say he stabilized, though he's got facial fractures and is "temporarily" blind. Jobrani just got a little shrapnel. But Mac didn't make it. Doc Rosen wouldn't say anything to anybody about it. The whole thing was fucked. We had a memorial service the next day.

Right before the convoy, I'd been joking with Mac. He'd got a care package with the shittiest candy known to man, stale Peeps and chocolate PEZ, which Mac said tasted like Satan's asshole. Harvey asked how he knew what Satan's asshole tasted like and Mac said, "Yo, son. You signed your enlistment papers. Don't act like you ain't have a taste." Then he stuck his tongue out of his mouth and waggled it around.

The ceremony was at the Camp Fallujah chapel. The H&S Company first sergeant did the roll call in front of Mac's boot camp graduation photo, which they'd had Combat Camera print out and stick on poster board. They also had his boots, rifle, dog tags, and helmet in a soldier's cross. Or maybe it wasn't his stuff. Maybe it was some boots, rifle, and helmet they keep in the back of the chapel for all the memorials they do.

First Sergeant stood up front and called out, "Corporal Landers."

"Here, First Sergeant."

"Lance Corporal Suba."

"Here, First Sergeant," I said, loud.

"Lance Corporal Jobrani."

"Here, First Sergeant."

"Lance Corporal MacClelland."

Everybody was quiet.

"Lance Corporal MacClelland."

I thought I heard First Sergeant's voice crack a bit.

Then, as if he were angry that there was no response, he shouted, "Lance Corporal James MacClelland."

They let the silence weigh on us a second, then they played Taps. I hadn't been close with Mac, but I had to hold both my forearms in my hands to stop from shaking.

Afterward, Jobrani came up to me. He had a bandage on the side of his head where he got peppered with shrapnel. Jobrani's got a baby face, but his teeth were gritted and his eyes were tight and he said, "At least you got one. One of those fucks."

I said, "Yeah."

He said, "That was for Mac."

"Yeah."

Except I killed hajji first. So it was more like Mac for hajji. And I didn't even kill hajji.

In our can, Timhead and I never talked much. We'd get back and I'd play *GTA* and he'd play *Pokémon* until we were too tired to stay up. Not much to talk about. Neither of us had a girlfriend and we both wanted one, but neither of us was dumb enough to marry some forty-year-old with two kids in Jacksonville, like Sergeant Kurtz did two weeks before deployment. So we didn't have anybody waiting for us at home other than our moms.

Timhead's dad was dead. That's all I knew about that. When we did talk, we talked mostly about video games. Except there was a lot more to talk about now. That's what I figured. Timhead figured different.

Sometimes I'd look at him, focused on the Nintendo, and I'd want to scream, "What's going on with you?" He didn't seem different, but he had to be. He'd killed somebody. He had to be feeling something. It weirded me out, and I hadn't even shot the kid.

The best I could get were little signs. One time in the chow hall we were sitting with Corporal Garza and Jobrani and Harvey when Sergeant Major walked up. She called me "killer," and after she passed, Timhead said, "Yeah, killer. The big fucking hero."

Jobrani said, "Yo? Jealous?"

Harvey said, "It's okay, Timhead. You just ain't quick enough on the draw. Ka-pow." He made a pistol with his thumb and finger and mimed shooting us. "Man, I'd have been up there so fast, bam bam, shot his fuckin' hajji mom, too."

"Yeah?" I said.

"Yeah, son. Ain't no more terrorist babies be poppin' out of that cunt."

Timhead was gripping the table. "Fuck you, Harvey."

"Yo," said Harvey, the smile dropping from his face. "I was just playing, man. I'm just playing."

I wasn't getting good sleep. Neither was Timhead.

Didn't matter if we had a mission in four hours, we'd be in our beds, on the video games. I'd tell myself, I need it to come down. Some brainless time on the PSP.

Except it was every day, time I could be sleeping spent coming down. Being so tired all the time makes everything a haze.

One convoy we stopped for two hours for an IED that turned out to just be random junk, wires not going anywhere but looking suspicious as hell. I was chugging Rip Its, jacked up so much on caffeine that my hands were shaking, but my eyelids kept sliding down like they were hung with weights. It's a crazy feeling when your heart rate is 150 miles per hour and your brain is sliding into sleep and you know when the convoy gets going that if you miss something, it will kill you. And your friends.

When I got back I smashed my PSP with a rock.

* * *

I told Timhead. "I never even liked people calling me 'killer' before this bullshit."

"Okay," he said, "so suck it up, vagina."

I tried a different tack. "You know what? You owe me."

"How's that?"

I didn't answer. I stared him down, and he looked away.

"You owe me," I said again.

He laughed a weak little laugh. "Well, I ain't gonna let you suck my dick."

"What's going on with you?" I said. "You okay?"

"I'm fine. What?"

"You know."

He looked down at his feet. "I signed up to kill hajjis."

"No, you fucking didn't," I said. Timhead signed up because his older brother had been in the MPs and got blown up in 2005, burns over his whole body, and Timhead joined to take his place.

Timhead looked away from me. I waited for him to respond.

"Yeah," he said. "Okay."

"You fucked in the head, man?"

"No," he said. "It's just weird."

"What do you mean?"

"My little brother's in juvie."

"I didn't know that."

There was a loud boom somewhere outside our can. Probably artillery going off.

"He's sixteen," said Timhead. "He set a couple fires."

"Okay."

"That's some dumb shit. But he's a kid, right?"

"Sixteen's only three years younger than me."

"Three years is a big difference."

"Sure."

"I was crazy when I was sixteen. Besides, my brother did it when he was fifteen."

We didn't say anything for a bit.

"How old you think that kid I shot was?"

"Old enough," I said.

"For what?"

"Old enough to know it's a bad fucking idea to shoot at U.S. Marines."

Timhead shrugged.

"He was trying to kill you. Us. He was trying to kill everybody."

"Here's what I see. Everything dust. And the flashes from the AK, going wild in circles."

I nod my head.

"And then I see the kid's face. Then the mom."

"Yeah," I said. "That's the shit, right there. I see that too."

Timhead shrugged. I didn't know what to say. After a minute, he went back to his game.

Two days later Jobrani and me opened up on a house after a SAF attack in Fallujah. I don't think I hit anything. I don't think Jobrani did either. When the convoy was done, Harvey gave Jobrani a high five and said, "Yeah, Jobrani. Jihad for America."

Timhead laughed and said, "I'm pretty sure you're still sleeper cell, Jobrani."

Afterward, I went and talked to Staff Sergeant. I told him everything Timhead said about the kid, but like it was me.

He said, "Look, it fucking sucks. Firefights are the scariest fucking thing you'll ever fucking face, but you handled it, right?"

"Right, Staff Sergeant."

"So, you're a man. Don't worry about that. Now all this other shit"—he shrugged—"it don't get easier. Fact you can even talk about it is a good thing."

"Thanks, Staff Sergeant."

"You want to go see the wizard about it?"

"No." There was no way I was going to let myself be seen going to Combat Stress over Timhead's bullshit. "No, I'm fine. Really, Staff Sergeant."

"Okay," he said. "You don't have to. Not a bad thing, but you don't have to." Then he gave me a grin. "But maybe you get religious, start hanging with the chaplain."

"I'm not religious, Staff Sergeant."

"I'm not saying really get religious. Just, Chaps is a smart guy. He's good to go. And hey, you start hanging with him, everybody's just, maybe you found Jesus or some bullshit."

A week later another IED hit. I heard the explosion and turned back. Garza was listening to the lieutenant screaming something on the radio. I couldn't see to where they were. Could have been a truck in the convoy, could have been a friend. Garza said Gun Truck Three, Harvey's. I swiveled the .50-cal. around, looking for targets, but nothing.

Garza said, "They're fine."

That didn't make me feel better. It just meant I didn't have to feel worse.

Somebody said combat is 99 percent sheer boredom and 1 percent pure terror. They weren't an MP in Iraq. On the roads I was scared all the time. Maybe not pure terror. That's for when the IED actually goes off. But a kind of low-grade terror that mixes with the boredom. So it's 50 percent boredom and 49 percent normal terror, which is a general feeling that you might die at any second and that everybody in this country wants to kill you. Then, of course, there's the 1 percent pure terror, when your heart rate skyrockets and your vision closes in and your hands are white and your body is humming. You can't think. You're just an animal, doing what you've been trained to do. And then you go back to normal terror, and you go back to being a human, and you go back to thinking.

I didn't go to the chaplain. But a few days after Harvey got hit the chaplain came to me. That day, we'd waited three hours outside of Fallujah while EOD defused a bomb I'd spotted. The whole time I sat there thinking, Daisy chains, daisy chains, ambush, even though we were in the middle of fuck-all nowhere desert with nowhere to ambush us from and if the IED had been daisychained to another one, it would have gone off already. Still, I was stressed by the end. More than usual. When Corporal Garza reached up to grab my balls, which he sometimes does to fuck with me, I threatened to shoot him.

Then we got back and the Chaps just happened to drop by the can, and I thought, I'm gonna shoot Staff Sergeant, too. We went and talked by the smoke pit, which is a little area sectioned off with cammie netting. Somebody' d put a wooden bench there, but neither of us sat down.

Chaplain Vega's a tall Mexican guy with a mustache that looks like it's about to jump off his face and fuck the first rodent it finds. Kind of mustache only a chaps could get away with in the military. Since he's a Catholic chaplain and a Navy lieutenant, I wasn't sure whether to call him "sir," "Chaps," or "Father."

After he tried to get me to open up for a bit, he said, "You're being unresponsive."

"Maybe," I said.

"Just trying to have a conversation."

"About what? That kid I shot? Did Staff Sergeant ask you to talk to me about it?"

He looked at the ground. "Do you want to talk about it?"

I didn't want to. I thought about telling him that. But I owed it to Timhead. "That kid was sixteen, Father. Maybe."

"I don't know," he said. "I know you did your job."

"I know," I said. "That's what's fucked with this country." I realized, a second too late, I'd used profanity with a priest.

"What's fucked?" he said.

I kicked at a rock in the dirt. "I don't even think that kid was crazy," I said. "Not by hajji standards. They're probably calling him a martyr."

"Lance Corporal, what's your first name?" he said.

"Sir?"

"What's your first name?"

"You don't know?" I said. I wasn't sure why, but I was angry about that. "You didn't, I don't know, look me up before you came over here?"

He didn't miss a beat. "Sure I did," he said. "I even know your nickname, Ozzie. And I know how you got it."

That stopped me. "Ozzie" came from a bet Harvey made after Mac's lizard died in a fight with Jobrani's scorpion. Fifty bucks that I wouldn't bite its head off. Stupid. Harvey still hadn't paid me.

"Paul," I said.

"Like the apostle."

"Sure."

"Okay, Paul. How are you?"

"I don't know," I said. How was Timhead doing? That was what he was really about, even though he didn't know it. "I usually don't feel like talking to anyone about it."

"Yeah," said the Chaps, "that's pretty normal."

"Yeah?"

"Sure," he said. "You're a Catholic, right?"

That's what's listed on my dog tags. I wondered what Timhead was. Apathetic Protestant? I couldn't tell him that. "Yeah, Father," I said. "I'm Catholic."

"You don't have to talk to me about it, but you can talk to God."

"Sure," I said, polite. "Okay, Father."

"I'm serious," he said. "Prayer does a lot."

I didn't know what to say to that. It sounded like a joke.

"Look, Father," I said. "I'm not that much for praying."

"Maybe you should be."

"Father, I don't even know if it's that kid that's messing with me."

"What else is there?"

I looked out at the row of cans, the little trailers they give us to sleep in. What else was there? I knew how I was feeling. I wasn't sure about Timhead. I decided to speak for myself. "Every time I hear an explosion, I'm like, That could be one of my friends. And when I'm on a convoy, every time I see a pile of trash or rocks or dirt, I'm like, That could be me. I don't want to go out anymore. But it's all there is. And I'm supposed to pray?"

"Yes." He sounded so confident.

"MacClelland wore a rosary wrapped into his flak, Father. He prayed more than you."

"Okay. What does that have to do with it?"

He stared at me. I started laughing.

"Why not?" I said. "Sure, Father, I'll pray. You're right. What else is there? Keep my fingers crossed? Get a rabbit's foot, like Garza? I don't even believe in that stuff, but I'm going crazy."

"How so?"

I stopped smiling. "Like, I was on a convoy, stretched my arms out wide, and a minute later a bomb went off. Not in the convoy. Somewhere in the city. But I don't stretch out like that anymore. And I patted the fifty, once, like a dog. And nothing happened that day. So now I do it every day. So, yeah, why not?"

"That's not what prayer is for."

"What?"

"It will not protect you."

I didn't know what to say to that. "Oh," I said.

"It's about your relationship with God."

I looked at the dirt. "Oh," I said again.

"It will not protect you. It will help your soul. It's for while you're alive." He paused. "It's for while you're dead, too, I guess."

We took different routes all the time. Don't be predictable. It's up to the convoy commander, and they're all lieutenants, but most of them are pretty good. There's one who can't give an Op Order for shit but tends not to fuck up too bad on the road. And there's one female lieutenant who's tiny and real cute but tough as balls and knows her shit cold, so it evens out. Still, there's only so many routes, and you got to use one.

It was at night and I was in the lead vehicle when I spotted two hajjis, looked like they were digging in the road. I said, "Hajjis digging," to Garza. They saw us and started running.

This was just getting into Fallujah. There were buildings on the left side of the road, but they must have been spooked stupid because they ran the other way, across a field.

Garza was on the radio, getting confirmation. I should have just shot them. But I waited for an order.

"They're running," Garza was saying, "yes..." He twisted and looked up at me. "Light 'em up."

I fired. They were on the edge of the field by then, and it was dark. The flash of the .50 going off killed my night vision. I couldn't see anything, and we kept driving. Maybe they were dead. Maybe they were body parts at the edge of the field. The .50 punches holes in humans you could put your fist through. Maybe they got away.

There's a joke Marines tell each other.

A liberal pussy journalist is trying to get the touchy-feely side of war and he asks a Marine sniper, "What is it like to kill a man? What do you feel when you pull the trigger?"

The Marine looks at him and says one word: "Recoil."

That's not quite what I felt, shooting. I felt a kind of wild thrill. Do I shoot? They're getting away.

The trigger was there, aching to be pushed. There aren't a lot of times in your life that come down to, Do I press this button?

It's like when you're with a girl and you realize neither of you has a condom. So no sex. Except you start fooling around and she gets on top of you and starts stressing you out. And you take each other's clothes off and you say, We're just gonna fool around. But you're hard and she's moving and she starts rubbing against you and your hips start bucking and you can feel your mind slipping, like, This is dangerous, you can't do this.

So that happened. It wasn't bad, though. Not like the kid. Maybe because it was so dark, and so far away, and because they were only shadows.

That night, I got Timhead to open up a bit. I started talking to him about how maybe I killed somebody.

"I'm bugging a little," I said. "Is this what it's like?"

He was quiet for a bit, and I let him think.

"For me," he said, "it's not that I killed a guy."

"Yeah?"

"It's like, his family was there. Right there."

"I know, man."

"Brothers and sisters in the window."

I didn't remember them. I'd seen all sorts of people around, eyes out of windows. But I hadn't focused in.

"They saw me," he said. "There was a little girl, like nine years old. I got a kid sister."

I definitely didn't remember that. I thought maybe Timhead had imagined it. I said, "It's a fucked-up country, man."

"Yeah," he said.

I almost went to the Chaps, but I went to Staff Sergeant instead. "It's not that I killed a guy," I told him. "It's that his family was there."

Staff Sergeant nodded.

"There was this nine-year-old girl," I said. "Just like my sister."

Staff Sergeant said, "Yeah, it's a son of a bitch." Then he stopped. "Wait, which sister?"

Both my sisters had been at my deployment. One's seventeen and the other's twenty-two.

"I mean . . ." I paused and looked around. "She reminded me of when my sister was little."

He had this look, like, "I don't know what to say to that," so I pressed.

"I'm really bugging."

"You know," he said, "I went and saw the wizard after my first deployment. Helped."

"Yeah, well, maybe I'll go after my first deployment."

He laughed.

"Look," he said, "it ain't like your sister. It's not the same."

"What do you mean?"

"This kid's Iraqi, right?"

"Sure."

"Then this might not even be the most fucked-up thing she's seen."

"Okay. "

"How long we been here?"

"Two and a half months."

"Right. And how much fucked-up shit have we seen? And she's been here for years."

I supposed that was true. But you don't just shrug off your brother getting shot in front of you.

"Look, this isn't even the wildest Fallujah's been. Al-Qaeda used to leave bodies in the street, cut off people's fingers for smoking. They ran torture houses in every district, all kinds of crazy shit, and you don't think the kids see? When I was a kid I knew about all the shit that was going on in my neighborhood. When I was ten this one guy raped a girl and the girl's brother was in a gang and they spread him out over the hood of a car and cut his balls off. That's what my brother said, anyway. It was all we talked about that summer. And Fallujah's way crazier than Newark."

"I guess so, Staff Sergeant."

"Shit. There's explosions in this city every fucking day. There's fire-fights in this city every fucking day. That's her home. That's in the streets where she plays. This girl is probably fucked up in ways we can't even imagine. She's not your sister. She's just not. She's seen it before."

"Still," I said. "It's her brother. And every little bit hurts."

He shrugged. "Until you're numb."

In the can the next night, after about thirty minutes of me staring at the ceiling while Timhead played *Pokémon*, I tried to bring it up again. I wanted to talk about what Staff Sergeant had said, but Timhead stopped me.

"Look," he said, "I'm over it."

"Yeah?"

He put both his hands in the air, like he was surrendering.

"Yeah," he said. "I'm over it."

A week later a sniper shot Harvey in the neck. It was crazy, because he wasn't even hurt bad. The bullet barely grazed him. A quarter inch to the right, he'd be dead.

Nobody got positive ID. We kept driving, primed and ready to kill, but no targets.

As we moved down the road, my hands jittery with adrenaline, I wanted to scream, *"Fuck!"* as loud as I could, and keep screaming it through the whole convoy until I got to let off a round in someone. I started gripping the sides of the .50. When my hands were white, I would let go. I did that for a half hour, and then the rage left me and I felt exhausted.

The road kept turning under our wheels, and my eyes kept scanning automatically for anything out of place, signs of digging or suspicious piles of trash. It doesn't stop. Tomorrow we would do this again. Maybe get blown up, or get injured, or die, or kill somebody. We couldn't know.

At the chow hall later that day, Harvey pulled the bandage back and showed everyone his wound.

He said, "Purple fucking Heart, bitches! You know how much pussy I'm gonna get back home?"

My mind was whirling, and I made it stop.

"This is gonna be a badass scar," he said. "Girls'll ask and I'll be like, 'Whatever, I just got shot one time in Iraq, it's cool.'"

When we got back to the can that night, Timhead didn't even pull out his Nintendo DS.

"Harvey's so full of shit," he said. "Mr. Tough Guy."

I ignored him and started pulling off my cammies.

"I thought he was dead," said Timhead. "Shit. *He* probably thought he was dead."

"Timhead," I said, "we got a convoy in five hours."

He scowled down at his bed. "Yeah. So?"

"So let it go," I said.

"He's full of shit," he said.

I got under the covers and closed my eyes. Timhead was right, but it wouldn't do either of us any good to think about it. "Fine," I said. I heard him moving around the room, and then he turned off the light.

"Hey," he said, quiet, "do you think—"

That did it. I sat up straight. "What do you want him to say?" I said. "He got shot in the neck and he's going out tomorrow, same as us. Let him say what he wants."

I could hear Timhead breathing in the dark. "Yeah," he said. "Whatever. It doesn't matter."

"No," I said. "It doesn't."

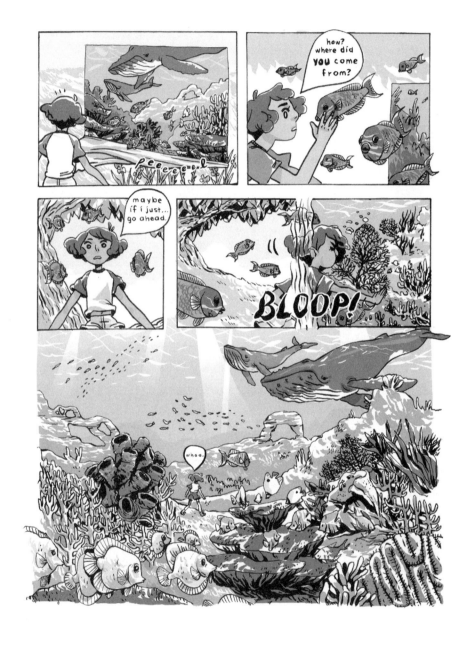

ROXANE GAY

Girls at the Bar

Before they venture out for the evening, they get ready together, standing in cramped bathrooms thick with the smell of burnt hair, deodorant, hand soap and lipstick. They wear silky thong panties and short denim skirts with frayed hems. They wear skimpy tank tops—the kind with the thin shoulder straps and open backs revealing their fancy bras. The polish on their toenails is chipping and cheap braids of gold circle their ankles. They coat their cleavage with perfume and glitter body spray and just before walking out the front door, they take a quick peek into their bedrooms to make sure they can bring someone home. They hide dirty underwear and scarves and flip flops and mascara tubes and paper plates beneath their beds. They wink at their reflections in the pane of glass next to the front door. They pile into cars, more bodies in the backseat than seat belts, their heavy purses shoved against the rear window. They roll the windows down and stick their heads out, their faces pressed into the wind. They turn the radio all the way up and they sing loudly, lustily. At the bar, they move in a pack, their bodies always touching. They find a table close enough to the bar they can shout drink orders over the music and the laughing and the men jostling for their attention. They sit around the table, the ugliest girl in the center, holding court. They complain about their jobs—they are in real estate; they are lawyers and doctors, an investment banker, a vulcanologist, a graduate student, a waitress. Their table quickly fills with empty glass bottles and shot glasses with just a trace of liquor pooling at the bottom. The peeled labels are pasted to their foreheads, wrinkling as they dry. They drink shots and straddle each other, thighs spread wide. They make out with each other, enjoying the taste of strawberry lip-gloss and tequila. When their favorite songs are played, they let loose a high-pitched shriek and exclaim, "That's my song." They bounce to the center of the bar, close their eyes and start dancing, first shaking their shoulders, then waists, finally hips. They jump on empty tables and throw their hands in the air, first left then right and laugh when a bouncer tosses them over his shoulder and sets them roughly on the floor. When a guy sends them a drink they look in his direction and conduct a quick assessment—looks, clothes, jewelry. They talk loudly, as if they're the only ones in the room. No one minds. There is something to be said for the spectacle of it all. They take pictures of themselves with their faces pressed together, using their phones held high, at the most flattering angle. They go to the bathroom where they apply fresh coats of lipstick and leave stall doors open as they hover over wet toilet seats to piss. When the bartender shouts, "Last call," they shout back in singsong voices, "For alcohol." Originality is not among their virtues. They down the last drinks of the night and make eye contact with dirty-looking boys who wear hemp bracelets, white t-shirts and Levi jeans. They kiss each other's cheeks, wiping lipstick prints away with their thumbs. They stumble to unfamiliar cars holding their heels in one hand, their clutches in the other. They bring home their bad boys and they fuck on top of their bedspreads. They fall asleep, their mouths dry and sour, their makeup smeared beautifully. When they wake, their heads aching and foggy, they groan at the stranger lying next to them, naked, his (or her, once in a while) head buried in a pillow, one arm hanging over the edge of the bed. They lie on their backs and stare at the ceiling. They smile.

JOY BAGLIO

Ron

I met Ron Myers at an amateur astronomers club, our identical Celestron SkyMaster binoculars slung around our necks—an unusual omen from the start. We clustered around the telescopes, listening to the lecture about Vega, faint and barely visible against the backdrop of light pollution. Ron was watching me, I could tell. Later, after most of the group members had left, we bonded over the moons of Jupiter. His favorite: Ganymede. Mine: Io. His name, Ron, was hardly of any interest, at first.

After that night, I waited two weeks. When Ron finally called, it was to suggest a free physics lecture at a science museum. We were both math nerds, although not by profession. When the lecture was over, we wandered into the main hall, through a narwhal exhibit where life-sized replicas lunged out of molded waves. We trekked up four flights of stairs to the space room, on the fifth and highest floor. The space room was outdated, stuffy, empty except for us. Ron gently backed me into a corner near a small model of Neptune and leaned his head in toward mine. The first time we kissed—the tiny orb of Neptune to my right, the dim lights of the space room flickering, the astronaut sounds playing mechanically in the background—it felt perfect.

We left the museum after dark, enveloped in a kind of wonder that happens rarely: last-day-of-school, first-kiss, foreign-city kind of wonder. The kind you wish you could stretch out like cellophane, over time and space, so it reaches all the far corners of your life. We talked endlessly about the universe, all the tidbits of science and astronomy gleaned from our day. The four-hundred-year-old raging storm of Jupiter's red spot. The scores of earthlike planets popping up through the newest search technology. The black hole in the center of our galaxy. He took my hand, nimbly danced his fingers over mine. The sidewalks were slick with September leaves, and everything was shadowed in a rain-drenched softness.

Ron's apartment was unlit, almost empty, as if he'd just moved in. He was a composer for a TV show, he said. He wrote the kind of scores that swelled when couples met, eye-rolling love scenes where the music was the only thing that made you feel anything. He laughed dryly.

"Here," he said. "This is what I really do." On a computer screen, tiny dots flashed and blinked, a sort of grid. It was a graph of orbital intersections in the Milky Way, and he had turned it into music. He pressed a button, and a syncopated orchestral hum began. "This is the sound of planets singing for you," he said.

"Explain," I said, fascinated.

"Planetary orbits, put into music. Based on their speed, when they cross. It's a lot of math, but, hey, music and math go together."

We sat in the dark, listening. I imagined the planets whizzing by and around us, blurred with speed, missing each other by a paper width, humming at their own frequencies. In the dark, our fingers found each other, our hands moved over the folds of clothing, shedding it like old skin.

If I could have choreographed my own life—designed each scene, staged each encounter with a director's omniscience—I'd have seen Ron Myers the next day, then the day after; I'd have seen him several times a week; we'd have fallen in love, learned everything about each other, met parents and families, moved in together, cooked pasta at midnight, and sat up late laughing at our favorite shows. There would have been no one else, and there wouldn't have needed to be. But Ron was distant, busy, and in the long stretches between our dates, I met someone else. He was an artisan whose storefront I browsed into one night after work. His business was a small, self-made venture, something he started reluctantly after failing to make great art. I walked around his display tables, tracing my fingers over the sanded smoothness of his walnut chairs and cutting boards, aware of him watching me from the back of the store. He had ideas about blue-collar work and the artist's life, about craft and concept, about our fragmented societal lives. We talked long into the night, and when he told me his name, Ron, I let out a shocked laugh, then covered my mouth, giddy at the coincidence.

"What's funny?" he asked, not knowing whether to smile or frown.

"Your name," I said. "It's one of my favorites."

I work at the Orion Theater in midtown, and that weekend I slipped my craftsman Ron a free ticket to our hot new comedy musical, *The BOOtiful Lives of Ghosts*. He had a penchant for campy horror, and he'd never been to Broadway, or off-off-Broadway for that matter. Later, he took me back to his studio behind his shop, where he showed me the power tools, how wood was hewn and cut and sanded. Together we ran our hands over the rough edges of raw oak planks. His last name, Wessell, was a musical cocktail of sounds and in the following days, I said it over and over in my head, envisioning his eyes, which creased at the corners when he smiled. I thought about him all week after that—imagined lying with him in an oak bed that he'd crafted, under the roof of our small cabin—and when Ron Myers called a week later, Ron Wessell's hands were still hot in my mind, moving over wood, over machinery, over my shoulders, hips, body.

I confided in my mother and sister over lunch. They'd had their share of fun, of scandal, of playing the game of courtship, the non-serious search for what we all crave.

"But they have the same name," my mother said, alarmed, as though this was an ominous sign, a dating taboo. To me, it felt exciting and sneaky, as if I were a time traveler, able to hop the light-years-apart distance between worlds. Somehow, the shared name was a kind of wormhole between them that only I could slip through.

My sister put it harshly: "You're two-timing and both of them are named Ron?" she sneered.

"I'm non-exclusively dating two men, casually," I said. "It's normal."

"It's not normal to date two men with the same name," she said.

"Why not?"

"It's like some weird fantasy, some name fetish."

"One of them could have easily been named something else," I said. "Maybe one of them was almost a Greg. Why does a name matter so much?"

"It does matter," my sister said. "At the very least, it's symbolic of something."

"Of what?" I asked, but my sister shrugged.

"How am I supposed to know?" she said.

It was when I met Ron Bardacci, who taught eighth-grade chemistry, that I felt the first suspicions of a conspiracy of a higher order. Whose conspiracy and how, I hadn't begun to hypothesize. For the first two weeks we dated, he flirtatiously quizzed me on the periodic table and taught me grams-to-mole conversions. His name was Ax, he told me. It wasn't until our third date, week number four, his driver's license forgotten on my kitchen table, that I learned his real name: Ron Axel Bardacci. For a second I thought: Walk away right now. Not another one. I will not be the butt of this cosmic joke, this symbolic charade. But then I stopped myself. A wave of what-the-hell and who-cares passed through me, and I knew what it really was—a highly unlikely act of chance, nothing more.

But it didn't stop there. Ron Wachowski, whom I met at a free wine tasting around the corner from the Orion, was a sous chef at Lizardo's: An Adventurous Eatery. That weekend, he brought me camel cricket custard, high in protein, which we sipped with reishi mushroom wine. On our second date, he cooked for me from the wasteland of my fridge and produced, as if by magic, wildflower risotto, green beans almondine, and a rustic pear tart. A week later, I met Ron Hebert, a guide for Escape to Nature!, an adventure company that led local expeditions into rugged areas. In our tent on the pinnacle of some low-grade mountain, we talked late into the night, listening to the pulsing chorus of tree frogs and whippoorwills. The list went on: Ron Walden, a proctologist with whom I carried on a whispered conversation in the hallway of the ER when I accompanied Ron Wessell, who was suffering from severe stomach pain, there late one night. Ron Getty, a historian who chatted with me over coffee. Ron Egglestein, a professional bird watcher I bumped into while jogging in the park. Ron Greenwald, a trombonist in a marching band. Ron Svenson, geologist. Ron Cory, jiu jitsu instructor. Even my postman was a Ron, who was courting me slowly through conversations linked with package deliveries.

And so it went on, all of my Rons, each delicately and unsuspectingly stepping in and out of the others' way, unaware of their paralleled existences. Why didn't I just stop saying yes? Weren't three or two, or even one, enough for me? How did I find the time? Why didn't I exempt myself from male attention, seal myself off in the land of "taken" or "exclusive"? The truth was, I couldn't contain my curiosity. And I was making real connections with each of them; with each, I was secretly hoping for something more. Still, I wondered how long I could sustain it. Each relationship was casual enough that it allowed the others to exist, and yet all of them inched slowly forward in the inevitable way relationships do.

And half the time I didn't know a newcomer was a Ron until we were past the point of turning back—an hour into the most interesting conversation I'd had all day. He'd be telling me about the work he did on the human genome or the strange story he'd heard last night in the ER, his trek through the arctic or down the entire length of the Great Wall, and then he'd let it drop, "By the way, I'm Ron." He'd slide it in there, nonchalant, and what could I do?

When I was up to twelve Rons, I realized the situation was serious. This was not how coincidence worked. Each wanted to see me on Friday or Saturday night, so I began a complicated system of rotation. I allocated all my after-work hours to Ron dates. The ones who saw me on Tuesday and Wednesday one week got prime weekend time the following week. Sometimes I felt that all the real joy in our outings had been crushed out, replaced by both a terror that they'd discover each other and a giddy performance anxiety, a need to impress them all equally, to win each one more deeply.

I toyed with the idea of cutting some from the continual audition process of our courtship, the not-quite-boyfriend status they each held in my life. But a drive to get to the bottom of this consumed me: I needed to see what part of the puzzle each one played, and my dating life took on the flavor of detective work. I made lists of all their hobbies and highlighted shared interests. I graphed their statistics, things like how much they earned, where they worked, body weight, age, past girlfriends, the sports they'd played in high school, their favorite actors. My kitchen table was cluttered with crudely sketched concept maps: flowcharts of their favorite foods; Sharpied Venn diagrams that aimed to make sense of their literary tastes. Wachowski liked Russian classics. Cory read the latest crime novels. Clarke could order bubble tea in Mandarin. Getty played the bagpipes.

I tried to find clues in the name itself. All of them were named simply Ron, not Ronald or Ronaldo. Numerology assigned Ron the number two, which was the most underestimated and feminine of all numbers. Anagrams and partial anagrams of the name included *nor*, *no*, *on*, and *or*, which told me nothing. It appeared three times in the first thunderword in James Joyce's *Finnegans Wake*, which seemed to portend . . . something.

I asked my friends what the name meant to them, what associations, feelings, thoughts came to mind.

"Sleazy," said my sister. "In a seventies porn-star kind of way. Greasy palms, drives a pickup truck."

"Quiet," one said. "Someone thoughtful, peaceful. An avid meditator."

"A serious name," said another. "Someone serious about life, about you."

But they were not serious. Not one. I waited and waited, each extravagant adventurous date after the next. Under the luminescent halo of moon or the blinking of stars or in summer fields under pyrotechnics of galactic proportions, they remained unflappable, neutral, compartmentalized, happy to laugh and joke, to probe into the depths of the intellect or the mysteries of the universe, yet somehow distant from me.

And the question remained: Why were they all drawn to *me*?

Gradually, like a badly choreographed dance, close calls began to occur. For my own sanity and under the guise of an old habit, I'd taken to calling each by his last name, a pattern that led to a moment of panic when I misheard Wasserman at the door and shouted my greetings to Wessell. Another time Greenwald was in my bed when Wachowski buzzed to ask if I was free to get dessert. And another time still, Carson was leaving my apartment as Bardacci entered, and they passed each other, gave a long side-glance, exchanging unspoken suspicions. Both seemed shaken in the ensuing days. Then there was the incident of Clarke's backpack, which he left under my couch just visible enough so that Hebert, who visited two hours later, pulled it out, unsuspectingly, and saw "Ron C." on the small airline ID tag that Clarke kept on all his possessions. "Oh, my cousin's a Ron, too," I lied, hating that I was forced to such baseness. "I told you it was my favorite name," though later I realized with a twinge of dread that it hadn't been Hebert with whom I'd discussed my favorite name, but Wessell.

Beyond the danger of my predicament, I started to notice unsettling overlaps: Hebert wanted to live in a tree house, and Egglestein said he had built one last year while Lewis doodled them in the margins of fantasy novels. Fitzgibbons made crème brûlée, which was Aaron's favorite. They all relished mint garnishes with shocking glee.

These connections did not feel meaningless. My thoughts ran wild: Maybe they were different angles of the same person. Slices of the same Ron. Perhaps together they formed the perfect man. Maybe the man I was in love with was somehow diffused throughout all of them, so that with each I was given excruciating joy and also the worst sense of unfulfillment. The thrill of them, the inimitable conversations, their depths of knowledge and experience was rivaled only by the unchartable void that seemed to separate me from them. And how might I bridge these chasms? I wondered.

I poured over my amateur astronomy manuals, over the layman's explanations of complex, paradigm-shifting hypotheses, things that no one really understood.

Then, one evening while I was cooking dinner and Ron Walden was reading to me from his *Collected Works of T. S. Eliot,* each line composed and perfectly ordered after the previous, I perked awake. The words of "The Lovesong of J. Alfred Prufrock" seemed startlingly clear and symbolic.

Yes, I thought. I must disturb the universe! I must dare. I must act. And then the idea entered my mind like a prophecy, and I stood at the stove, wooden spatula in hand suspended over sautéing eggplant, feeling something ineffable.

Ron Myers had told me that when galaxies collide it's actually elegant, a billions of years' long cosmic dance, like a drop of paint dissolving over eons into another. They drift, over light-years, closer and closer, until one tendril of stars, like a long and delicate arm, brushes the other, and *whoosh*, a gentle surge of energy emanates from those worlds colliding, shifting around each other, melding into one another. And you're left not with chaos, but with one galaxy, spinning and bright and whole.

I hatched a plan.

Yesterday, I had what might be my final date with Ron Myers. The first Ron. I wanted to tell him of the others, let him in on the secret before it came crashing down, but all I did was talk excited astro-babble about parallel universes and identities splayed and spliced. He smiled at me curiously and stared with neutral infatuation. We walked around the block to a gelato food cart and sat on a stone wall overlooking the river, his fingers trailing through mine.

"You know," he said. "Ever since I played the singing planets for you, I've had this crazy idea."

"Do tell," I said.

For a moment, I thought that he would move beyond our perpetual distance. A flutter of energy zinged through me, and I felt, fleetingly, that he was so close to perfection. I imagined him across centuries: the different ways the times would have chopped and swelled his hair, the way his body would have widened or shrunk according to his means, the shifting blur of fashions and styles and fabrics over his lean shoulders—the loose tunics and tight-ruffed shirts—yet there was something rooted and familiar in his gaze, as if I had lived lifetimes with him. He held my hand, his fingers sweaty and clenched over mine. His eyes bored into me—neutron stars, it seemed—and I stared back, unflinching, my breath bated.

"Do you ever—" he stopped, laughed. "It's absolutely crazy."

"I like crazy," I said. "Please go on."

He held his breath, laughed again. "No, it's not the time for this," he said. "Let's get more gelato."

And he was up, pulling me back into the world.

Tonight, the chosen night of my plan, it's raining, a slick drizzle that makes me feel as though everything solid is unspooling. It's November, the tail end of the Leonid meteor shower, dark at 5:00 pm, and I pull the curtains closed and light a candle to create a warming glow. I've stuck a bunch of glow-in-the-dark stars to the ceiling—for added mystique—and brewed a pot of mint tea. They are all on their way, thinking it's a party at my place, and I don't know what will ensue; if they'll turn on me, a pack of men named Ron, all embittered and deceived, or if they'll merge, like galaxies, into a single form, applaud and thank me for resolving their fractured existences. Or maybe they'll squirm under the scrutiny, answerless just like me. My Celestron SkyMaster binoculars sit on the mantel in the hall, homage to that first meeting. I stand by the door, waiting.

The first to arrive is Svenson. When I see him, carrying a bottle of wine, my stomach flips with guilt. I kiss him hurriedly, and after he's inside, I hold the door for Wessell, who's trailing like a shadow. One by one they arrive, each courteous and polite.

They sit shyly around my living room, smiling and greeting each other. They haven't figured it out yet, although Bardacci and Carlson, who first glimpsed each other in my hallway, exchange knowing glances. Some of them graciously take a mug of tea, others pick a grape with careful fingers. They smile and wait. I stand in the center of the room, clink my water glass as if I'm making a toast at a wedding, but of course I'm not. I'm aware of the familiar look in their eyes, the wondering, the straining to figure it out, just as I am. I pause before I say it: "I am dating all of you, that's why you're here." It's what I'd planned to say, nothing more. I want to see their responses to that one simple fact. They don't react like you'd think. Hebert chews thoughtfully, nodding as though I'm revealing some logical truth. Wachowski listens patiently, eyes on me. They wait for me to go on, to elaborate, as though there must be some explanation, some reason why, or as if they've known all along.

"All of you are my boyfriends," I say, then sit, watching, waiting for them to react, to turn angry, jealous. Or maybe I'm waiting for some spell to break, for some magical snap of the universe to whisk them all together into one body.

They stare at me. Then one laughs. Then another.

"Well, you've got good taste," Campo de Leon says, gesturing to the men in the room. They laugh, until I am the only one staring mutely, angrily, at all of them. They seem even more like strangers to me at that moment—foreign, mysterious. These were the men to whom I had hoped to bare my soul, dreamed of families and futures. I flit my eyes around, watching for signs, hints of a conspiracy, foreknowledge of this strange happening. But they shake hands with each other as if it is the first time, and I'm left baffled, furious. I pace indignantly to the cupboard and lay out more teacups, then begin a passive-aggressive tea-pouring trance. They introduce themselves and the name ricochets around the room, until the peculiarity is undeniable.

Finally, my voice shaking, I ask them: "What is it with that name? Why are you all Ron?"

"No idea," Carson says. "You must have a thing for it."

"Name fetish?" Wachowski says, and several grin.

"My grandfather had the name," Lewis says. "It's been in my family for years."

Others share their stories, and I wait—somewhere between despair and hopefulness—for some kind of revelation.

"How could this happen?" Greenwald asks.

Fitzgibbons, a Dante scholar, jokingly proposes he figure out in which ring of *The Inferno* we'd each find ourselves, to see if there is some karmic, literary overlap, and several get excited and begin confessing cardinal sins. Wasserman, a yoga instructor, suggests that maybe there is some energetic reason, a higher connection, and Bardacci, whose mother is a Reiki master, offers to tune in to everyone's energy.

The Rons who believe in God attest to some higher truth.

The science-oriented ones talk of parallax.

Several want to know why I didn't tell them sooner.

"I'm sorry," I say. "I'm not sure why." And my voice becomes very weak, and I stop talking, because if I keep going, I might cry.

Only Egglestein comes over, takes my hand, and whispers that he hopes, very much, we still have a future together in some way, how much he enjoys our time. "Though, I understand that your life is complicated now," he says.

I can barely hear him through my own flurry of thoughts, through the dozen chattering voices, but I smile absently, half-numb to his tenderness.

Around 9:30 pm my sister calls. She knows of the plan, of the gathering. She disapproves in theory, but supports me with a kind of begrudging zeal. I move into the hallway, where the Rons' coats are piled high on a chair.

"Are they still there?" she asks in a fierce whisper.

I peek around the corner: Some have removed pillows from the couch and are sitting cross-legged on the floor, end tables crowded with mugs of mint tea. They are loud, vigorous in their discussion, some standing and gesticulating, others nestled into the maternal softness of the couch.

"Yes," I say, unable to tell her more. From the background, I hear the gurgles of her toddler, the soft cooing voice of her husband when he speaks to the baby.

"So you can't talk?"

"Right," I say.

"Well then." I can tell she's disappointed. "Maybe you can hang on to at least one of them at the end of the night? One is better than none, right? The one who wants to build a tree house. I like him."

The Rons have fragmented into small groups. Some are still discussing *The Inferno*, while Bardacci, who lived abroad in Italy in college, is slapping Fitzgibbons on the back as though congratulating him.

Then, one by one, as the night draws on, they leave, kissing me on the cheek, smiling, pressing my hand, telling me that they've truly enjoyed knowing me. Getty winks at me across the room before collecting his coat. Lewis takes me aside, holds me a moment, then kisses my forehead. With each composed farewell my questions multiply exponentially. My frustration mounts as I smile and thank each for coming.

"Will I see you again?" I ask Wessell, knowing I have no right to expect I will.

"It will work out, all of this," he says, then blows me a kiss. There is nothing bad about any of them, I realize, and I wonder if it is the last time we'll be together, any of us.

Ron Myers is the last to leave. He steps out into the night, smiling, telling me to look up. The clouds have cleared, and the moon is full, glowing.

"How many miles away is it, do you know?" he asks me.

My voice feels like a solid glob in my throat, but I manage the words "Too many." Then, "Two hundred thousand, I think."

"You know what a full moon means, right?"

"End of a cycle?" I say. "End of the month? End of something."

"It means magic," he says. "Let go, let love, make music." Then his hand is on my shoulder, gentle, warm. "I'll see you later. It's been a long day."

The formal goodwill is too much to bear. I hate the silence, the serene moon, my own strength or lack of it, the smile on his face. Something in me snaps, and I gust my breath out.

"Why don't you stay tonight?" I say. "If you're not offended that I have so many other men in my life, all with your name, why don't you stay?"

He laughs, tense, noncommittal. "You know I can't."

"You never can," I say. Then I narrow my eyes, holding him with the sheer power of my gaze. "What was the crazy thought?" I say.

"What are you talking about?"

"The crazy thought you wouldn't tell me yesterday afternoon. At the gelato cart."

He stares back, the blankness of his eyes disarming and cold, even in their familiarity.

I press on, squeezing my voice into the confines of gentleness. "Please," I say. "You can tell me."

We're silent, staring in some kind of face-off for what feels like whole minutes; finally he laughs. "I don't know how to say it," he says. "Do you ever feel like you're a planet set loose, spinning through space, orbiting different suns, glimpsing so many different worlds, but always set back at a distance from them, like each on its own is missing something?"

I'm thinking: That sounds about right.

"Before I even knew of your situation," he continues, "I started feeling this, mostly while composing. It started when I showed you the singing planets—remember that night? It was the closest I ever felt to you, the most—I don't know—whole. But after that night, I kept waiting for more. More you, more something. Know what I mean?"

I do know, and it terrifies me, and I don't want to say, "I showed you my cards, so show me yours," so instead I say, with all the multifaceted depth I can summon: "What if I choose you. Over the others."

He looks at me, laughs. "Don't," he says. "That would be a wasted choice."

"Why?" I say and step closer, so close my nose is a hair's breath from him. He looks at me, beyond me, pulls me near, so that my face is pressed to the absorbent flannel of his shoulder. I smell museum and spices and sage deodorant; I breathe in his infuriating strength, strain to hold on to the solid warmth of him, a solidity that doesn't need any particle of me.

"Because," he says, "I'm still waiting."

Something vibrates in his pocket, and he shifts, uncomfortable. "Sorry," he says. "I need to get this." Then he turns away into the darkness of the park, his phone open and glowing.

The moon is behind a lone cloud, and I stare up at the light-polluted sky, scanning the night for the last of the Leonids. I am searching with only half my senses, listening with the other half. I can hear, faintly, the melodic tones of a girl's voice. Ron Myers laughs. I can tell from his voice that he's smiling, though I can't hear what he's saying, not the sentences. It's just one word that catches in my ear, like a clue I've been waiting for: my name, said sweetly into the phone, whispered almost, as though that is the one word he does not want me to hear.

BY MISTER LOKI

A PLACE
like
HOME

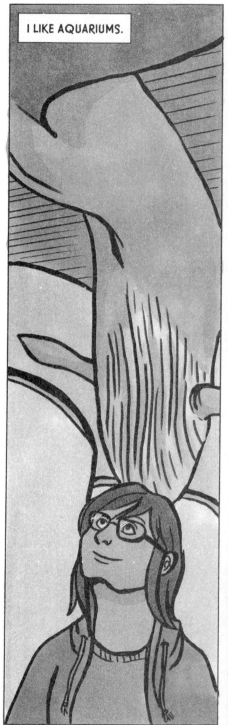

I LIKE AQUARIUMS.

IN IT, I FEEL WELCOME AMONG CREATURES THAT OTHERWISE ARE CONSIDERED GROTESQUE AND ALIEN,

REFERRED TO AS BEAUTIFUL AND GRACEFUL IN WATER.

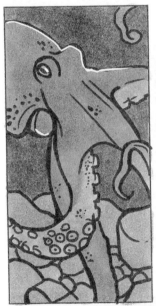

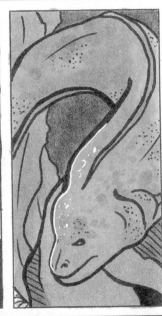

SOCIETY HAS TOLD ME THAT I AM BROKEN, A THING TO BE REPAIRED.

IT IS HERE THAT I AM PROVEN...

I WAS MASTERFULLY CREATED TO BE ME,

DESIGNED FOR A UNIQUE PURPOSE.

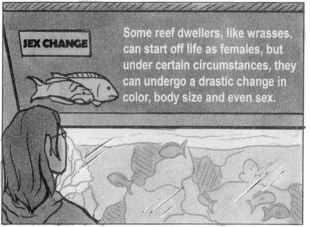

SEX CHANGE

Some reef dwellers, like wrasses, can start off life as females, but under certain circumstances, they can undergo a drastic change in color, body size and even sex.

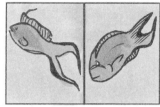

NO ONE TELLS A FISH THEIR BRIGHT COLORS HAVE NO PLACE IN OCEAN BLUES.

THOUGH THEY MIGHT ENVY THE RARE GLOW,

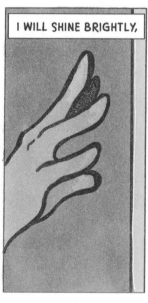

I WILL SHINE BRIGHTLY,

FOR I AM NO MISTAKE.

The Devil's Grip

Rusty Serrano woke with a jerk, sweating, writhing, gasping for breath. Again, that damn dream—a baby squeezed in a vise, in a grip, too smothered to scream. He steadied his breathing. The first morning rays of West Texas summer sun were flooding the room, casting flickers of lilac and crimson through the crystals on his dresser, blue calcite and rosy quartz.

Last night, he'd heard his mom's keys jangling as she came in late from her job at the café. He knew she would sleep in. His older brother Tate would be up any minute for his job at the car shop. Rusty, nineteen and out of school, had no job, nowhere to go. At least not today. But he had a plan.

He pulled out the bottom dresser drawer, where he'd hidden the papers he'd brought back from Alpine, the college town nearby. *Sul Ross State University. So close, yet so far...until now.* He hadn't told anyone his secret plans. Not his mom. Not even Tate. Especially not Tate, who treated him like a burden, at best.

He listened for dishes clinking in the kitchen. Silence. *Good, no one's around.*

Rusty had cerebral palsy. One of those baby birthing things, they said. Couldn't get out. He never got why. Was he not allowed to be born or something? His legs lurched this way and that, but his hands were steady and his mind was sharp. And another blessing—his good looks, with his straight black hair, blue eyes, and lean physique.

Rusty yanked on his jeans, hoisted himself off the bed, and walked down the hall to the kitchen on two legs that carried him like clumsy stilts, his arms sweeping the air for balance—*like swimming...or drowning.*

He opened the back door. The desert heat rolled in. He caught a glimpse of the lazy semi-rural roads of Marathon, his small, stifling town. *Aptly named, too. Marathon—my life.*

He grabbed one of his mom's Coors from the fridge and downed half of it. "C-Can't let T-Taaaate see this." His CP put a twist to his tongue, to his lips, pulling at his words like putty. "M-Mr. Perfect T-Taaate."

Tate, with his dark brown hair and eyes, his easy smile, looked like their dad. Or so he'd heard. He only knew his dad from photos and stories—stories about his dad's drinking, his lost jobs, his fights.

Then baby Rusty's diagnosis had arrived—cerebral palsy. *That must have been the last straw for the coward,* Rusty often thought. *The chicken up and ran. Not even a trickle of kid support from the bastard—not from the bank and not from the heart.*

Rusty took a few more swigs. He heard footsteps.

"Rusty!" Tate yelled. "What the hell are you doing? Put that beer down!"

"N-Not your b-buuusiness!"

"That's Mom's beer."

"Sh-Sheee said I could have sooome."

"It's mine too. I pay the bills, don't I?" Tate was a mechanic now, helping his mom who could barely cover the rent. "And I say you can't have it."

"W-Waaatch me," Rusty said, and chugged the last half of the cold beer.

"At breakfast? Geez! What a lush. How are you ever going to get a job?"

"I-I'll get a job. You waaatch. I'll do better. I'll get a *careeeer.*"

"A career? You barely finished high school."

"Y-Yeah, but—"

"But nothing, you stupid drunk."

The beer can went flying and hit Tate on the side of the face. Tate lunged at Rusty and wrestled him to the kitchen floor. Rusty grabbed at Tate's leg and Tate shook him off.

"You brainless baby," Tate muttered. "Mama's boy."

Rusty lay on the floor cradling a bruised elbow. Tate headed for the door. "Forget breakfast," Tate said. "I'm going to work. And don't expect me at dinner. I'll be at Sissy's." Tate always had his arm around some girl, though lately it had just been Sissy. Tate let the door slam behind him and headed for his motorcycle.

Rusty wrenched himself up on a kitchen chair, balanced on his legs, and shook his fist. "B-Bastard!" he yelled. "I'm g-going tonight. To the desert. N-Not j-juuust to the d-desert. T-To the cave! And you're c-coming too, T-Taaate."

* * *

That evening, Rusty donned his blue jean jacket and drove his pickup to Sissy's *casita,* her little white cottage with blue trim, hoping to surprise them. Tate had rigged Rusty's used pickup with a steering knob and a joystick hand pedal: push to go, pull to stop. Rusty's legs were useless for driving, but his hands were deft. He veered the vehicle onto the circular drive to her porch, his tires crunching the dusty gravel, and shoved the joystick forward, screeching the brakes a little just for fun.

"Uh, oh." He noticed empty beer cans on the floor and tossed them behind the seat. Sliding down from his truck, he struggled his way up the two wooden steps, feeling the folded paper in his jeans back pocket, and knocked on the white wooden door.

"Hey, Rusty," Sissy said, smiling from the doorway. "What's up?"

Rusty sighed. *She's stunning,* he thought, and stood staring at her tousled dark blonde hair, laughing blue eyes, and curves in all the right places. *Sweet. Like Sandra, in Alpine yesterday.*

In the library, he'd sat at a table across from two young women who were moving their hands in a rapid rhythm like a salsa dance, like a rumba. They'd peered at him and giggled. One flipped back her brown hair and, lifting two straight fingers, drew a circle around her face and pointed at him. Rusty shrugged and shook his head. She retrieved a pencil from her purse, scribbled a note, and pushed the paper to him: *face nice = handsome.* Rusty blinked, incredulous. *What? Who, me?* Below that, she'd written *Sandra.* She pointed to herself, reached across the table, and patted his hand. Her touch felt silky, like a cool desert breeze in the heat of the day. He inhaled slowly, seeking her scent. Then, glancing at her watch, she'd tossed him a wink, waved bye to her friend and left. No one had ever called him handsome. Certainly not in sign language.

Sweet, he thought again, still staring at Sissy in the doorway. He broke his gaze and looked away.

The TV blared from the living room. "Tate," Sissy called over her shoulder, "it's your brother."

"What the . . . ?" Tate shouted over the TV noise. Before he could get off the couch, Rusty leaned toward Sissy, close enough to catch her lingering fragrance, like a blue sage blossom. "H-Hey, S-Sissy," he whispered, "you wanna g-go to a c-cave?"

"What do you mean? A real cave?" she asked. "Awesome. When?"

"L-Like, n-now." Rusty's voice felt tight, trying to sound casual.

Tate joined her at the door in his jeans and T-shirt. "A cave? You got to be kidding. We have to work tomorrow."

"Oh, please, honey," Sissy whined, her lips in a pout. "It's early."

"At night?" Tate shot Rusty a glare.

"Come on, baby," she murmured, stroking Tate's cheek. "Out there under the stars." She leaned into him and whispered, "My caveman." Tate rolled his eyes.

They squeezed into the cab of Rusty's pickup and headed south on a remote desert highway, in silence, for miles. The sun hung low in the west. Tate grasped the window ledge and wrapped his left arm around Sissy who sat wedged in the middle. Rusty darted a quick side-glance and saw her smirk and kiss and nibble on Tate's ear. "Tate," she whispered, her voice like molasses, "my caveman," as if Rusty weren't there, as if he didn't have feelings like other guys.

Tate stared ahead, didn't even answer Sissy. *He didn't have to*, Rusty thought. *Tate's cool, a lady's man. Tate answers to no one.*

Finally, Rusty veered off the road, and jounced the truck down a dry, sandy arroyo and into the creosote flats. The summer sun disappeared behind the crusty peaks of the Santiagos, casting an orange glow on the Davis Mountains to the north. Dusty pinks and blues emerged along the eastern horizon. Rusty spotted the distant high mesa and its red sloping ridge. Swerving around a cluster of prickly pear cactus, he slowed, flicked on the headlights, and weaved a path among the mesquite trees and the spiky cholla. "Whoa!" He dodged a rocky outcrop and jerked on the joystick to pick up speed.

"Jesus, Rusty!" Tate yelled. "I didn't rig this truck for you to get us killed. Use that stick nice and slow!" Rusty felt his face flush. "What's gotten into you lately?" Tate persisted. "Just 'cause you got your own wheels now, thanks to Mom. Must be Easy Street being the baby of the family."

"I'm n-not the b-baaaby," Rusty said.

"Well, you act like it. If she only knew how you drive. Man, the stuff you get away with!"

Rusty stared at the jagged landscape, his jaw clenched. He gripped the wheel and veered around a big barrel cactus. On every bounce, Sissy's thigh rubbed against Rusty's leg, but neither she nor Tate seemed to notice. Rusty stole a side-glimpse of Sissy's blue eyes and the purple cloisonné barrette that hung onto her flaxen hair fluttering in the dusty wind.

Near the high mesa, he headed for a rocky butte, screeched the brake, and skidded to a stop by a lone juniper a few yards from a rocky outcrop. "Damn you!" Tate yelled. His hands grabbed the windowsill, and Sissy's hands flew to the dash. Sissy let go a stifled screech and laughed. "Where the hell are we?" she muttered, as she wrapped her arms around Tate.

"Rusty's favorite hangout, the middle of nowhere." Tate gestured toward the sandy basin. "I don't care how cool the cave is, desert is boring."

"N-no, it's not b-boring." Rusty reached into his jeans pocket and fingered the folded paper. *Good, it's still there.* "Look." He pulled a piece of violet amethyst crystal from the front pocket of his blue jeans jacket and handed it carefully to Sissy. She rolled it in her hands and offered it to Tate, who looked away.

"Besides, you could get hurt out here." Tate brushed the dust off his T-shirt. "The wilds of West Texas is no place for a kid with crippled legs. It's just you and the buzzards. And for what? A bunch of stupid rocks? Jesus!"

"Y-You caaan't tell me whaaat to do." Rusty's throat tightened.

"Like hell I can't. Somebody needs to."

Rusty shot him a silent glare. He stepped to the ground, hung a flashlight on his belt, and walked around the rocky butte with that spastic, jerky gait he hated.

Tate and Sissy joined him, the volcanic cobbles crunching underfoot. A bloody glow had settled on the land. At the base of the butte, almost invisible behind the spiky leaves of a towering yucca, an earthy hole gaped like a small, private wound.

"Oh, my God." Sissy groaned.

"That's no cave," Tate said, standing back. "That's a rat hole!"

Rusty tossed the flashlight into the hole, slid his legs in, and pushed until the rock felt like fingers closing on his waist. He felt the sweat break out as he shoved himself deeper inside, until he was sitting in a small granite room the size of his bedroom. The ceiling hung low. The cold musty scent of damp soil penetrated his lungs.

Rusty flicked on the flashlight. Tate and Sissy squeezed in and scooted over to join him. The granite walls were rough and speckled black and gold. He darted the light beam around. Shadows rose and lunged along the walls.

"Wow!" Sissy squealed. "A real cave." She touched the ceiling. "I can't believe it."

"This is the Devil's Porch," Rusty announced. "Found it m-myself. B-But wait till you see the D-Devil's *Grip*." Rusty shone the flashlight under his chin, making a ghoul face.

"Give me that." Tate took the flashlight and peered around. "You've been down here alone? You could've gotten stuck. For days. And died! For a bunch of rocks!"

"No. N-Not rocks—rhyolite, mica, limestone. L-Look." Rusty placed his palm on the wall. "T-Touch it." He took Sissy's hand and set her palm on the dark rock. "That's g-granite. Igneous rock. R-Rough, l-like a man's b-beard in the morning. H-Here." Rusty guided Sissy's hand to his chin and moved her fingers gently across his thick, black stubble. She allowed the touch for a moment and withdrew her hand.

"It's *what*-neous rock?" Sissy ran her fingertips along the wall.

"Igneous r-rock, from *ignite*—f-formed by fire."

She smiled at him in the dim light. "How come you know so much about caves and rocks and stuff?"

Rusty grinned. "'C-Cause they're so cool. B-Besides, I have a s-secret." He shifted his body toward her. "Y-You'll be the first to hear it, you and T-Taaate. I haven't even told M-Mom, or anyone."

"So, what is it?" Tate asked impatiently. "You found another crystal?"

"No." Rusty took a deep breath. He leaned toward Sissy and paused for effect. "I w-want to b-be a geologist."

"A geologist?" Tate exclaimed. "Oh, come on! You barely squeaked by in high school!"

"And why n-not?" Rusty seethed.

"Because you're not a college egghead. That's why not."

"They g-got claaaasses in Alpine," Rusty replied. Then he looked away and mumbled, "and g-girls . . ."

"Girls? What do you mean, *girls*?"

"I m-met one at the college," Rusty blurted, and aimed his angry eyes on Tate. "In Alpine. S-Sandra."

"Oh, my God. Now it's girls? What will you come up with next?"

Sissy broke in. "Aw, Tate, come on. That's sweet. He can have a girl-friend if he wants."

"You don't know him." Tate insisted.

"Just b-because you didn't get into c-college!" Rusty bellowed.

"Tate . . . ? You applied to college?" Sissy stared at Tate. "You never told me that."

"So? It was stupid. Thought I wanted to be an engineer. You know, design stuff." Tate turned his head away, looked into the shadows

"No, no, no. Not stupid!" Sissy insisted. "So, what happened?"

Tate shrugged. "Sul Ross. In Alpine. Got on the waiting list. *Pre-engineering*, they called it." He exhaled a long sigh. "But I couldn't wait. Had to start mechanic's school. Mom lost her job and couldn't make the rent. So I withdrew my application."

Sissy shook her head. "Well, she's working now. Maybe there's still a way."

"Naw…" Tate hesitated. "Besides, I'm not a college egghead either." Tate narrowed his eyes at Rusty and clenched his jaw. "But if *I* can't get in, *you* sure as *hell* can't!"

"Oh yeah? W-Well, what's this?" Rusty yanked the folded paper from his back pocket, snapped it open, and threw it at Tate. "An application. And I've still got t-two days to g-get it in." He felt glad that the semi-dark concealed his shaking hands.

"Besides, college costs money, if you didn't know. Lots of it."

"They g-got scholarships. And l-loans. And work study j-jobs."

"Work *and* study? Ridiculous! Then go ahead," Tate yelled, "fall on your face."

"Tate, honey," Sissy broke in. "Why couldn't he go to—?"

"Don't coddle him, Sissy. He'll get his hopes up for nothing. Like that stock boy job. After that fell apart, he moped for months. Don't let him fool you, Sissy. He's a dreamer."

"Yeah, but… dreams are…" Sissy began.

"Look, he doesn't have to worry. Mom and I can take care of him. We always have and we always will." Tate turned to his brother. "Okay," he said, "here's my offer. I'll see if they can use you at the shop. You know, errands, or something. Office work. Filing maybe."

"Tate, hon," Sissy added, "can't he study too? He's sharp as a—"

"Sissy, you stay out of this! It's not your business!"

Sissy rolled her eyes and crawled off, clutching the flashlight.

"Y-You think I'm n-no good for nothing, d-don't you?"

"Of course, you're not no good," Tate said, shaking his head. "But be realistic."

"Y-You go to h-hell!" Rusty and Tate glared at each other in the dim light.

"Hey!" Sissy's voice came from the far end of the cave. "What's that?" Sissy aimed the light at a small hole. "It looks like a tunnel."

"I t-told you," Rusty said. "It's a whole 'nother r-room. But there's n-no way you can g-get through there." He pointed to the hole and cleared this throat loudly. "*That* is the D-Devil's Grip."

"Oh, cool." Sissy stuck her head into the hole and looked down the tunnel. "Oooh, you think there's skeletons in there? You know, like old miners and stuff? Bones and picks, and ... whoa ... maybe gold?"

"Of course not," Tate said.

"Let's see." Sissy tossed the flashlight down the shaft, pushed her shoulders through, squirmed and pulled, and disappeared into the Devil's Grip. "Hey, I made it." Her muffled voice echoed up the tunnel. "It's creepy in here, like a dungeon."

"Damn you, Sissy! Hold on!" Tate followed her, cramming his shoulders in, sliding and twisting until he, too, vanished into the hole.

Rusty began to sweat, thinking of Tate and Sissy being squeezed, being gripped in a vise. Whisperings floated from the tunnel, like mumblings from the underworld.

After a while, Rusty heard scrapes and groans, as Tate emerged from the dungeon. Sissy eased through the hole, slapped the dust off her pants, and tucked in her shirt.

Tate crawled across the Devil's Porch to the exit. "We're out of here."

"Hey," Sissy said, stroking her hair, "where's my barrette? My purple cloisonné? Damn!" She felt around on the ground. "It must be in the dungeon."

"Can't go back now," Tate said. "Let's go." And he crawled out of the cave.

"But wait, dammit!" she called after him. "My friend Lee brought it all the way from China! Huffing an aggravated sigh, she scrambled from the cave with Rusty close behind. They followed Tate to the pickup, the gravel crunching under their feet. "But Tate," she tried one more time, "My barrette ... the gift ... my friend!"

"Your BFF?" Tate teased, his hand on the door. "Come on. It's just a silly trinket."

Rusty slid into the driver's seat and tossed his flashlight on the floor. As Sissy scooted into the cab, she happened to spot the empty beer cans piled behind the seat. "Whoa," she murmured. She turned swiftly to Tate at the cab door. "Tate, sugar, can you see if I left my purse in the back?"

Tate stepped away to the truck bed. Sissy grabbed Rusty's jacket and pulled him close. Rusty gasped in surprise. "Rusty, hon," she whispered. "I see those beer cans. A whole pile of 'em. Sweetheart, that's gonna get you nowhere. What about your caves and your crystals? What about your mom? And Sandra? And all the other Sandras out there waiting for you?" Rusty's face flushed.

Tate appeared at the door. Sissy and Rusty sat in a stiff pose, facing straight ahead, as Tate joined them on the seat. "Didn't see any purse," he grouched.

"Whoops . . . found it." Sissy grinned, holding up her handbag. "Now, Tate . . . hon. How are you gonna get me another cloisonné barrette? All the way from China?"

"I'll get you one somewhere." Tate sounded impatient.

That's when the idea struck Rusty like a volcanic blast.

They rode home in silence. Sissy snuggled against Tate, and Tate stared out the window. Rusty gripped the steering knob, his head spinning. He knew now what he had to do. He would brave the Devil's Grip and retrieve the barrette. He would go to Sissy, open his hand, and there it would be—the lovely cloisonné, its gold border glistening. And Tate had to be there. Rusty had to see his face. Surprise them both. *Be realistic,* Tate had said. Well, Rusty would show them reality, a new reality.

The next evening, Tate was at Sissy's and Rusty's mom was working late at the café. Near midnight, Rusty shrugged his jacket on, laced his hiking boots, and grabbed his flashlight and a six-pack of Coors.

He drove to the sandy arroyo, parked by the lone juniper at the outcrop, and chugged a cold beer. A coyote yipped close by. He cranked open another beer and downed it, easing his breath to calm his nerves. Then he walked to the yucca by the high butte under a star-studded sky.

Rusty felt full to bursting. He took a piss by the yucca. Tossing the flashlight into the "rat hole," he squeezed through the first shaft to the Devil's Porch and crawled across the gravel to the Devil's Grip on all fours like a supplicant. The tunnel loomed before him like an extended maw— longer than he remembered, a ghastly six or eight feet. But it slanted downhill. That would help. He felt the sweat break out. His heart pulsed. A lump in his throat choked him. He thought he heard a movement, a scurrying. *What was that?* he wondered. *A rat? A snake? A rattler?*

He inhaled deeply until his breathing slowed. *Man, I'm thirsty. Wish I'd brought a beer.*

Removing his jacket, he dropped the flashlight into the tunnel, inserted both arms, and jammed in his shoulders, forcing, squirming, gliding on pea gravel, bit by bit. His shoulders landed on the other side.

Rusty gathered his quivering legs from the tunnel and darted the light beam around. The "dungeon" was a small room with a low granite ceiling that grazed his head, its slab walls leaning in like a condemned building. Shadows danced along the walls, the flakes of feldspar as luminous as a shattered moon. He scanned the reddish-brown dirt floor and found the scuffed spot where Tate and Sissy had been. And there it was—the barrette, its gold trim gleaming in the dirt. *Ha! Too cool!* He wiped the barrette on his jeans, watched it flicker in the flashlight beam, and stuck it in his back pocket. *Yes, Tate, this is reality. Rusty Serrano is not no good for nothin'.*

He scooted back to the tunnel—to the Devil's Grip—eager to exit, and reached up and in with both arms, the flashlight in his fist. Shoving and wriggling, he forced his shoulders. But they didn't fit. They had to fit. The tunnel was the only way out.

He tried forcing his shoulders again and thrusting his spastic legs. *Damn. It's uphill now.* This time, the loose dirt and pebbles worked against him, sliding him down. He pushed his trembling feet and wormed his way toward the top until his fingers touched the outer ridge of the tunnel. *Got it!* And that's when his body reached the worst of the bottleneck. The Devil's Grip closed around his torso like a cinch. He could go no farther. His reaching arms were stuck and his legs stretched way down, unable to push or pull. His sweating hands twisted and turned, but couldn't dislodge his chest. The earth had him in a vise.

The flashlight grew dim. He struggled and crammed his body until his shoulders and hips were jammed like a plug. His throat clenched down on the rising panic. He pressed again with his feet. His legs convulsed. The jerky rhythms jolted his hips and jarred his chest, his neck, shaking free the sobs that had snagged in his throat.

"H-Help me!" he yelled to no one. The spasms grew stronger. He heard screams, screams from his own throat, bouncing back at him like a hammer. He felt a hand close tightly around his middle.

The dream . . . the damn dream! His body twisted and writhed, gasping for air. The earth, the world, had him in a Devil's hand, a Devil's Grip. Squeezing him. Binding him. He couldn't breathe, he couldn't move, he needed to scream . . . he needed to be let-go-of.

Breathe, keep breathing. He imagined a tether, a tie, wrapped around his ankles, his knees, and felt it coil and twine around his hips, his waist, pinning his arms to his side. He saw himself walking, sleeping, talking, with this cord ramming his parts together, jamming him, pinching him, crowding him. All his life! Yes, he knew it—he could hardly breathe, his whole goddamn life!

"L-Let me go!" he screamed, his breaths coming quick and shallow. His shouts echoed back. Sweat poured down his neck. He pushed again. His legs jerked and quivered, jostling him loose. His body slipped down and his feet hit the dungeon floor. "Oh, G-God . . ." His spasms triggered, shaking his thighs in a terrible rhythm. "N-No," he sobbed. "L-Let go!"

The flashlight went dark. Rusty shivered. He licked his grimy lips, felt the grit in his teeth. The cave smelled of blackness, of death. So, the Grip had won. He would never be free. This was reality. He was helpless.

"No!" he screamed. He sucked air into his frantic lungs and heaved. But the Grip, the cinch, closed on his middle again, like a demon. Sweat poured from his arms, his chest. His breath came in gasps. He forced his hips forward and reached until his hand grasped the far end of the tunnel. He felt another squeeze of the vise.

Rusty closed his eyes, inhaled a long breath, and tried once more, easing into the hole slowly, smoothly, squeezing himself thin. His body moved upward a bit, then some more. He tugged his way until his fingertips felt the upper edge of the shaft. "L-Let me g-go!" he screamed.

No, no, no! Breathe deep. This time, Rusty opened his lungs, and released his breath like the bleeding of bile, until he was empty, clear, drained. He closed his eyes and lay a long while as visions drifted by: his home . . . his bed . . . his crystals. He thought of his mother, María, forever dragging, tired, and alone. He imagined Sissy's sweet whisperings . . . and Tate, how he'd rigged the joystick, covered the rent, and rose early for work each morning—for him and for Mom—his engineering dreams diminishing, year by year. Rusty opened his eyes in the dark, feeling thinner . . . lighter, as if floating, limp, and loose.

Sensing a calmer strength, he reached toward the tunnel entry, and wriggled and tugged. His knuckles ached. He eased himself upward, upward, dragging fingers, shoving feet, scraping his limp body along the rocks. His elbows caught the edge and dragged, prying his torso another few inches. The granite tore at his shirt, ripping shreds away and scuffing skin. Streaks of blood and sweat smeared across his chest as he slid farther and farther and, finally, out and free. Free of the Devil's Grip.

Rusty lay on the gravel in the Devil's Porch, the rocks rough against his chest and cheek. He slept a long while, sucking sweet air into his lungs with cadence and calm.

When he awoke, he gathered his jacket and crawled from the cave as the chilly night air stroked his face. He hiked to the high mesa, his boots crunching on the steep, rocky trail, to the flat crest on top of the world. The moonlit mountains—the Davis peaks and the Santiagos—stretched their jagged silhouettes along the horizon to the south, to the west, to the north. Rusty sat on a pile of broken breccia, held his knees, and shivered at the beauty of the vast midnight sky, the rich, rugged landscape he loved, made more mysterious by a half-moon on the rise. He stood tall, stretched his hands high, and breathed deeply, taking in the scents of the desert—pungent, bittersweet. "Not boring," he said aloud.

Rusty slid the folded paper from his jeans pocket, snapped it out flat, and read the heading in the celestial light: *Sul Ross State University, Admissions Application.* In the dim glow, he peered at the blank line "Name," where tomorrow he would fill in *Rusty Serrano.*

Rusty dug in his back pocket and retrieved the cloisonné barrette. He caressed the jewel, the purple, the gold, as it glistened in the half-moon-light. Clutching the application, he hiked down the rocky trail with that lurching gait he'd always hated, and smiled. *I'm not drowning*, he thought as he inhaled the crisp night air deep into his lungs. *I'm not drowning at all!*

In the first light of dawn, Rusty pulled into a recycling center, dumped his pile of empty beer cans, and headed to Sissy's. He climbed the porch steps, strolled casually to her door, and knocked, the four remaining cans of the six-pack dangling in plastic rings from his fingers.

Sissy opened the door in her yellow robe, tying the cloth belt. "Hey, what are you—?"

Rusty slipped past her and walked to the kitchen table as Sissy followed. Tate stood at the counter stirring coffee, dressed in jeans and T-shirt.

Rusty slammed the four beers on the table. "I d-don't n-need these anymore," he announced. "I'm d-done."

Tate and Sissy stared back at Rusty. "Well ..." Tate began.

Rusty pulled Sissy's cloisonné barrette from his pocket and tossed the "trinket" to the table where it bounced and clinked and glistened among the breakfast dishes. Sissy gasped. Tate starred at the barrette, then at Rusty.

Rusty broke the silence. "T-Tate. You're c-coming with me."

Tate smirked. "Where the hell to now? The damn cave? The Devil's Grip?"

Rusty walked to Tate and hooked his elbow. "N-No. T-To Alpine."

Tate shook him off. "What for?"

"The d-deadline is t-today. They g-got night c-classes."

"Night classes?" Tate hurled his stirring spoon to the table. "Persistent bastard, aren't you?"

Tate chugged his coffee, grabbed his wallet from the counter, and stomped out the door and down the steps. "I'm just going for the ride," he said with a shrug. "To help you out." Rusty followed behind, keeping his silence.

Sissy followed and watched them from the porch, her hands on her hips.

Tate yelled to her, "Call the shop, hon. Tell 'em I'll be late!" Then he slid into the truck and stared straight ahead, his jaw clenching.

Rusty slipped behind the wheel and fired the ignition. On the dashboard, a chunk of quartz gleamed, a crystal of lilac and rose. He peered past Tate at Sissy, who gave him a wink.

Rusty wrenched the car around the driveway and sped down Avenue D toward the highway.

"Jesus, Rusty!" Tate hollered. "Use that stick slow and easy! You're gonna get us killed!"

Rusty smirked.

"What's so funny?" Tate asked, pausing to look at his brother. "So, you think I can do this?"

"You idiot," Rusty replied, smiling, "w-what d-do you think?"

Tate offered a silent shrug.

Rusty swerved onto the highway. The morning sun rose behind them, burning the scrubby flats. It flooded the jagged landscape with dusty greens and golds. "L-look at those hills," he announced. "Feldspar and g-granite and ..." The old truck shuddered and shook, and jiggled the crystal to the floor.

Tate retrieved the rock at his feet and held it firmly in his palm. "A geologist, huh?"

Rusty rolled down his window, letting in a rush of hot wild wind. He jerked forward on the joystick and gunned it for Alpine.

ALICE HOFFMAN

In the Trees

America the plum blossoms are falling.

When you have a secret in our town, you have to carry it close to your heart. You have to be careful even when you sleep to make sure you don't announce your crimes while you're dreaming. Everything is a crime here, even falling in love. That is what happened to me. My mother had warned me that being a woman could bring you sorrow, but I didn't listen. Not then. It was July, the time of year when the river is so blue it hurts to look at it. Fishermen come here from all across the country. My father owns a bait store, and everyone stops there, people from California and New York and Chicago. Men who are ruined, and those who are so rich they can't even count their money anymore. There's only one motel in town, but local folks open their houses, put their kids in tents in the yard, then rent out their bedrooms. You have to catch visitors from out of state while you can, my father says. We have a sort of trout that cannot be found anywhere else, called a blue rainbow. In school we've been told it was the original fish, the one that fed the multitudes, and that all other trout are descended from our rainbows. But we are taught many things I no longer believe. Less than a hundred years ago, there were countless wolves in our hills; now the last one to be caught is in the historical museum. I go there sometimes just to stare at him. You can see the stitches in his pelt, and his eyes are made of yellow glass. How can something so beautiful come to an end so quickly? Now we have hundreds of rabbits. It's the penance we pay. When I walk to school in the morning they're on everyone's lawn. There's not much grass left anymore, just patches of dirt. Sometimes the rabbits refuse to

move out of the way; they block the sidewalk, and when I run, they
chase me.

I fell in love with a boy who came from Chicago in July. His name was
Will and his dream was to catch one of our rainbows, or so he said. Then
after a while he said I was his dream. Maybe that was why I let him do
things to me I'd never let anyone do before, but it was only part of the
reason. I felt caught up in something when I looked in his eyes. I didn't
understand that love is something that can ambush you, and there you
are at the mercy of the forces of nature, like the wolves that had continued to come to the river to drink when they should have run as far as
they could.

We met at night, in the parking lot of the motel, where he and his
father and brothers were staying. I'd worked there one summer clean-
ing rooms, but I complained about some of the things I found, and they
didn't hire me back. After that, I just worked in my father's shop. I'd
wash my hands with lemon juice at the end of the day. I'd take off my
clothes and change into clean jeans and a T-shirt that smelled of soap
instead of fish. I'd let my hair out of the tight braids I usually wore and
brush it till it shone. Then I'd walk to the motel. I'd try to walk slowly,
so as not to give my heart away, but I'd always wind up running. I was
fifteen, an age when a girl can be stupid and smart at the same time.
We would go to his father's truck to be alone. The nights were starry in
July and the trees whispered. There was a plum tree I knew about and
sometimes, after we were done in his father's truck, we would walk to
that tree and steal plums. Will believed things that I didn't. He was glad
that the wolves had disappeared and he didn't care that polar bears
were now found wandering down the streets in northern Scotland, and
that the bees were all but gone. He didn't pay any attention to the lasts
of things, but I did. I figured my little sister wouldn't even know honey
had ever existed. Will had his eye on the future, he said. I, myself, didn't
like to think about what would happen next. I was here now, with him,
at the plum tree, listening to the cicadas and wondering why their song
was so hard to hear. When I was a little girl they were so loud you could
barely talk to each other outside at night. Now we could whisper and
hear each other just fine.

I was in love with Will and with July and I never wanted the night
to end. I dreaded the next day, which would force us further into the
future. When I walked home alone on the dirt road that led to our
house I was often dizzy. It was love that had done that to me, and

the stars, and the way I knew that something would happen to ruin everything.

My mind is made up there's going to be trouble.

Will's father caught the biggest trout on record. I cried when I saw him on the dock, being photographed by the newspaper, with Will and his brothers flanking him. The fish was every color blue from sapphire to turquoise to cobalt. It shimmered in the sunlight, but its eyes were white. People said it was the granddaddy, the ancestor of all the other fish. Our mayor took Will's family to dinner. I was in the crowd but Will didn't wave. The truth is I don't think he even saw me. I was no one, after all. A girl he'd met by accident. I didn't go meet Will that night. Instead I went down to the river. My father always said it would take a day and a night to swim all the way across and that a person who tried to do so would likely drown. I took off all my clothes and I dove in. It was dark and the water looked black and I realized I was crying. I thought about a girl I knew who had once ruined her life with love. Ten years later, no one talked to her, although I always did.

Will came looking for me and told me I was wrong to think he'd forget me. He was still here, wasn't he? We held each other in the woods. I knew he would be leaving, but I did it anyway, as if this were the only day we would ever have. Still, I knew I'd have a price to pay.

My father found a letter I was writing to Will and he took me out and beat me with his belt. He told me I would thank him someday, but I doubted it. Someday didn't matter to me. I had welts on my skin and something had broken inside me. I packed a bag and ran down the dirt road, ready to leave town and everything I had ever known, but when I got to the motel, Will's father's truck was gone. I went into the office. Anna was there, the woman I worked with when I cleaned rooms. She was the one no one talked to, unless they were from out of town.

"Off to Chicago," she said. "You couldn't have thought he'd stay?"

I went to the river instead of going home. I knew what happened to girls like me. Everybody did. My secret hurt me, like a stone in my shoe. But worse. Much worse, because it was my heart

I sit in my house far days on end and stare at the roses in the closet.

I did nothing for as long as I could, and then I went to the doctor. I'd known him all my life, so I kept my eyes lowered as I spoke to him. I told him I wanted to go to Chicago, where I'd heard they could free me of my misfortune. I knew someone who had been there, and she'd told me the address. I didn't tell him it was Anna, and that I had the address written down in my notebook. The doctor listened to my secret, then he told me to wait where I was. Instead of helping me, he called my father.

My father came in like a storm, cursing. He told me I had no right to do what I wanted to do. I was underage and my body belonged to him and he should have known I would turn out this way.

My father locked me in my room. I sat in the closet, thinking things over. When it was dark, I climbed out my window. I took the money my mother had buried in the yard in a coffee can. I felt bad, but not too bad, because she always said she was saving it for me and this was my time of need. I don't think about what happened after that. I don't think of the men in the cars, or the place I went to where they locked you in a room so you couldn't make a phone call, or the man they called Doc who wasn't a doctor. There were other girls there, but we didn't speak to each other. I heard them crying, but I swallowed my tears. I wished I weren't fifteen. I wished none of this had ever happened. I never think about the pain now, except when I still have it. They said that due to the circumstances, I would not be able to have children. I don't think about that either.

When I went home my father didn't speak to me, but my mother let me in. I didn't go back to school, I sat in my closet and thought about things that had passed. In time it was April and I could see the plum tree blossoms from my room. I thought of myself as the plum tree, standing alone in the woods. I would be sixteen eventually, not that I cared. When it was July again people started coming to the river, but not Will, which was just as well. The trout were gone. People searched for them, they rented boats and came from all over the country, but there were no blue rainbows to be found. We didn't even have the last one in the historical museum. That one was on Will's father's wall in Chicago.

After that the future crept up on all of us, though I still try to keep it from my thoughts. Now when you go to the market, they sell trout that they paint with blue dye, but it doesn't fool anyone any more than the honey they make from sugar water and molasses. These things are lost. I know what it's like to disappear. I go to the river at night. It's mostly deserted now, but I swim out as far as I can. I swim until I'm hurting. I think about not going back, but I do. I can always find my way because the stars are still there.

AKHIL SHARMA

Surrounded By Sleep

One August afternoon, when Ajay was ten years old, his elder brother, Birju, dove into a pool and struck his head on the cement bottom. For three minutes, he lay there unconscious. Two boys continued to swim, kicking and splashing, until finally Birju was spotted below them. Water had entered through his nose and mouth. It had filled his stomach. His lungs had collapsed. By the time he was pulled out, he could no longer think, talk, chew, or roll over in his sleep.

Ajay's family had moved from India to Queens, New York, two years earlier. The accident occurred during the boys' summer vacation, on a visit with their aunt and uncle in Arlington, Virginia. After the accident, Ajay's mother came to Arlington, where she waited to see if Birju would recover. At the hospital, she told the doctors and nurses that her son had been accepted into the Bronx High School of Science, in the hope that by highlighting his intelligence she would move them to make a greater effort on his behalf. Within a few weeks of the accident, the insurance company said that Birju should be transferred to a less expensive care facility, a long-term one. But only a few of these were any good, and those were full, and Ajay's mother refused to move Birju until a space opened in one of them. So she remained in Arlington, and Ajay stayed, too, and his father visited from Queens on the weekends when he wasn't working. Ajay was enrolled at the local public school and in September he started fifth grade.

Before the accident, Ajay had never prayed much. In India, he and his brother used to go with their mother to the temple every Tuesday night, but that was mostly because there was a good dosa restaurant nearby. In America, his family went to a temple only on important holy days and birthdays. But shortly after Ajay's mother came to Arlington, she moved into the room that he and his brother had shared during the summer and made an altar in a corner. She threw an old flowered sheet over a cardboard box that had once held a television. On top, she put a clay lamp, an incense-stick holder, and postcards depicting various gods. There was also a postcard of Mahatma Gandhi. She explained to Ajay that God could take any form; the picture of Mahatma Gandhi was there because he had appeared to her in a dream after the accident and told her that Birju would recover and become a surgeon. Now she and Ajay prayed for at least half an hour before the altar every morning and night.

At first, she prayed with absolute humility. "Whatever you do will be good because you are doing it," she murmured to post cards of Ram and Shivaji, daubing their lips with water and rice. Mahatma Gandhi got only water, because he did not like to eat. As weeks passed and Birju did not recover in time to go to the Bronx High School of Science for the first day of classes, his mother began doing things that called attention to her piety. She sometimes held the prayer lamp until it blistered her palms. Instead of kneeling before the altar, she lay face down. She fasted twice a week. Her attempts to sway God were not so different from Ajay's performing somersaults to amuse his aunt, and they made God seem human to Ajay.

One morning, as Ajay knelt before the altar, he traced an Om, a cross, and a Star of David into he pile of the carpet. Beneath these, he traced an S, for Superman, inside an upside down triangle. His mother came up beside him.

"What are you praying for?" she asked. She had her hat on, a thick gray knitted one that a man might wear. The tracings went against the weave of the carpet and were darker than the surrounding nap. Pretending to examine them, Ajay leaned forward and put his hand over the S. His mother did not mind the Christian and Jewish symbols—they were for commonly recognized gods, after all—but she could not tolerate his praying to Superman. She'd caught him doing so once, several weeks earlier, and had become very angry, as if Ajay's faith in Superman made her faith in Ram ridiculous. "Right in front of God," she had said several times.

Ajay, in his nervousness, spoke the truth. "I'm asking God to give me a hundred percent on the math test."

His mother was silent for a moment.

"What if God says you can have the math grade but then Birju will have to be sick a little while longer?" she asked.

Ajay kept quiet. He could hear cars on the road outside. He knew that his mother wanted to bewail her misfortune before God so that

God would feel guilty. He looked at the postcard of Mahatma Gandhi. It was a black-and-white photo of him walking down a city street with an enormous crowd trailing behind him. Ajay thought of how, before the accident, Birju had been so modest that he would not leave the bathroom until he was fully dressed. Now he had rashes on his penis from the catheter that carried his urine into a translucent bag hanging from the guardrail of his bed.

His mother asked again, "Would you say, 'Let him be sick a little while longer'?"

"Are you going to tell me the story about Uncle Naveen again?" he asked.

"Why shouldn't I? When I was sick, as a girl, your uncle walked seven times around the temple and asked God to let him fail his exams just as long as I got better."

"If I failed the math test and told you that story, you'd slap me and ask what one has to do with the other."

His mother turned to the altar.

"What sort of sons did you give me, God?" she asked. "One you drown, the other is this selfish fool."

"I will fast today so that God puts some sense in me," Ajay said, glancing away from the altar and up at his mother. He liked the drama of fasting.

"No, you are a growing boy." His mother knelt down beside him and said to the altar, "He is stupid, but he has a good heart."

PRAYER, AJAY THOUGHT, should appeal with humility and an open heart to some greater force. But the praying that he and his mother did felt sly and confused. By treating God as someone to bargain with, it seemed to him they prayed as if they were casting a spell.

This meant that it was possible to do away with the presence of God entirely. For example, Ajay's mother had recently asked a relative in India to drive a nail into a holy tree and tie a saffron thread to the nail on Birju's behalf. Ajay invented his own ritual. On his way to school each morning, he passed a thick tree rooted half on the sidewalk and half on the road. One day, Ajay got the idea that if he circled the tree seven times, touching the north side every other time, he would have a lucky day. From then on, he did it every morning, although he felt embarrassed and always looked around beforehand to make sure no one was watching.

One night, Ajay asked God whether he minded being prayed to only in need.

"You think of your toe only when you stub it," God replied. God looked like Clark Kent. He wore a gray cardigan, slacks, and thick glasses, and had a forelock that curled just as Ajay's did.

God and Ajay had begun talking occasionally after Birju drowned. Now they talked most nights while Ajay lay in bed and waited for sleep. God sat at the foot of Ajay's mattress. His mother's mattress lay parallel to his, a few feet away. Originally, God had appeared to Ajay as Krishna, but Ajay had felt foolish discussing brain damage with a blue God who held a flute and wore a dhoti.

"You're not angry with me for touching the tree and all that?"

"No. I'm flexible."

"I respect you. The tree is just a way of praying to you," Ajay assured God.

God laughed. "I am not too caught up in formalities."

Ajay was quiet. He was convinced that he had been marked as special by Birju's accident. The beginnings of all heroes are distinguished by misfortune. Superman and Batman were both orphans. Krishna was separated from his parents at birth. The god Ram had to spend fourteen years in a forest. Ajay waited to speak until it would not appear improper to begin talking about himself.

"How famous will I be?" he asked, finally.

"I can't tell you the future," God answered.

Ajay asked, "Why not?"

"Even if I told you something, later I might change my mind."

"But it might be harder to change your mind after you have said something will happen."

God laughed again. "You'll be so famous that fame will be a problem."

Ajay sighed. His mother snorted and rolled over.

"I want Birju's drowning to lead to something," he said to God.

"He won't be forgotten."

"I can't just be famous, though. I need to be rich too, to take care of Mummy and Daddy and pay for Birju's hospital bills."

"You are always practical." God had a soulful and pitying voice and God's sympathy made Ajay imagine himself as a truly tragic figure, like Amitabh Bachchan in the movie *Trishul.*

"I have responsibilities," Ajay said. He was so excited at the thought of his possible greatness that he knew he would have difficulty sleeping. Perhaps he would have to go read in the bathroom.

"You can hardly imagine the life ahead," God said.

Even though God's tone promised greatness, the idea of the future frightened Ajay. He opened his eyes. There was light coming from the street. The room was cold and had a smell of must and incense. His aunt and uncle's house was a narrow two-story home next to a four-lane road. The apartment building with the pool where Birju had drowned was a few blocks up the road, one in a cluster of tall brick buildings with stucco fronts. Ajay pulled the blanket tighter around him. In India, he could not have imagined the reality of his life in America: the thick smell of meat in the school cafeteria, the many television channels. And, of course, he could not have imagined Birju's accident, or the hospital where he spent so much time.

THE HOSPITAL WAS BORING. Vinod, Ajay's cousin, picked him up after school and dropped him off there almost every day. Vinod was twenty-two. In addition to attending county college and studying computer programming, he worked at a 7-Eleven near Ajay's school. He often brought Ajay hot chocolate and a comic from the store, which had to be returned, so Ajay was not allowed to open it until he had wiped his hands.

Vinod usually asked him a riddle on the way to the hospital. "Why are manhole covers round?" It took Ajay half the ride to admit that he did not know. He was having difficulty talking. He didn't know why. The only time he could talk easily was when he was with God. The explanation he gave himself for this was that, just as he couldn't chew when there was too much in his mouth, he couldn't talk when there were too many thoughts in his head.

When Ajay got to Birju's room, he greeted him as if he were all right. "Hello, lazy. How much longer are you going to sleep?" His mother was always there. She got up and hugged Ajay. She asked how school had been, and he didn't know what to say. In music class, the teacher sang a song about a sailor who had bared his breast before jumping into the sea. This had caused the other students to giggle. But Ajay could not say the word "breast" to his mother without blushing. He had also cried. He'd been thinking of how Birju's accident had made his own life mysterious and confused. What would happen next? Would Birju die or would he go on as he was? Where would they live? Usually when Ajay cried in school, he was told to go outside. But it had been raining, and the teacher had sent him into the hallway. He sat on the floor and wept.

Any mention of this would upset his mother. And so he said nothing had happened that day.

Sometimes when Ajay arrived his mother was on the phone, telling his father that she missed him and was expecting to see him on Friday. His father took a Greyhound bus most Fridays from Queens to Arlington, returning on Sunday night in time to work the next day. He was a book-keeper for a department store. Before the accident, Ajay had thought of his parents as the same person: MummyDaddy. Now, when he saw his father praying stiffly or when his father failed to say hello to Birju in his hospital bed, Ajay sensed that his mother and father were quite different people. After his mother got off the phone, she always went to the cafeteria to get coffee for herself and Jell-O or cookies for him. He knew that if she took her coat with her it meant that she was especially sad. Instead of going directly to the cafeteria, she was going to go outside and walk around the hospital parking lot.

That day, while she was gone, Ajay stood beside the hospital bed and balanced a comic book on Birju's chest. He read to him very slowly. Before turning each page, he said. "OK, Birju?"

Birju was fourteen. He was thin and had curly hair. Immediately after the accident, there had been so many machines around his bed that only one person could stand beside him at a time. Now there was just a single waxy, yellow tube. One end of this went into his abdomen; the other, blocked by a green, bullet-shaped plug, was what his Isocal milk was poured through. When not being used, the tube was rolled up and bound by a rubber band and tucked beneath Birju's hospital gown. But even with the tube hidden it was obvious that there was something wrong with Birju. It was in his stillness and his open eyes. Once, in their house in Queens, Ajay had left a plastic bowl on a radiator overnight and the sides had drooped and sagged so that the bowl looked a little like an eye. Birju reminded Ajay of that bowl.

Ajay had not gone with his brother to the swimming pool on the day of the accident, because he had been reading a book and wanted to finish it. But he heard the ambulance siren from his aunt and uncle's house. The pool was only a few minutes away, and when he got there a crowd had gathered around the ambulance. Ajay saw his uncle first, in shorts and an undershirt, talking to a man inside the ambulance. His aunt was standing beside him. Then Ajay saw Birju on a stretcher, in blue shorts with a plastic mask over his nose and mouth. His aunt hurried over to take Ajay home. He cried as they walked, although he had been certain that Birju would be fine in a few days: in a Spider-Man comic he had just read, Aunt May had fallen into a coma and she had woken up perfectly fine. Ajay had cried simply because he felt crying was called for by the seriousness of the occasion. Perhaps this moment would mark the beginning of his future greatness. From that day on, Ajay found it hard to cry in front of his family. Whenever tears started coming, he felt like a liar. If he loved his brother, he knew, he would not have thought about himself as the ambulance had pulled away, nor would he talk with God at night about becoming famous.

When Ajay's mother returned to Birju's room with coffee and cookies, she sometimes talked to Ajay about Birju. She told him that when Birju was six he had seen a children's television show that had a character named Chunu, which was Birju's nickname, and he had thought the show was based on his own life. But most days Ajay went into the lounge to read. There was a TV in the corner and a lamp near a window that looked out over a parking lot. It was the perfect place to read. Ajay liked fantasy novels where the hero, who was preferably under the age of twenty-five, had an undiscovered talent that made him famous when it was revealed. He could read for hours without interruption, and sometimes when Vinod came to drive Ajay and his mother home from the hospital it was hard for him to remember the details of the real day that had passed.

One evening, when he was in the lounge, he saw a rock star being interviewed on *Entertainment Tonight*. The musician, dressed in a sleeveless undershirt that revealed a swarm of tattoos on his arms and shoulders, had begun to shout at the audience, over his interviewer, "Don't watch me! Live your life! I'm not you!" Filled with a sudden desire to do something, Ajay hurried out of the television lounge and stood on the sidewalk in front of the hospital entrance. But he did not know what to do. It was cold and dark and there was an enormous moon. Cars leaving the parking lot stopped one by one at the edge of the road. Ajay watched as they waited for an opening in the traffic, their brake lights glowing.

"ARE THINGS GETTING WORSE?" Ajay asked God. The weekend before had been Thanksgiving. Christmas would come soon, and a new year would start, a year during which Birju would not have talked or walked. Suddenly, Ajay understood hopelessness. Hopelessness felt very much like fear. It involved a clutching in the stomach and a numbness in the arms and legs.

"What do you think?" God answered.

"They seem to be."

"At least Birju's hospital hasn't forced him out."

"At least Birju isn't dead. At least Daddy's Greyhound bus has never skidded off a bridge." Lately, Ajay had begun talking much more quickly to God than he used to. Before, when he had talked to God, Ajay would think of what God would say in response before he said anything. Now, Ajay spoke without knowing how God might respond.

"You shouldn't be angry at me." God sighed. God was wearing his usual cardigan. "You can't understand why I do what I do."

"You should explain better then."

"Christ was my son. I loved Job. How long did Ram have to live in a forest?"

"What does that have to do with me?" This was usually the cue for discussing Ajay's prospects. But hopelessness made the future feel even more frightening than the present.

"I can't tell you what the connection is, but you'll be proud of yourself."

They were silent for a while.

"Do you love me truly?" Ajay asked.

"Yes."

"Will you make Birju normal?" As soon as Ajay asked the question, God ceased to be real. Ajay knew then that he was alone, lying under his blankets, his face exposed to the cold dark.

"I can't tell you the future," God said softly. These were words that Ajay already knew.

"Just get rid of the minutes when Birju lay on the bottom of the pool. What are three minutes to you?"

"Presidents die in less time than that. Planes crash in less time than that."

Ajay opened his eyes. His mother was on her side and she had a blanket pulled up to her neck. She looked like an ordinary woman. It surprised him that you couldn't tell, looking at her, that she had a son who was brain-dead.

○─○─○

IN FACT, THINGS WERE getting worse. Putting away his mother's mattress and his own in a closet in the morning, getting up very early so he could use the bathroom before his aunt or uncle did, spending so many hours in the hospital—all this had given Ajay the reassuring sense that

real life was in abeyance, and that what was happening was unreal. He
and his mother and brother were just waiting to make a long-delayed bus
trip. The bus would come eventually to carry them to Queens, where he
would return to school at P.S. 20 and to Sunday afternoons spent at the
Hindi movie theater under the trestle for the 7 train. But now Ajay was
starting to understand that the world was always real, whether you were
reading a book or sleeping, and that it eroded you every day.

He saw the evidence of this erosion in his mother, who had grown
severe and unforgiving. Usually when Vinod brought her and Ajay home
from the hospital, she had dinner with the rest of the family. After his
mother helped his aunt wash the dishes, the two women watched theo-
logical action movies. One night, in spite of a headache that had made
her sit with her eyes closed all afternoon, she ate dinner, washed dishes,
sat down in front of the TV. As soon as the movie was over, she went
upstairs, vomited, and lay on her mattress with a wet towel over her forehead. She asked Ajay to massage her neck and shoulders. As he did so,
Ajay noticed that she was crying. The tears frightened Ajay and made
him angry. "You shouldn't have watched TV," he said accusingly.

"I have to," she said. "People will cry with you once, and they will cry
with you a second time. But if you cry a third time, people will say you are
boring and always crying."

Ajay did not want to believe what she had said, but her cynicism made
him think that she must have had conversations with his aunt and uncle
that he did not know about. "That's not true," he told her, massaging her
scalp. "Uncle is kind. Auntie Aruna is always kind."

"What do you know?" She shook her head, freeing herself from Ajay's
fingers. She stared at him. Upside down, her face looked unfamiliar and
terrifying. "If God lets Birju live long enough, you will become a stranger,
too. You will say, 'I have been unhappy for so long because of Birju, now
I don't want to talk about him or look at him.' Don't think I don't know
you," she said.

Suddenly, Ajay hated himself. To hate himself was to see himself
as the opposite of everything he wanted to be: short instead of tall, fat
instead of thin. When he brushed his teeth that night, he looked at his
face: his chin was round and fat as a heel. His nose was so broad that he
had once been able to fit a small rock in one nostril.

His father was also being eroded. Before the accident, Ajay's father
loved jokes—he could do perfect imitations—and Ajay had felt lucky to
have him as a father. (Once, Ajay's father had convinced his own mother

that he was possessed by the ghost of a British man.) And after the accident, his father had impressed Ajay with the patient loyalty of his weekly bus journeys. But now his father was different.

One Saturday afternoon, as Ajay and his father were returning from the hospital, his father slowed the car without warning and turned into the dirt parking lot of a bar that looked as though it had originally been a small house. It had a pitched roof with a black tarp. At the edge of the lot stood a tall neon sign of an orange hand lifting a mug of sudsy golden beer. Ajay had never seen anybody drink except in the movies. He wondered whether his father was going to ask for directions to somewhere, and if so, to where.

His father said, "One minute," and they climbed out of the car.

They went up wooden steps into the bar. Inside, it was dark and smelled of cigarette smoke and something stale and sweet. The floor was linoleum like the kitchen at his aunt and uncle's. There was a bar with stools around it, and a basketball game played on a television bolted against the ceiling, like the one in Birju's hospital room.

His father stood by the bar waiting for the bartender to notice him. His father had a round face and was wearing a white shirt and dark dress pants, as he often did on the weekend, since it was more economical to have the same clothes for the office and home.

The bartender came over. "How much for a Budweiser?" his father asked. It was a dollar fifty. "Can I buy a single cigarette?" He did not have to buy; the bartender would just give him one. His father helped Ajay up onto a stool and sat down himself. Ajay looked around and wondered what would happen if somebody started a knife fight. When his father had drunk half his beer, he carefully lit the cigarette. The bartender was standing at the end of the bar. There were only two other men in the place. Ajay was disappointed that there were no women wearing dresses slit all the way up their thighs. Perhaps they came in the evenings.

His father asked him if he had ever watched a basketball game all the way through.

"I've seen the Harlem Globetrotters."

His father smiled and took a sip. "I've heard they don't play other teams, because they can defeat everyone else so easily."

"They only play against each other, unless there is an emergency—like in the cartoon, when they play against the aliens to save the Earth," Ajay said.

"Aliens?"

Ajay blushed as he realized his father was teasing him.

When they left, the light outside felt too bright. As his father opened the car door for Ajay, he said, 'Tm sorry."

That's when Ajay first felt that his father might have done something wrong. The thought made him worry. Once they were on the road, his father said gently, "Don't tell your mother."

Fear made Ajay feel cruel. He asked his father, "What do you think about when you think of Birju?"

Instead of becoming sad, Ajay's father smiled. "I am surprised by how strong he is. It's not easy for him to keep living. But, even before, he was strong. When he was interviewing for high school scholarships, one interviewer asked him, 'Are you a thinker or a doer?' He laughed and said, 'That's like asking, 'Are you an idiot or a moron?'"

From then on, they often stopped at the bar on the way back from the hospital. Ajay's father always asked the bartender for a cigarette before he sat down, and during the ride home he always reminded Ajay not to tell his mother.

Ajay found that he himself was changing. His superstitions were becoming extreme. Now when he walked around the good-luck tree he punched it, every other time, hard, so that his knuckles hurt. Afterward, he would hold his breath for a moment longer than he thought he could bear, and ask God to give the unused breaths to Birju.

○─○─○

IN DECEMBER, A PLACE opened in one of the good long-term care facilities. It was in New Jersey. This meant that Ajay and his mother could move back to New York and live with his father again. This was the news Ajay's father brought when he arrived for a two-week holiday at Christmas.

Ajay felt the clarity of panic. Life would be the same as before the accident but also unimaginably different. He would return to P.S. 20, while Birju continued to be fed through a tube in his abdomen. Life would be Birju's getting older and growing taller than their parents but having less consciousness than even a dog, which can become excited or afraid.

Ajay decided to use his devotion to shame God into fixing Birju. The fact that two religions regarded the coming December days as holy ones suggested to Ajay that prayers during this time would be especially potent. So he prayed whenever he thought of it—at his locker, even in the middle of a quiz. His mother wouldn't let him fast, but he started throwing away the lunch he took to school. And when his mother prayed in the morning, Ajay watched to make sure that she bowed at least once toward each of the postcards of deities. If she did not, he bowed three times to the possibly offended god on the postcard. He had noticed that his father finished his prayers in less time than it took to brush his teeth. And so now, when his father began praying in the morning, Ajay immediately crouched down beside him, because he knew his father would be embarrassed to get up first. But Ajay found it harder and harder to drift into the rhythm of sung prayers or into his nightly conversations with God. How could chanting and burning incense undo three minutes of a sunny August afternoon? It was like trying to move a sheet of blank paper from one end of a table to the other by blinking so fast that you started a breeze.

o—o—o

ON CHRISTMAS EVE, his mother asked the hospital chaplain to come to Birju's room and pray with them. The family knelt together beside Birju's bed. Afterward, the chaplain asked her whether she would be attending Christmas services. "Of course, Father," she said.

"I'm also coming," Ajay said.

The chaplain turned toward Ajay's father, who was sitting in a wheelchair because there was nowhere else to sit. "I'll wait for God at home," he said. That night, Ajay watched *It's a Wonderful Life* on television. To him, the movie meant that happiness arrived late, if ever. Later, when he got in bed and closed his eyes, God appeared. There was little to say.

"Will Birju be better in the morning?"

"No."

"Why not?"

"When you prayed for the math exam, you could have asked for Birju to get better and, instead of your getting an A, Birju would have woken."

This was so ridiculous that Ajay opened his eyes. His father was sleeping nearby on folded-up blankets. Ajay felt disappointed at not feeling guilt. Guilt might have contained some hope that God existed.

When Ajay arrived at the hospital with his father and mother the next morning, Birju was asleep, breathing through his mouth while a nurse poured a can of Isocal into his stomach through the yellow tube. Ajay had not expected that Birju would have recovered; nevertheless, seeing him that way put a weight in Ajay's chest.

The Christmas prayers were held in a large, mostly empty room; people in chairs sat next to people in wheelchairs. His father walked out in the middle of the service.

Later, Ajay sat in a corner of Birju's room and watched his parents. His mother was reading a Hindi women's magazine to Birju while she shelled peanuts into her lap. His father was reading a thick red book in preparation for a civil-service exam. The day wore on. The sky outside grew dark. At some point, Ajay began to cry. He tried to be quiet. He did not want his parents to notice his tears and think that he was crying for Birju, because in reality he was crying for how difficult his own life was.

His father noticed first. "What's the matter, hero?"

His mother shouted, "What happened?" and she sounded so alarmed it was as if Ajay were bleeding.

"I didn't get any Christmas presents! I need a Christmas present!" Ajay shouted. "You didn't buy me a Christmas present!" And then, because he had revealed his own selfishness, Ajay let himself sob. "You have to give me something. I should get something for all this." Ajay clenched his hands and wiped his face with his fists. "Each time I come here I should get something."

His mother pulled him up and pressed him into her stomach. His father came and stood beside them. "What do you want?" his father asked.

Ajay had no prepared answer for this. "What do you want?" his mother repeated.

The only thing he could think was, "'I want to eat pizza and I want candy."

His mother stroked his hair and called him her little baby. She kept wiping his face with a fold of her sari. When at last he stopped crying, they decided that Ajay's father should take him back to his aunt and uncle's. On the way they stopped at a mini-mall. It was a little after five, and the streetlights were on. Ajay and his father did not take off their winter coats as they ate in a pizzeria staffed by Chinese people. While he chewed, Ajay closed his eyes and tried to imagine God looking like Clark Kent, wearing a cardigan and eyeglasses, but he could not. Afterward, Ajay and his father went next door to a magazine shop and Ajay got a bag of Three Musketeers bars and a bag of Reese's Peanut Butter Cups, and then he was tired and ready for home.

He held the candy in his lap while his father drove in silence. Even through the plastic, he could smell the sugar and chocolate. Some of the houses outside were dark and others were outlined in Christmas lights.

After a while, Ajay rolled down the window slightly. The car filled with wind. They passed the building where Birju's accident had occurred. Ajay had not walked past it since the accident. When they drove by, he usually looked away. Now he tried to spot the fenced swimming pool at the building's side. He wondered whether the pool that had pressed itself into Birju's mouth and lungs and stomach had been drained, so that nobody would be touched by its unlucky waters. Probably it had not been emptied until fall. All summer long, people must have swum in the pool and sat on its sides, splashing their feet in the water, and not known that his brother had lain for three minutes on its concrete bottom one August afternoon.

BENJAMIN ALIRE SÁENZ

The Art of Translation

There were moments when I sensed my mother and father at my side, staring at me as if they were trying to sift through the wreckage of a storm, trying to find my remains. My mother would touch me, hold my hand, whisper words to me, words I couldn't understand. I felt as if I was no longer in control of my own voice, my own body. When my mother looked into my eyes and kissed my forehead, I stared back into her almost familiar face. I could see the hurt in her eyes as she whispered my name and I felt as if I had become a wound, the source of all her hurt.

My brothers and sisters came to visit. I looked at all of them as though they were perfect strangers. I stared into their eyes, listened to their voices. I felt as if they must have all been hiding somewhere in my memory. I would look at my fingers and whisper their names and count them when I was lying in bed in the dark: *Cecilia, Angela, Monica, Alfredo, Ricardo. One, two, three, four, five.* And then I would repeat the names again and again and again. And count *one, two, three, four, five.* I must have loved them once, and I tried to remember that love but there was nothing there. Only their names remained and their expectant faces. Angela kept repeating, *How could they have done this? How could they do this to you?* But didn't she know? She was eight years older. How could she not know how cruel the world was? No, not the world, the world was neither cruel nor kind. But the boys in the world—it was the boys that were cruel—that's how they translated the world, with fists, with rage, with violence. And what good did it do to think about all these things, to ask why when there was no answer?

And wasn't their last name Guerra? And didn't that name mean war? And didn't that mean that they were born to fight? But being born to fight did not mean that they were born to win the battles they fought. As I repeated the names of my brothers and sisters and felt each syllable on my tongue, I wondered what their names meant and wondered if they had scars too, scars that they were hiding from me and hiding from my mom and dad and from the world. And wasn't that the way it should be? Shouldn't everyone's scars be silent and hidden? Shouldn't we all pretend perfection and beauty and the optimism of a perfect day in spring? Why not? This was America, the country of happiness, and we had come from Mexico, the most tragic country in the world. And the only thing me—and those like me—were allowed to feel was gratitude. The boys who had hurt me, they spoke a different language and it was not a language I understood and maybe never would understand.

My brothers and sisters came in the evenings, all of them, as I lay in the hospital room. And I was trying, really trying, and I spoke to them softly but I wasn't really aware of the words I was speaking and what did it matter if what I was saying didn't mean anything at all? I felt as if it was someone else who was uttering words in an unknown language. And they were kind, my brothers and sisters, so kind, and they said I was looking better and I was surprised that I understood what they were saying. I smiled and squeezed their hands when they squeezed mine and I wondered what they felt because all I felt was that I was left for dead on the outskirts of Albuquerque on a warm night when I had stepped out to mail a letter. That was all I was doing, mailing a letter at the post office and then I heard someone yelling names at me and then I was being dragged away and kicked and everything changed. And here I was in a hospital room, not dead, *not dead.* But I knew that something in me had died. I did not know the name for that something.

I felt like an impersonator. I found it disconcerting that everyone still remembered who I was. But I knew that whoever it was they remembered was gone and I did not believe that the boy they had loved would ever come back.

I looked at my father and touched his face as if I were a boy who was staring at a man for the first time in his life. There was something sad about my father's face, and yet there was something hard and angry about it too. It seemed to me that the hospital room was suffering from a chronic silence. It was as though all sound had been banished from the world and the words and the laughter had been sent back to Mexico and I had been forced to stay in this foreign land that hated me. That's what they had said when I'd felt the knife slicing into my back *Why don't you go back to where you came from? Motherfucker, motherfucker, go back, go back.* But not knowing my way back, I was forced to stay.

The doctor asked me if I knew my name.

I looked back at the doctor. I was trying to decide if he was real or if he was just a dream I was having.

The doctor looked back at me, stubbornly waiting for an answer.

I didn't want to talk to him. But I decided he wasn't a dream and that he wasn't going to go away. "Yes," I said, "I know my name."

"You want to tell me what it is?"

"Don't you know?"

"Can you just tell me?"

"My name is Nick."

"What's your last name?"

"Guerra."

"What year is it?"

I decided the doctor wasn't a bad man. He wasn't like the boys. He wasn't going to hurt me. I think I might have smiled at him.

"What year is it, Nick?"

"1985."

The doctor nodded and smiled and I wondered if he had a son.

"Who's the president?"

I closed my eyes. "Ronald Reagan."

"Who's the vice president?"

"Bush? Is it Bush? Does it matter?"

The doctor smiled. "You've suffered quite a shock, Nick."

"Is that what it was?"

The doctor touched my shoulder and I flinched, a reflex. "Steady," the doctor whispered. "No one's going to hurt you here." His smile was kind and it almost made me want to cry. "You're going to be just fine, Nick."

I wanted to believe him. I shut my eyes. I wanted to sleep.

When I woke in the darkness of the hospital room, I thought I heard the sound of my own voice. A nurse rushed into the room. I looked at her with a question on my face. "You were screaming," she said.

"Oh," I said. "I'm thirsty."

She gave me a glass of water.

"I'm sorry they did this to you," she said.

"You're sure I was screaming?"

"Yes."

"I was dreaming," I said. "It rhymes with screaming."

"What do you remember, Nick?" It was the doctor again. It wasn't night anymore and I was glad.

"Do you remember being transferred here from the hospital in Albuquerque?"

"Albuquerque?" I whispered. "Is that an English word?"

The doctor had a puzzled look on his face. "No, I don't think it is."

"What does it mean?"

"I don't know, Nick."

He was quiet for a moment. His eyes were green and silent and I didn't know what his silence meant.

"Nick, do you remember arriving here?"

"No."

"What do you remember?"

"Why does it matter?"

"Do you know what city you're in?"

"Home."

"Home?"

"El Paso."

"Is that a guess?"

I shook my head. "When will you let me out of here?"

"I'm worried about you, Nick."

"I thought you said I was going to be fine."

When the doctor left, I wondered what the word for worry was in Spanish. I couldn't think of the word. It was gone. In order to translate words from one language to another, you had to know both languages. The languages I knew were disappearing. I wondered if I would have to find a way to live without words.

When my mother told me I was being released, I smiled at her.

"We're taking you home," she said.

I nodded.

"Why won't you talk, Nick?"

"I talk," I said.

"You don't."

I remember the trip back to my old neighborhood, the familiar houses. It was as if I was watching myself get down from the car, watching myself as I stared at my father's neat and perfect lawn. My mother's roses were in bloom and I thought they were very beautiful and I spelled out the word beautiful to myself and I wondered about the origins of that word and what kind of dreamer had dragged it into the world.

I wandered the rooms of the house. Nothing seemed foreign. But nothing seemed familiar. I stared at the pictures on the wall. There was a picture of me as a boy and I held an Easter basket and my sister Angela was kissing me.

I wanted to sleep. I was tired.

The bandages on my back were gone. I wondered if the words they wrote on my skin had disappeared—but I knew they were still there. They would always be there. And then I laughed to myself. What if they had misspelled the words?

The newspapers started calling almost immediately after I was released from the hospital. How did they know I was home? I watched my parents as they struggled to answer everyone's hungry questions. *No, they couldn't speak to me, yes, it was outrageous, no, the family had no comment, please, please, no, no, describe how you feel. Describe how you feel?*

I didn't like that my mother and father hovered over me as if I was a bird born with a broken wing.

I noticed how my mother would flinch every time the phone rang. A reporter from one of the TV stations showed up at our front door, cameraman in tow, and smiled sympathetically at my mother as she stood at the door. "We'd like to feature you," she said. "Would you mind saying something, just a short interview? Actually, would the boy like to say something?"

"His name is Nick," my mother said stiffly. "And he's a man, *not* a boy." She shut the door. I studied the look on her face. I thought she was going to cry—but she didn't and I was glad she didn't because I didn't know how to calm her. I could see her lips trembling and I knew it was because of me. When the reporter began taping her segment using our house as a background, I stood in quiet awe of my sister Angela who stormed out into the yard, grabbed the reporter's microphone, looked into the camera and yelled: "Someone used my brother's back like a goddamned chalkboard. You want to know what they wrote on his back? Is that what you want? You want to know how we feel? We fucking feel like dancing." She tossed the microphone into the neighbor's yard and stared at them until they drove away.

I watched her from the doorway. I wondered how it was that she came to be the owner of that rage. I wanted it for myself but there was nothing in me. I was a tree who had lost its leaves in the middle of spring. When Angela came back into the house, she was shaking. I put my hand on her back and felt the sobs washing through her body. I wanted to beg her to give me her tears.

A magazine from Chicago called. Would it be possible to interview me over the phone. "No," my mother said. The reporter pushed, wanting to know how I was doing. Would I be permanently scarred? Was I returning to college in the fall? Did I hate the boys who'd done this? What did I think about the Hispanic community's reaction? Did I support the student demonstrators? My mother listened patiently to all her question— then hung up the phone.

The phone calls became routine—calls from friends, from acquaintances, from people we didn't know, most of them offering sympathy. I asked myself if sympathy was a good word or a bad word. But there were other phone calls too, calls that were not related to the word sympathy. *Wasn't it true that the boy had done something to those other boys? He must have provoked them, goaded them into attacking him. Surely the boys must have had a reason. Couldn't it be true that the boy wanted to start some kind of race war? Did the boy have papers? What was an illegal doing at a public university?*

I looked up the word *illegal.*

An anonymous caller said that I was lucky. "They didn't exactly lynch him, did they?"

My father had our phone number changed.

But even after that, when the phone rang, my parents gave each other tentative glances before they answered it.

Everything felt like it was happening to someone else. The newspaper people and the journalists, they didn't want to speak to me. They wanted to speak to a Nick who no longer existed. The dead couldn't speak. Didn't they know that? The thought occurred to me that the living were exhausted from the weight of the words they were forced to carry with them everywhere they went.

I at least felt free of the weight of words. *Why don't you talk, Nick?*

If I lay still in my bed, maybe I would dissolve like dry ice in a glass of water. To melt, to turn into a gas, to float away. To disappear.

But my mother's food—and the smell of it—reminded me that having a body wasn't always a bad thing. The odor of her *sopas* and *caldillos* and *guisados*. The garlic, the onion, the cumin, the cilantro, the roasted chiles. Sometimes, the odors that came out of my mother's kitchen made me want to live.

Taste lies on the tongue but it is beyond the reach of language. That's what I wrote down on a piece of paper. I stared at what I had written. I ripped up the piece of paper until all the words were indecipherable.

My mother came into my room one night. She sat on my bed. "I thought you'd be reading," she said.

"I don't want to read anymore."

"You told me you couldn't live without books. You said you wanted to learn all the meanings of every word that existed in the world."

"I don't remember saying that. It must have been a long time ago."

"No, Nick, it wasn't long ago at all."

"I don't feel that way anymore."

"What were you thinking about?"

"What?"

She kissed my forehead. "When I walked in the room, Nick, you were thinking about something."

"My scars." I didn't know why I said that.

"They're not just places of hurt, Nick. They're places of healing." My mother and I disagreed about how to translate the words on my back.

I felt the soundless tears running down my face.

I let her rock me to sleep.

I woke to the sound of thunder. I'd been having the same dream, the white sun beating down on me, the blood on my back as purple as Lenten vestments. But the morning storm was stronger than the dream. I opened my eyes, heard the drops pounding the house, smelled the pungent odor of the thirsty creosote.

I ran my hands under my T-shirt, feeling my own smooth chest. I caught myself reaching for the scars on my back, the tough, raised skin. I rose from my bed and stared out the window. I watched as my father's peach trees swayed to the rhythm of the wind and the water.

Days, weeks, months of nothing but sun.

The learning to live without water.

The parched land.

The waiting.

And then the rain.

When I was a child, the whole world stopped at the sound of the thunder. I had a memory of people stepping out of their houses. The people would watch and listen closely as if each drop that fell to the ground was a whisper of a loved one come back from the dead.

I tried to picture my brothers and sisters playing outside, their laughter distant and lost amid the thunder, their bodies glowing in the bolts of lightning. I saw myself running toward them. Together, me, my brothers and sisters, all of us laughing, happy, together.

The storm stopped as suddenly as it began. The image of my brothers and sisters disappeared. I looked up at the immaculate, clearing sky.

I moved away from the window then sat on my bed. I decided to go for a run. I was sick of feeling the presence of three white boys that had occupied my body. Their hate sat inside me like a bird who was nesting—waiting for her eggs to hatch. I decided I could get used to hating, could even learn to love it in the same way that I'd learned to love the desert.

You could learn to love anything.

I yawned, stretched my arms upwards and left them reaching towards the sky until they hurt. I looked in the closet for my running shoes and found that all of my shoes were neatly arranged. My mother must have unpacked and organized everything. She was good at turning chaos into order.

I grabbed my running shoes, opened a drawer and found a pair of socks. I changed into my running clothes, then walked into the kitchen. My mother and father were drinking coffee and reading the newspaper. They looked up at me carefully—as if they were afraid I might break if they said the wrong thing. A part of me wanted to laugh, but the other part had forgotten how to laugh.

"Hi," I said.

I thought I saw something in my mother's eyes. She was either happy or sad—I couldn't decide.

"I'm going running," I said.

"Be careful," my mother said. "You're still a little weak."

"Just a short run, Mom."

"You want breakfast when you come back?"

"Sounds nice." I looked at my father. "You were right, Dad."

"About what?"

"You said I should have stayed home and gone to college here. You were right."

He didn't say anything. He ran his fingers through his thick, graying hair. "It doesn't matter. You're going to be okay. You're home now."

I nodded and kissed my father on the top of his head as I walked out the door. I wondered why I had done that but it seemed like the right thing to do. The old Nick would have done that. *You're home now.* Home. I thought that word was just a dream.

I half expected the ground to give, open up and swallow me whole. But every time I took a step, nothing happened. I found myself heading toward the desert, but as I reached it, I stopped as if I had reached a line I was not allowed to cross. I looked toward the houses behind me, all in neat rows, all with numbers and mailboxes and sidewalks. I wondered why people had such a need to make the desert into something tame. Green lawns and flowers. It was all so futile—and such a waste of water. I sat down and looked at the well-trimmed hedges, the flowers struggling to survive.

I walked past all the homes and stood at the edge of the desert. I looked out at the mesquites and chamizos and the cacti. They always caught me there in the dream, caught me in the desert. They lived there, those boys, the three of them, the white boys who had hurt me. They lived in all the deserts of the earth. Death. That was the new word for desert. So that's where they lived now, in every desert, in every dream I would ever have. I knew they would find me someday, catch me, cut me up again. I turned my back on the desert I once loved and ran home.

Breakfast was waiting for me when I walked into the house. "I'm out of shape." I smiled at my mother. "Smells good."

"Huevos con chorizo."

I washed my hands at the sink.

My mother pushed the plate in front of me. "You're too thin."

I nodded, began eating, then looked around the room. "When did you paint the kitchen?"

"Two weeks ago."

"Guess I haven't been much help around here."

"You're looking better, *mi'jo. Y no se te quita lo bonito.*"

"Mom, I'm plain as a row of cotton."

"A row of cotton is anything but plain."

"You want me to argue with you, Mom?"

"It would make me feel better if you did."

I shrugged, took a tortilla and scooped my eggs up into my mouth. "Good," I said. "This is really good."

My mom looked almost happy. "What are you going to do now, Nick?"

I forced a smile as I looked into my father's dark eyes. I thought they looked like a winter night. "Now? Today?"

"Yes. Now."

"Now?"

"Now that you're alive again."

"Oh," I said. "So that's it. I'm alive?" I rolled my eyes.

"See, you always did that before—" She took a drink from her cup of coffee. "You always used to do that. You're home now, Nick. You're home."

I looked up the old words in the dictionary, words I'd once known the meanings of: *home, desert, death, knife, skin, blood, knife, hate.*

Waiting tables is not what I had dreamed of doing. Not that I minded the job. Café Central. My oldest brother knew the owner. It was the nicest restaurant in the city. The food was as good as it was expensive. And the money was even better than the food. Not that I gave a damn. What was I going to do with the money?

I liked my new routine. Running in the morning, going to work in the evening. It almost didn't matter that nothing happened in between.

Sometimes, I wanted to go out after work. Going out sounded like something normal. I wanted normal, but something about normal scared me. Walking down streets at night. Something bad would happen. But there was this bar that all the waiters talked about, some dive called the Regal Beagle. I wanted to go. Normal.

One Saturday, I made up my mind. The bar was walking distance from the restaurant—but I decided to drive. I parked half a block away. I walked into the bar and smiled nervously as I looked around. I sat on a stool and ordered a drink. I polished off my bourbon in three gulps. I ordered another. As I finished my second drink, I thought about having a third—but already I felt lightheaded.

I didn't notice her sitting next to me—until she spoke. "What's your name?" Her voice was deep and raspy as if she had a cold. I stared at her cigarette, the smoke coming out of her mouth. "I'm Sylvia."

I nodded.

"Quiet, huh?"

"Not much to say."

"So what's your name?" She smiled. She was pretty when she smiled. I guessed she was in her thirties—maybe older. It was hard to tell in the dim light of the bar.

"Nicholas," I said. "My name is Nicholas." I tried to pretend it was normal for me to be sitting in a dark bar having a couple of drinks and talking to a woman. Men did it all the time. Normal.

"You look nervous." She offered me a cigarette.

"I don't smoke."

She laughed. "Maybe you should."

"No thanks." I caught the bartender's eyes, lifted my glass.

"Aren't you going to offer me one too?"

I smiled. "Sure." Men sat at bars and bought women drinks all the time. Normal. I caught the bartender's eye and tapped her glass.

The bartender placed a beer in front of her. "He's a little young for you, isn't he, Sylvia?"

She laughed, then she looked at me. "Are you too young?"

"I'm old enough to drink," I said.

"Well, if you're old enough to drink." She laughed.

"You laugh a lot."

"Well, there's a lot to laugh about." She took a sip of her beer.

"So what kind of beer do you drink?"

"Bud."

I watched her lips move as she talked. I liked the sound of her voice— what she was saying didn't matter so much. And anyway, men weren't good at translating what women said. Something about her job and her ex-husband. We had another drink. I felt strange, like I was someone else. I wanted to know what it was like to kiss her, thought I'd like to try. But it didn't seem right. "I better go," I said. "It's late."

"We're just getting started."

"Are we?"

"What do you say we go to Juárez?"

I thought a moment. I'd already had too much to drink and then I heard myself saying, "What the fuck."

She laughed. "Yeah, what the fuck."

She held my hand as we walked over the Santa Fe Bridge. I found myself sitting at a booth in the Kentucky Club. It was strange. I should have felt drunker than I felt. She asked me questions. I answered them and I smiled to myself because I knew the answers weren't true. Men lied to women all the time. *Normal.*

We weren't there long. She said she liked the Florida better. So we walked down the street and had another drink. Maybe two. It was late and I was tired but she was kissing me as we sat there and I was kissing her back. "We should go," I said.

"Where to?" She was smiling. "My place? Your place?"

"Your place," I said.

She was still smiling. "I don't live so far."

She must have seen something in my expression.

"You don't have to be so shy. "

"It's the way I am."

When I took her hand, I thought that it was as warm as the night. I could feel myself trembling.

"I won't hurt you," she said.

Her apartment was small and bare—but it was clean. She offered me a beer. I told her I should go, didn't know what I was doing there, but when she reached over and kissed me again, I kissed her back and didn't want to stop. It was strange, her tongue, the taste of cigarette and beer, but it was sweet, and I wanted to tell her I'd never done this before but words didn't matter. They had never mattered. She unbuttoned my shirt, laughed because I was wearing a T-shirt underneath, and when my shirt was off, she tried to take off my T-shirt. I stopped her. "Not my T-shirt." I hadn't meant to sound angry, but that's the way it came out. She looked at me, said everything was okay. "Then how about your pants?" I kissed her again, then let her take off my pants, then my underwear. I felt her warm hands on my legs, on my penis. I groaned softly.

"Nice," she said. She stood in front of me and took off her clothes. I reached over and felt her body. I pulled her close to me and when I felt her back, it was smooth and unscarred.

"What do you like?" she asked.

"Just don't touch my back."

I woke to the sound of her breathing. I felt still and serene, and yet I felt worn out and hungover. I'd never woken up in someone else's bed. In the dim light of the lamp, I could make out her features, the wrinkles around her eyes. She was forty—at least forty, maybe older. But she had felt young when I was inside her, and I had felt something I had no name for—and there hadn't been any dreams. When we had been having sex, I had almost felt happy to be the owner of a body, happy, and I'd liked that moment of almost happiness. I had liked it so much.

I wondered if I'd pleased her. Maybe I hadn't. Maybe she didn't care. I lay there, the steady rhythm of her breathing like a lullaby. I felt stupid and guilty. But she hadn't cared. She was used to this, had placed the condom on me as if it was just another simple and ordinary task—like drinking a glass of water. I stared at the white of my T-shirt, wondered if her smell would be on it when I went back home.

I looked at my watch. Three o'clock in the morning, and I was lying in a stranger's bed. I wanted to leave, but I liked looking at her in the dim light of the lamp on her nightstand. I just kept staring. Suddenly I wondered if I owed her any money. It had all been too easy. Why would anybody want to sleep with me if it wasn't for money? I sat up on the bed. My clothes were in the other room. I heard her voice.

"Going home, Mr. T-shirt?"

I turned around and looked at her. "Yeah," I said. "Gotta get some sleep and go to work. Do I owe—"

"I'm not a fucking prostitute."

"Sorry," I said. "I just thought that—"

"Doesn't matter."

"It does matter. Look, I don't do—I mean why would anybody want to sleep—I mean—"

"You don't get out much."

"No, I don't."

"I could tell."

"That bad, huh?"

"No. You're nice. Last night was nice."

"And I'm young enough to be your son."

"So what? What's wrong with sleeping with someone you want to sleep with?"

"Nothing."

"Well, then?"

"You're not mad?"

"Go home. I bet you live with your parents."

"So what?"

"Don't get mad."

"I gotta go."

"Want my phone number?"

I got up from the bed. I didn't like feeling stupid. So stupid. I walked into the living room, put on my pants, then carried my shoes and socks back into the bedroom. I sat on the bed and put on my shoes and socks. "Yeah," I whispered.

"Yeah what?"

"Yeah, I want your phone number."

"Good boy. Next time can I see your back?"

"No."

"What's wrong with it?"

"Nothing."

"Nothing?"

"I don't like to talk about it."

"Talking never hurt anybody. "

"Look, it's private."

"So's your dick."

"Forget it, then." I put on my shoes, then stood up. "I'm sorry. I'm being an asshole. But that's the way it is with me."

"Fuck you," she said.

"Yeah, right." I slammed the door on my way out.

I looked up more words: *sex, kiss, hands, tongue.* No dictionary could define, could translate, the needs of the human body. I looked up the name Sylvia. It was Latin for forest. Maybe it was a place I could get lost in.

A week later, I found her at the Regal Beagle again, smoking her cigarette, drinking her beer. I wanted to apologize. I wanted to explain to her about my back. But I'd never spoken to anyone about what happened, not to my brothers and sisters, not to my parents, not to anyone. Well, except for the police—but that didn't count.

I sat next to her at the bar. "I'm sorry," I said.

She smiled.

I went home with her. Our sex was angry—more like a fight than sex. And even though there was plenty of life in the sex, there was no love. There was no love at all. Not that I was surprised. When I fell asleep, I woke up as she was trying to take off my T-shirt.

"I fucking said no," I said.

"Just get out!" she yelled. "Just get the fuck out! You're a fucked-up kid."

I didn't say a word as I finished putting on my clothes. She was right. I was fucked up.

"You're fucked up," she said again.

"I heard you the first time."

I felt a sharp pain on my back as I moved toward the door. I tried not to wince, tried not to show any sign of pain as I started at the glass ashtray that had bounced off my back and had fallen to the floor with a thud. "Who's more fucked up—me or you?"

"Is it a contest?" The look on her face, it reminded me of the look on the faces of those boys, the rage in it, the hate.

I took a deep breath and walked out the door.

I thought my back would have another bruise by the time I woke up in the morning. I started the engine, then sat in the idling car for a long time. Finally, I put the car in drive. As I drove home in the morning light, I found myself repeating basic Spanish grammar: *yo soy, tu eres, el es, nosotros somos, ustedes son, ellos son.* I whispered the word for the sun, *sol,* then whispered the word for night, *noche.* I liked night better than sun. *Yo soy una noche sin estrellas.*

It was a sentence. A real sentence. The words did not feel foreign on my tongue.

As I lay in bed, words from my youth came back to me. *Fuego. Lluvia. Desierto. Coraje. Odio. Trabajo. Sangre. Corazón. Muerte.* I repeated the words to myself, used each one in a simple sentence, then translated it to myself: *Tengo la sangre de mi hermana.* I have my sister's blood. *En el desierto no cae lluvia.* Rain does not fall in the desert. *Tengo odio en mi corazón.* I have hate in my heart. I wondered if my translations were accurate. I fell asleep translating, trying to make sense of what was inside me—but how could I translate the words on my back? How could I translate what had happened?

I woke up in the afternoon.

I went for a run in the desert.

The boys were there. They would always be there. They would be everywhere I went. There was nothing to do but outrun them. But their hate was a bullet. And who could outrun a bullet?

When I got back home, I took a shower. I knew that nothing could wash away the scars. I looked at myself in the mirror. My eyes were as black as a starless night.

My mother asked me if I was okay.

I nodded.

"You don't look okay."

"It's just a hangover," I said.

"You never used to drink," she said.

There's a lot of things I never used to do. That's what I wanted to say. But I didn't bother. I understood that my mom felt the presence of those words in the room.

I went to work. I waited tables.

I came home and went to my room and prayed for sleep. I remembered me as a boy, leaning into my mother's shoulder during mass and wondering if God saw us. I remembered watching my father work in the sun, his skin glowing in his own sweat. I remembered the boy I had been in high school, looking up words in a dictionary. I fell asleep trying to think of the word for what I felt.

When I woke in the morning, I told myself that the scars on my back had always been there. They were nothing more than birthmarks. I thought of that night. I told myself I should *not* have yelled; I should *not* have been outraged as if that act had been undeserved and violent and indecent; I should *not* have begged them to stop in the name of a god I did not even believe in. What I should have done—when they were holding me down—what I should have done when they took that knife and wrote on me as if the knife was merely a pen and my own blood nothing more than ink—what I should have done—I should have looked at my attackers and told them I had been waiting for them. I should have looked them all in the eyes and told them I knew their hate, understood it, embraced its awful necessity. I should have offered up my body as a sacrifice to their cruel and hungry gods. It was a war, after all, and sacrifices were necessary in a war—though I had never acknowledged that the war existed.

War. *Guerra.* That was me. That was my name.

And then I knew that I would have to relearn the meaning of every word I had ever learned. I would have to learn how to translate all those words. Thousands of them. Millions of them. And then I smiled and felt the tears running down my face. Finally I understood. It wasn't the words that mattered. *It was me. I mattered.* So now I would have to fight to translate myself back into the world of the living.

NANCY FULDA

Movement

It is sunset. The sky is splendid through the panes of my bedroom window; billowing layers of cumulus blazing with refracted oranges and reds. I think if only it weren't for the glass, I could reach out and touch the cloudscape, perhaps leave my own trail of turbulence in the swirling patterns that will soon deepen to indigo.

But the window is there, and I feel trapped.

Behind me my parents and a specialist from the neurological research institute are sitting on folding chairs they've brought in from the kitchen, quietly discussing my future. They do not know I am listening. They think that, because I do not choose to respond, I do not notice they are there.

"Would there be side effects?" My father asks. In the oppressive heat of the evening, I hear the quiet *Zzzap* of his shoulder laser as it targets mosquitoes. The device is not as effective as it was two years ago: the mosquitoes are getting faster.

My father is a believer in technology, and that is why he contacted the research institute. He wants to fix me. He is certain there is a way.

"There would be no side effects in the traditional sense," the specialist says. I like him even though his presence makes me uncomfortable. He chooses his words very precisely. "We're talking about direct synaptic grafting, not drugs. The process is akin to bending a sapling to influence the shape of the grown tree. We boost the strength of key dendritic connections and allow brain development to continue naturally. Young neurons are very malleable."

"And you've done this before?" I do not have to look to know my mother is frowning.

* * *

My mother does not trust technology. She has spent the last ten years trying to coax me into social behavior by gentler means. She loves me, but she does not understand me. She thinks I cannot be happy unless I am smiling and laughing and running along the beach with other teenagers.

"The procedure is still new, but our first subject was a young woman about the same age as your daughter. Afterwards, she integrated wonderfully. She was never an exceptional student, but she began speaking more and had an easier time following classroom procedure."

"What about Hannah's...talents?" my mother asks. I know she is thinking about my dancing; also the way I remember facts and numbers without trying. "Would she lose those?"

The specialist's voice is very firm, and I like the way he delivers the facts without trying to cushion them. "It's a matter of trade-offs, Mrs. Didier. The brain cannot be optimized for everything at once. Without treatment, some children like Hannah develop into extraordinary individuals. They become famous, change the world, learn to integrate their abilities into the structures of society. But only a very few are that lucky. The others never learn to make friends, hold a job, or live outside of institutions."

"And...with treatment?"

"I cannot promise anything, but the chances are very good that Hannah will lead a normal life."

* * *

I have pressed my hand to the window. The glass feels cold and smooth beneath my palm. It appears motionless although I know at the molecular level it is flowing. Its atoms slide past each other slowly, so slowly; a transformation no less inevitable for its tempo. I like glass—also stone—because it does not change very quickly. I will be dead, and so will all of my relatives and their descendants, before the deformations will be visible without a microscope.

I feel my mother's hands on my shoulders. She has come up behind me and now she turns me so that I must either look in her eyes or pull away. I look in her eyes because I love her and because I am calm enough right now to handle it. She speaks softly and slowly.

"Would you like that, Hannah? Would you like to be more like other teenagers?"

* * *

Neither yes nor no seems appropriate, so I do not say anything. Words are such fleeting, indefinite things. They slip through the spaces between my thoughts and are lost.

She keeps looking at me, and I consider giving her an answer I've been saving. Two weeks ago she asked me whether I would like a new pair of dancing shoes and if so, what color. I have collected the proper words in my mind, smooth and firm like pebbles, but I decide it is not worth speaking them. Usually by the time I answer a question, people have forgotten that they asked it.

The word they have made for my condition is temporal autism. I do not like it, both because it is a word and because I am not certain I have anything in common with autists beyond a disinclination for speech.

They are right about the temporal part, though.

My mother waits twelve-point-five seconds before releasing my shoulders and returning to sit on the folding chair. I can tell she is unhappy with me, so I climb down from the window ledge and reach for the paper sack I keep tucked under my bed. The handles are made of twine, rough and real against my fingers. I press the sack to my chest and slip past the people conversing in my bedroom.

Downstairs I open the front door and stare into the breathtaking sky. I know I am not supposed to leave the house on my own, but I do not want to stay inside, either. Above me the heavens are moving. The clouds swirl like leaves in a hurricane: billowing, vanishing, tumbling apart and restructuring themselves; a lethargic yet incontrovertible chaos.

I can almost feel the earth spinning beneath my feet. I am hurtling through space, a speck too small to resist the immensity of the forces that surround me. I tighten my fingers around the twine handles of the sack to keep myself from spinning away into the stratosphere. I wonder what it's like to be cheerfully oblivious of the way time shapes our existence. I wonder what it's like to be like everyone else.

* * *

I am under the brilliant sky now, the thick paper of the sack crackling as it swings against my legs. I am holding the handles so tightly that the twine bites into my fingers.

At my feet the flytraps are opening, their spiny blossoms stretching upwards from chips and cracks in the pavement. They are a domestic variety gone wild, and they are thriving in the nurturing environment provided by this part of town. Our street hosts a flurry of sidewalk cafes, and the fist-sized blossoms open every evening to snare crumbs of baguettes or sausage fragments carried by the wind from nearby tables.

The flytraps make me nervous, although I doubt I could communicate to anyone why this is so. They feel very much like the clouds that stream overhead in glowing shades of orange and amber: always changing, always taking on new forms.

The plants have even outgrown their own name. They seldom feed on flies anymore. The game of out-evolving prey has become unrewarding, and so they have learned to survive by seeming pleasant to humanity. The speckled patterns along the blossoms grow more intricate each year. The spines snap closed so dramatically when a bit of protein or carbohydrate falls within their grasp that children giggle and hasten to fetch more.

One flytrap, in particular, catches my attention. It has a magnificent blossom, larger and more colorful than any I have seen before, but the ordinary stem is too spindly to support this innovation. The blossom lies crushed against the sidewalk, overshadowed by the smaller, sturdier plants that crowd above it.

It is a critical juncture in the evolutionary chain, and I want to watch and see whether the plant will live to pass on its genes. Although the flytraps as a whole disquiet me, this single plant is comforting. It is like the space between one section of music and another; something is about to happen, but no one knows exactly what. The plant may quietly extinguish, or it may live to spawn the next generation of flytraps; a generation more uniquely suited to survival than any that has come before.

I want the flytrap to survive, but I can tell from the sickly color of its leaves that this is unlikely. I wonder, if the plant had been offered the certainty of mediocrity rather than the chance of greatness, would it have accepted?

I start walking again because I am afraid I will start crying.

I am too young. It is not fair to ask me to make such a decision. It is also not fair if someone else makes it for me.

I do not know what I should want.

* * *

The old cathedral, when it appears at the end of the avenue, soothes me. It is like a stone in the midst of a swirling river, worn smooth at the edges but mostly immune to time's capricious currents. Looking at it makes me think of Daniel Tammet. Tammet was an autistic savant in the twenty-first century who recognized every prime from 2 to 9,973 by the pebble-like quality they elicited in his mind. Historical architecture feels to me the way I think Tammet's primes must have felt to him.

The priest inside the building greets me kindly, but does not expect a response. He is used to me, and I am comfortable with him. He does not demand that I waste my effort on fleeting things—pointless things—like specks of conversation that are swept away by the great rush of time without leaving any lasting impact. I slip past him into the empty room where the colored windows cast shadows of light on the walls.

My footsteps echo as I pass through the doorway, and I feel suddenly alone.

I know that there are other people like me, most of them from the same ethnic background, which implies we are the result of a recent mutation. I have never asked to meet them. It has not seemed important. Now, as I sit against the dusty walls and remove my street shoes, I think maybe that has been a mistake.

The paper sack rustles as I pull from it a pair of dancing slippers. They are pointe shoes, reinforced for a type of dancing that human anatomy cannot achieve on its own. I slide my feet into position along the shank, my toes nestling into the familiar shape of the toe box. I wrap the ribbons carefully, making sure my foot is properly supported.

Other people do not see the shoes the same way I do. They see only the faded satin, battered so much that it has grown threadbare, and the rough wood of the toe box where it juts through the gaps. They do not see how the worn leather has matched itself to the shape of my foot. They do not know what it is like to dance in shoes that feel like a part of your body.

I begin to warm my muscles, keenly aware of the paths the shadows trace along the walls as sunset fades into darkness. When I have finished the last of my pliés and jetés, stars glimmer through the colored glass of the windows, dizzying me with their progress. I am hurtling through space, part of a solar system flung towards the outer rim of its galaxy. It is difficult to breathe.

*   *   *

Often, when the flow of time becomes too strong, I crawl into the dark space beneath my bed and run my fingers along the rough stones and jagged glass fragments that I have collected there. But today the pointe shoes are connecting me to the ground. I move to the center of the room, rise to full *pointe* . . .

And wait.

Time stretches and spins like molasses, pulling me in all directions at once. I am like the silence between one movement of music and the next, like a water droplet trapped halfway down a waterfall that stands frozen in time. Forces press against me, churning, swirling, roaring with the sound of reality changing. I hear my heart beating in the empty chamber. I wonder if this is how Daniel Tammet felt when he contemplated infinity.

Finally I find it; the pattern in the chaos. It is not music, precisely, but it is very like it. It unlocks the terror that has tightened my muscles and I am no longer a mote in a hurricane. I am the hurricane itself. My feet stir up dust along the floor. My body moves in concordance with my will. There are no words here. There is only me and the motion, whirling in patterns as complex as they are inconstant.

Life is not the only thing that evolves. My dancing changes every day, sometimes every second, each sequence repeating or extinguishing based on how well it pleases me. At a higher level in the fractal, forms of dance also mutate and die. People call ballet a timeless art, but the dance performed in modern theatres is very different from the ballet that originally emerged in Italy and France.

Mine is an endangered species in the performance hierarchy; a neoclassical variant that no one remembers, no one pays to watch, and only a few small groups of dancers ever mimic. It is solitary, beautiful, and doomed to destruction. I love it because its fate is certain. Time has no more hold on it.

When my muscles lose their strength I will relinquish the illusion of control and return to being yet another particle in the rushing chaos of the universe, a spectator to my own existence. But for now I am aware of nothing except my own movement and the energy rushing through my blood vessels. Were it not for physical limitations, I would keep dancing forever.

* * *

My brother is the one who finds me. He has often brought me here and waits with electronics flickering at his temples while I dance. I like my brother. I feel comfortable with him because he does not expect me to be anything other than what I am.

By the time I have knelt to unlace my dance shoes my parents have arrived also. They are not calm and quiet like my brother. They are sweaty from the night air and speak in tense sentences that all jumble on top of each other. If they would bother to wait I might find words to soothe their frantic babble. But they do not know how to speak on my time scale. Their conversations are paced in seconds, sometimes in minutes. It is like the buzzing of mosquitoes in my ears. I need days, sometimes weeks to sort my thoughts and find the perfect answer.

My mother is close to my face and seems distressed. I try to calm her with the answer I've been saving.

"No new shoes,"I say. "I couldn't dance the same in new shoes."

I can tell that these are not the words she was looking for, but she has stopped scolding me for leaving the house unaccompanied.

My father is also angry. Or perhaps he is afraid. His voice is too loud for me, and I tighten my fingers around the paper sack in my hands.

"Stars above, Hannah, do you have any idea how long we've been looking for you? Gina, we're going to have to do something soon. She might have wandered into the Red District, or been hit by a car, or—"

"I don't want to be rushed into this!" Mother's voice is angry. "Dr. Renoit is starting a new therapy group next month. We should—"

"I don't know why you're so stubborn about this. We're not talking about drugs or surgery. It's a simple, noninvasive procedure."

"One that hasn't been tested yet! We've been seeing progress with the ABA program. I'm not willing to throw that away just because . . ."

I hear the *Zzzap* of father's shoulder laser. Because I have not heard the whine of a mosquito, I know that it has targeted a spec of dust. This does not surprise me. In the years since father bought the laser the mosquitoes have changed, but the dust is the same as it was millennia ago.

A moment later I hear mother swear and swat at her shirt. The mosquito whizzes past my ear as it escapes. I have been keeping track of the statistics over the years. Mother's traditional approach to mosquitoes is no more effective than Father's hi-tech solution.

* * *

My brother takes me home while my parents argue about the future. I sit in his room while he lies down and activates the implants at his temples. Pinpricks of light gleam across his forehead, flickering because he's connected to the Vastness. His mind is wide, now. Wide and broadening; horizons without end. Each pulse of his neurons flares across the thoughtnets to stimulate the neurons of others, just as theirs are stimulating his.

Forty minutes later my grandparents pause by the open doorway. My grandparents do not understand the Vastness. They do not know that the drool pools at his cheek because it is hard to perceive the faint messages from the body when the mind is ablaze with stimuli. They see the slackness of his face, the glassy eyes staring upwards, and they know only that he is far away from us, gone somewhere they cannot follow, and that they think must be evil.

"It isn't right," they mutter, "letting the mind decay like that. His parents shouldn't let him spend so much time on that thing."

"Remember how it was when we were young? The way we'd all crowd around the same game console? Everyone in the same room. Everyone seeing the same screen. Now that was bonding. That was healthy entertainment."

They shake their heads. "It's a shame young people don't know how to connect with each other anymore."

I do not want to listen to them talk, so I stand up and close the door in their faces. I know they will consider the action unprovoked, but I do not care. They know the words for temporal autism, but they do not understand what it means. Deep inside, they still believe that I am just bad mannered.

Faintly, beyond the door, I hear them telling each other how different young people are from the way they used to be. Their frustration mystifies me. I do not understand why old people expect the younger generations to hold still, why they think, in a world so full of tumult, children should play the same games their grandparents did.

I watch the lights flare at my brother's temples, a stochastic pattern that reminds me of the birth and death of suns. Right now, he is using a higher percentage of his neural tissue than anyone born a hundred years ago could conceive of. He is communicating with more people than my father has met in his entire lifetime.

How was it, I wonder, when Homo habilis first uttered the noises that would lead to modern language? Were those odd-sounding infants considered defective, asocial, unsuitable to interact with their peers? How many genetic variations bordered on language before one found enough acceptance to perpetuate?

My grandparents say the Vastness is distorting my brother's mind, but

I think it is really the opposite. His mind is built to seek out the Vastness, just like mine is attuned to the dizzying flow of seconds and centuries.

*   *   *

Night collides into morning, and somewhere along the way I fall asleep. When I wake the sky beyond my brother's window is bright with sunlight. If I bring my face close to the glass, I can just see the flytrap with the magnificent blossom and the crumpled stem. It is too early to tell whether it will survive the day.

Outside the neighbors greet each other; the elderly with polite nods or handshakes, the teenagers with shouts and gestured slang. I wonder which of the new greetings used this morning will entrench themselves into the vocabulary of tomorrow.

Social structures follow their own path of evolution—variations infinitely emerging, competing, and fading into the tumult. The cathedral at the end of our street will one day host humans speaking a different language, with entirely different customs than ours.

Everything changes. Everything is always changing. To me, the process is very much like waves hitting the tidal rocks: Churn, swirl, splash, churn . . . Chaos, inevitable in its consistency.

It should not be surprising that, on the way from what we are to what we are becoming, there should be friction and false starts along the way. Noise is intrinsic to change. Progression is inherently chaotic.

Mother calls me for breakfast, then attempts to make conversation while I eat my buttered toast. She thinks that I do not answer because I haven't heard her, or perhaps because I do not care. But it's not that. I'm like my brother when he's connected to the Vastness. How can I play the game of dredging up memorized answers to questions that have no meaning when the world is changing so rapidly? The heavens stream past outside the windows, the crustal plates are shifting beneath my feet. Everything around me is either growing or falling apart. Words feel flat and insignificant by comparison.

Mother and father have avoided discussing synaptic grafting with each other all morning, a clear indication that their communication strategies must once again evolve. Their conversations about me have always been strained. Disputed phrases have died out of our family vocabulary, and my parents must constantly invent new ones to fill the gaps.

I am evolving too, in my own small way. Connections within my brain are forming, surviving, and perishing, and with each choice I make I alter the genotype of my soul. This is the thing, I think, the my parents most fail to see. I am not static, no more than the large glass window that lights the breakfast table. Day by day I am learning to mold myself to a world that does not welcome me.

I press my hands to the window and feel its cool smoothness beneath my skin. If I close my eyes I can almost feel the molecules shifting. Let it continue long enough, and the pane will someday find its own shape, one constrained not by the hand of humans but by the laws of the universe, and by its own nature.

I find that I have decided something.

I do not want to live small. I do not want to be like everyone else, ignorant of the great rush of time, trapped in frantic racing sentences. I want something else, something that I cannot find a word for.

I pull on mother's arm and tap at the glass, to show her that I am fluid inside. As usual, she does not understand what I am trying to tell her. I would like to clarify, but I cannot find the way. I pull my ballet slippers from the rustling paper bag and place them on top of the information packet left by the neuroscientist.

"I do not want new shoes," I say. "I do not want new shoes."

BRYAN HURT

Moonless

It took some doing but I finally made a white dwarf star like they'd been making out in Santa Fe. I made mine in my basement because basements are the perfect place to compress time and space. I slammed together some very high-frequency energy waves and—ZAP!—a perfect miniature white dwarf. Even though it was very small for its type, no larger than a pushpin, it was extremely dense and incredibly bright. The star was so bright that you couldn't look directly at it. Had to look above or below or off to the side and squint. One time I set myself the challenge of just staring at it for thirty seconds. Got a big headache, huge mistake.

Density was a problem too. The star was dense enough that it drew small objects toward it. Tissue paper, curtains, the tail of my cat. Of course they all burst into flames. But at the same time it wasn't so dense that it just hovered there above my table, an object fixed in space. It wobbled this way and that, wandering the basement, knocking against the walls, the floor, the ceiling, leaving burn marks everywhere. The last straw was when it set fire to my favorite Einstein poster—the one with his tongue sticking out, his messed-up hair and goofy grin. I trapped the star in a box, put a padlock on the heavy lid.

But stars are not meant to be kept in boxes. At night I could hear it down in my basement bumping against the walls of its prison. My dreams were soundtracked by a million leaden pings. The only solution was to make another one. A second white dwarf that matched the first one exactly and set both of them into a stable binary orbit. The two stars dancing around their common center of gravity. It was a simple and elegant solution, as most solutions from nature are.

But once I had the stars locked in equilibrium, I couldn't help but notice how shabby the rest of their surroundings were. The basement's dull walls, spiderwebs hanging from the ceiling beams, boxes stacked and packed with old LPs and moth-eaten sweaters and love letters from girlfriends who'd liked me first for my ambition and then called it neglect. So I went to the art store and bought black poster board, which I glued together and strung with Christmas lights. I called the finished product the universe even though it was more like a diorama of. Still I felt the display added some dignity to the scene, my white dwarves floating there in front of all that blackness, the holiday lights shining behind. My cat liked it too. He rubbed his cheeks against the sharp corners of the universe and purred.

Exactly when it happened, I don't know. But soon little globes of matter began forming around my stars. The globes were made of drops of water from the glass I'd spilled, Einstein ashes, and fur that the stars pulled from the back of my cat, who liked to nap underneath them. There were two of them, two globes. They were more like tiny planets really, each one orbiting its own star. I put my elbows on the table and squinted at them from behind my welder's mask (for by then I'd learned my lesson). One planet was slightly larger than the other, had its own miniature moon, so I named it after a moony ex-girlfriend who liked to stare at the night sky and ask why our love wasn't as dark and infinite. The other one had no moon, so I called it Moonless.

The next time I checked on my cardboard universe even more had changed. There was a tiny flag planted on the tiny moon. Microscopic satellites orbited the planet and miniature airplanes flew to miniature cities. Each city swarmed with tiny cars with subatomic red-faced drivers inside. Moonless was doing even better; its civilization had become even more advanced. There were hovercars, biodomes, black glass buildings that swooped and curved as if they'd been painted into existence. On top of its tallest mountain was an enormous telescope that was pointing at its neighbor. Operating the telescope was a tiny scientist in a tiny white lab coat, her hair twisted into a tiny but perfect black knot.

But I was not in the right mood to appreciate the wonders of my universe. I could not force myself to feel the requisite joy or awe or whatever I should have felt at that particular moment in time. I had just returned home from my laboratory, it had been a not-so-great day. First I'd been rejected by one of my lab assistants. Not even formally rejected. Asked her out and she just jammed her eyes into a microscope and hummed. Then I'd lost out on a big government grant to my chief rival, the smug molecular astrophysicist Dr. Hu. I patted him on the back and ate his celebratory cake, forced a smile with icing on my lips. Someone had dented my car in the parking lot. My cat had made a hairball in one of my loafers, which I stepped in as soon as I got home.

So no. I could not muster the enthusiasm to celebrate the triumph of my dwarves, the impossibility of their little people. What I felt instead, primarily, was annoyed.

Because take for example the planet named after the moony ex-girl-friend: here was a brand-new world, unlimited potential, infinite possi-bilities, and it was basically just a smaller copy of this one. Same cars, same space junk, same flag on the moon. Pretty much all the same crap except played out on an even smaller, more insignificant scale. Pathetic, really. Boring. Much like the girlfriend I'd named the planet after. After a promising start—exciting, sexy—it was a movie on the couch every Friday night, maybe with a little petting mixed in. But when I'd start taking her pants off, she'd yawn and say she liked it better in the morning when she was not tired but still half asleep. As if sex were something that happened only once a day, like breakfast or sunsets. In the end she was the one who said I didn't love her. Said that if I didn't like what she had to offer, I'd never be happy. So I flicked the moony planet into the universe's back-drop, watched it explode against the cardboard and Christmas lights. The explosion was so small that it barely even registered as a blip.

But the tiny scientist on Moonless saw it too. She blinked into her viewfinder, pushed her glasses up the bridge of her nose, then turned the telescope in the opposite direction, a full half circle, so that when it stopped it was pointing directly up at me. She wrote something in her tiny notebook, her tiny hand trembling. I didn't go back into the base-ment for a while after that.

But basements can't be avoided forever. When I did return—with a basket of laundry so ripe you could practically see the wafterons rising off it—I saw that the tiny scientist had built a gigantic ray gun. She was taking potshots at my Christmas lights. Zapped a light and tiny glass tin-kled onto cardboard. I told her to knock it off. She zapped another one. "Or what?" she said. "You're going to destroy this planet too?" Maybe I was. I told her not to test me. "Oh I'll test you," she said. She wheeled the gun around and fired a shot that skimmed my nose. The second one hit me dead on. It stung a lot. I ducked the next salvo and raised my hand to swipe her planet out of existence. She set her chin, bracing for the blow.

But I was not a destroyer of worlds. Not really. I had destroyed one world, singular, and it was just a very small one. I hadn't even meant to create it. What I'd intended to do was make a star, a modest white dwarf, something beautiful just to see if I could do it. Maybe I also wanted to have something to show off to girlfriends when I brought them down to my basement, something that would help get them to hop into my bed. I didn't want to contribute to the grand unhappiness. There was already too much of it in this world. Just today I'd read about a kid in Ohio who shot another kid in school. In Japan someone had taken a knife into the subway and stabbed five people to death. At work I'd found Dr. Hu crying alone in a bathroom stall. He had stage four prostate cancer, inoperable, spreading.

Still, perhaps it was all unavoidable. Maybe whenever you made something—stars, planets, people, whatever—you always made a little sadness, a little death. There was no such thing as pure creation. I told the tiny scientist that I was sorry about the planet but either I was going to destroy it or I was going to be destroyed by something else. That's how it worked: that was science, that was the natural order of things.

"That's bullshit," she said. She said that I was a coward and a chicken shit. She said that her husband had been on that other planet on an expedition. I had killed him. She asked how I wasn't responsible for that. "Look," I said. "I'll make it up." I pulled some fur from the back of my cat, dunked it in some water and rolled it into a ball, which I set in orbit around the dwarf.

The ball came undone. It drifted into the star and burned to ash. "Pathetic," she said. She looked at me, angry and disappointed, just like every moony Lindsay or Sarah or Kara or Jen looked at me when something came undone between us. But it was just a little thing, an insignificant thing, barely worth dwelling on because it hardly even existed. A small planet; her husband, a small man.

"I'm sorry," I said and I guess I was. "But what do you want from me? I can't fix everything. I'm not a god."

Even then I think we both knew that wasn't true, not entirely. For after the tiny scientist grew old and died, and her children died, and her planet's sun died, and everyone died, I continued making new stars. I made white dwarves but also other types because my techniques had become more advanced. Sometimes new planets coalesced around these stars and sometimes the planets made life. I continued to flick away the inferior or disappointing ones, or I'd feed them to my cat. Of those that remained I watched tiny people spread out and inhabit all the corners of my tiny universe, until the universe became too full to contain them and so I'd wipe them all away. Sometimes there were other tiny scientists with very powerful telescopes who would look up and out at me. When they saw me there were always questions about who I was and what I wanted. Was I good or malevolent? Omnipotent or indifferent? A god of death? I was just a man, I'd say to them, just as I'd told the original scientist. But like the original scientist, the more they studied me, the more they watched, the more they became unconvinced. Not because I had power over life and death, destruction and creation—which I did. But because there was only one of me. The god of my own isolation, my own unhappiness. A man with a cat in a basement. What is a god if not alone?

ABOUT THE AUTHORS

CHIMAMANDA NGOZI ADICHIE is the author of the prize-winning novels *Purple Hibiscus* (Commonwealth Writers' Prize and Hurston-Wright Legacy Award), *Half of a Yellow Sun* (Orange Prize), and *Americanah* (National Book Critics Circle Award). She is also the author of the acclaimed story collection, *The Thing Around Your Neck*. Her writing has appeared in various publications, including *The New Yorker, Granta, The O. Henry Prize Stories, The Financial Times*, and *Zoetrope*. A recipient of a MacArthur Foundation Fellowship, Adichie divides her time between the United States and Nigeria.

MARIA ANDERSON is from Three Forks, Montana. Her stories have recently appeared in *Sewanee Review, McSweeney's, Alpinist, Iowa Review,* and *Best American Short Stories 2018*. She has been awarded residencies from Jentel, the Helene Wurlitzer Foundation, and Joshua Tree National Park. Her story, "Water Moccasin," won *Sewanee Review's* Walter Sullivan Award.

RYKA AOKI writes poetry, fiction, and essays. Among her published books are *He Mele a Hilo* (A Hilo Song) and two Lambda Award finalists, *Seasonal Velocities* and *Why Dust Shall Never Settle Upon This Soul*. Her most recent novel is *Light from Uncommon Stars*. Aoki's work has appeared or been recognized in *Vogue, Elle, Bustle, Autostraddle, PopSugar,* and *Buzzfeed*. Her poetry was featured at the Smithsonian Asian Pacific American Center, and she was honored by the California State Senate for her "extraordinary commitment to the visibility and well-being of Transgender people." Ryka Aoki is a professor of English at Santa Monica College.

JOY BAGLIO is a writer of speculative literary fiction currently living and teaching in Northampton, Massachusetts. Her short stories have appeared in *Tin House, American Short Fiction, The Iowa Review, Gulf Coast, TriQuarterly,* and elsewhere. She's the recipient of fellowships from Yaddo, The Vermont Studio Center, and the Speculative Literature

Foundation. She is presently at work on a genre-bending collection of short stories and a novel about ghosts.

KALI FAJARDO-ANSTINE's widely acclaimed debut collection of short stories, *Sabrina & Corina,* was a finalist for the National Book Award and the PEN/Bingham Prize and winner of an American Book Award and the 2021 Addison M. Metcalf Award from the American Academy of Arts and Letters. Her writing has been published in *The New York Times, Harper's Bazaar, Elle, The American Scholar, Boston Review, Bellevue Literary Review, The Idaho Review, Southwestern American Literature,* and elsewhere. She has received fellowships from MacDowell Colony, Yaddo, and Hedgebrook. Originally from Denver, Colorado, she has lived across the country, from San Diego, California to Key West, Florida.

NANCY FULDA is a past Hugo and Nebula Nominee, a Vera Hinckley Mayhew Award winner, and a recipient of the Asimov's Readers' Choice Award. She is the author of the collection, *Dead Men Don't Cry: 11 Stories.* Fulda holds a PhD in Computer Science and currently leads an Artificial Intelligence research lab at Brigham Young University.

ROXANE GAY is a writer, editor, cultural critic. and author of *Ayiti, An Untamed State,* and the bestsellers *Bad Feminist* (essays), *Difficult Women* (stories), and *Hunger* (memoir). Her writing has appeared in *Best American Mystery Stories 2014, Best American Short Stories 2012, Best Sex Writing 2012, A Public Space, McSweeney's, Tin House, Oxford American, American Short Fiction, Virginia Quarterly Review,* and in many other publications. Gay is from Omaha, Nebraska, and currently divides her time between Los Angeles and New York.

ALICE HOFFMAN is the author of more than thirty novels, three books of short stories, and eight books for children and young adults. Among her many critically acclaimed and bestselling novels, the most recent are: *The Rules of Magic, The Museum of Extraordinary Things, The Marriage of Opposites, Faithful, The World That We Knew, The Red Garden,* and *The Dovekeepers,* which is often considered her masterpiece. Hoffman grew up on Long Island (NY) and lives near Boston.

VANESSA HUA, a columnist for the *San Francisco Chronicle,* is the author of the bestselling novel, *A River of Stars,* named a Best Book of 2018 by the *Washington Post* and National Public Radio, and of a short story collection, *Deceit and Other Possibilities,* a *New York Times* Editors' Choice and recipient of an Asian/Pacific American Award in Literature. As a journalist she has filed stories from China, Burma, South Korea, Panama, and Ecuador that have appeared in *The New York Times, Washington Post, The Atlantic,* and elsewhere. Her short fiction has been published in *The Atlantic, Guernica, The Sun,* and other periodicals. She teaches in the Warren Wilson College MFA Program and at the Writers' Grotto.

BRYAN HURT has published two books, the novel *Everyone Wants to Be Ambassador to France,* selected as the winner of the 10th Annual Starcherone Prize for Innovative Fiction, and the anthology *Watchlist: 32 Stories by Persons of Interest.* He is also Midwest editor for *Joyland,* an international literary journal. His work has been nominated for the Pushcart Prize and named finalist for the Calvino Prize and Horatio Nelson Prize in Fiction. He has received fellowships from the Sewanee and Tin House Writers' Conferences and is presently an assistant professor at the University of Arkansas.

PHIL KLAY is a veteran of the U.S. Marine Corps and the author of two books, *Redeployment,* a collection of short stories, winner of the 2014 National Book Award for Fiction, the National Book Critics Circle John Leonard Award, given for a best first book in any genre, and The National Book Foundation's 5 Under 35 Award. *Missionaries,* a novel, was a *New York Times* Notable Book and chosen as one of the Ten Best Books of 2020 by the *Wall Street Journal.* His writing has appeared in *Granta, The New York Times, The Washington Post, The Wall Street Journal, The Atlantic,* and elsewhere. He currently teaches fiction at Fairfield University and is a Board member for Arts in the Armed Forces.

MISTER LOKI is a queer, self-taught illustrator residing in Los Angeles, after graduating from University of California, Los Angeles, with a BSN. He is a pediatric bone marrow transplant nurse by night and a published comic illustrator and science illustrator by day. He has a passion for telling multifaceted historical and fantasy stories for queer youth.

CASEY ROBB's careers have included physical therapy and civil engineering. Her poetry has won awards and her short stories have appeared in numerous journals, including *Menda City Review, Foliate Oak, Foundling Review, Kaleidoscope,* and *Poydras Review.* Casey is a Texan who lives in Northern California with her two adopted daughters.

BENJAMIN ALIRE SÁENZ is an author of poetry and prose for adults and teens. He is the winner of the PEN/Faulkner Award and the American Book Award for his books for adults. His Young Adult novel *Aristotle and Dante Discover the Secrets of the Universe* was a Printz Honor Book and winner of the Stonewall Award, the Pura Belpré Award, and the Lambda Literary Award. He teaches creative writing at the University of Texas, El Paso.

RION AMILCAR SCOTT is the author of two short story collections, *Insurrections,* winner of the 2017 PEN/Bingham Prize for Debut Fiction and the Hillsdale Award from the Fellowship of Southern Writers, and *The World Doesn't Require You,* a finalist for the PEN/Jean Stein Book Award and winner of the 2020 Towson Prize for Literature. His work has been published in *The New Yorker, The Kenyon Review, Crab Orchard Review, Best Small Fictions 2020, Best American Science Fiction and Fantasy 2020,* and *The Rumpus,* among others. Presently he teaches Creative Writing at the University of Maryland.

AKHIL SHARMA is the author of the novels *An Obedient Father* and *Family Life,* a *New York Times* Best Book of the Year, as well as the critically acclaimed story collection, *A Life of Adventure and Delight.* His writing has appeared in *the New Yorker, The Atlantic, Best American Short Stories,* and *O. Henry Award Stories.* A native of Delhi, he lives in New York City and teaches English at Rutgers University-Newark.

ROBERT ANTHONY SIEGEL is the author of a memoir, *Criminals,* and two novels, *All Will Be Revealed* and *All the Money in the World.* His work has appeared in *The Paris Review, The Oxford American, Ploughshares,* and in other publications. He has been a Fulbright Scholar in Taiwan and a Mombukagakusho Fellow in Japan. He lives in New York City.

SHIVANA SOOKDEO is an Ignatz and Eisner winning cartoonist and a designer with Scholastic's comics imprint, Graphix. She is known for simple, eye-catching visuals paired with thoughtful, quietly dense narratives. She is presently located in Brooklyn, New York.

BRYAN WASHINGTON is the author of *Lot,* a highly acclaimed story collection, as well as the bestselling novel, *Memorial,* chosen as a Notable Book of 2020 by *The New York Times, Washington Post, Los Angeles Times,* and others. His work has appeared in *The New Yorker, Tin House, Vulture, The Believer,* and *Catapult.* Among his many honors are a Lambda Literary Award, the National Book Foundation's 5 Under 35 Award, and having been named a National Book Critics Circle Award Finalist. Washington is from Houston and presently the Writer-In-Residence at Rice University.

ABOUT THE EDITOR

BRICE PARTICELLI teaches writing at the University of California (Berkeley) and was named a 2022 Creative Writing Fellow in Literature by the National Endowment for the Arts. He earned his Ph.D. in education from Columbia University, where he was the director of a literacy-focused not-for-profit. His work has recently been published in *Harper's*, *Guernica, Salmagundi,* and *The Smart Set,* as well as in peer-reviewed academic journals. Dr. Particelli is the co-editor (with Anne Mazer) of the multicultural anthology of short stories, *America Street,* and is currently working on his first book.

ACKNOWLEDGMENTS

The editor and the publisher gratefully acknowledge the authors, artists, literary agents, and publishers who granted permission to include the stories and comics in this volume.

"The Thing Around Your Neck" by Chimamanda Ngozi Adichie, currently collected in *The Thing Around Your Neck,* copyright © 2009 by Chimamanda Ngozi Adichie. Used by permission of The Wylie Agency LLC and Penguin Canada.

"Cougar" by Maria Anderson. Copyright © 2016, 2022 by Maria Anderson. First published in *The Iowa Review.* Reprinted in *Best American Short Stories* in 2018. Reprinted here in a slightly different form, by permission of the author. All rights reserved by the author.

"To the New World" by Ryka Aoki, copyright © 2009, 2021 by Ryka Aoki. All rights reserved. First published in a slightly different form in *The Collection: Short Fiction from the Transgender Vanguard,* Leger P & MacLeod, eds. Published here by permission of Ryka Aoki.

"Ron" by Jo Baglio. Copyright © 2012, 2021 by Jo Baglio. First published in 2012 by *Tin House.* Published here by permission of the author. All rights reserved.

"Sugar Babies," from *Sabrina & Corina: Stories* by Kali Fajardo-Anstine, copyright © 2019 by Kali Fajardo-Anstine. Used by permission of One World, an imprint of Random House, a division of Penguin Random House LLC. All rights reserved.

"Movement" by Nancy Fulda, copyright © 2011 by Nancy Fulda. Originally printed in the March 2011 issue of *Asimov's Science Fiction Magazine.* Used by permission of the author. All rights reserved.

"Girls at the Bar" by Roxane Gay, copyright © 2010 by Roxane Gay, from *Northville Review* (2010). Used by permission of the author.

"In the Trees" by Alice Hoffman. Copyright © 2018 by Alice Hoffman. First published in Jonathan Santlofer's *It Occurs to Me That I Am America: New Stories and Art* (Touchstone, 2018). Used by permission of the author.

"Accepted," from *Deceit and Other Possibilities* by Vanessa Hua, copyright © 2016 by Vanessa Hua, (Detroit: Willow Books, 2016). Reprinted by Counterpoint, 2020. Used by permission of Counterpoint.